THE DALAI LAMA'S CAT

AWAKEN
THE KITTEN
WITHIN

ALSO BY DAVID MICHIE

THE DALAI LAMA'S CAT

AWAKEN THE KITTEN WITHIN

DAVID MICHIE

CONCH
CONCH BOOKS

First published in 2021

CONCH

Conch Books, an imprint of Mosaic Reputation Management (Pty) Ltd

Cover design: Sue Campbell Book Design
Author photo: Janmarie Michie

Cataloguing-in-Publication details are available from the National
Library of Australia www.trove.nla.gov.au

ISBN 978-0-6488665-4-1 (print)
ISBN 978-0-6488665-5-8 (e-book)

HOMAGE

With heartfelt gratitude to my precious gurus:
Les Sheehy, extraordinary source of inspiration and wisdom;
Geshe Acharya Thubten Loden, peerless master and
embodiment of the Dharma; and
Zasep Tulku Rinpoche, precious Vajra Acharya and yogi.

Guru is Buddha, Guru is Dharma, Guru is Sangha,
Guru is the source of all happiness.
To all gurus I prostrate, make offerings and go for refuge.

May this book carry waves of inspiration from my own gurus
To the hearts and minds of countless living beings.

May all beings have happiness and the true causes of happiness.
May all beings be free from suffering and the true causes
of suffering;
May all beings never be parted from the happiness that is
without suffering, the great joy of nirvana liberation; and
May all beings abide in peace and equanimity, their minds free
from attachment and aversion, and free from indifference.

The Owl and the Pussycat went to sea
In a beautiful pea-green boat,
They took some honey, and plenty of money,
Wrapped up in a five-pound note.

—Edward Lear, poet

Every man's world picture is and always
remains a construct of his mind
and cannot be proved to have any other
existence.

—Erwin Schrödinger, physicist

PROLOGUE

MONSOON. NOT MY FAVORITE SEASON, DEAR READER. FOR A feline with a coat as sumptuously absorbent as mine, and being somewhat wonky of gait, venturing out in wild weather is an exercise fraught with danger. Which is why interminable rains and fog keep me trapped inside, with little choice but to spend day after day on the first-floor windowsill of His Holiness's room, deprived even of my special view. No longer is the courtyard of Namgyal Monastery bustling with maroon robes and enchanted tourists, hoping that His Holiness might appear in their midst at any moment. It is, instead, as gray and unappealing as a saucer of last night's dinner.

So on that particular morning, when a familiar knock on the door was followed by the appearance of Tenzin, I looked up with special interest. His Holiness's adviser on diplomatic matters, Tenzin was suave and suited as always as he conferred with the Dalai Lama, the two of them glancing at a clock. Novice monks were slipping into the room to dust flowerpots and plump up cushions – all a well-rehearsed prelude to the arrival of a visitor. Reaching out first my two front legs, then my back two, I stretched tremulously, pleased that the tedium was about to be broken.

But by whom?

One of the many intrigues of being His Holiness's Cat is the steady stream of celebrities who beat a path to the

Himalayas, and indeed to this particular room. Presidents and pop stars, sages and scientists, all find their way to our door. The stated reasons for their visits are many and varied, but you and I know the real reasons, do we not?

First and foremost, visitors come to experience the *feeling* of being in the presence of the Dalai Lama. That benevolent, energetic field in which he envelops all who perceive him. The understanding he conveys, spontaneously and without apparent effort, that whatever may be going on in our lives and the world around us, all is well beneath the surface.

In recent years there has been an additional reason why discerning visitors do their utmost to secure an audience. It may seem brazen for me to suggest it – but false modesty is such a deeply unattractive quality, is it not, dear reader? It's certainly not one I would wish to be accused of. You see, the other compelling reason why people come from all around the world to this room is to discover, for themselves, if it really is true. Does the Dalai Lama really "have a cat", to use that common if misleading expression? Is His Holiness's Cat – HHC in official circles – simply a beguiling myth or a dazzling, blue-eyed reality? Was that shimmer of gray glimpsed on a Zoom teaching the end of a bushy tail belonging to his much-fabled feline, or was it simply a play of light, a chimera, the source of which must remain shrouded in mystery?

ON THAT PARTICULARLY BLEAK MORNING, AS HEADLIGHTS appeared at the gates of Namgyal Monastery, I looked into the fog, but could perceive very little beyond the slow approach of a vehicle. The low drone of an engine increasing in volume before coming to a standstill. Silence, followed by the opening and shutting of car doors. It was some minutes before Tenzin showed a woman into the room.

As you will have correctly assumed, I am a cat of the utmost discretion and can't possibly divulge the identity of His Holiness's VIP guests. In this particular case, however, it's probably important for you to know that she is a very well-known pop star. You know, the one whose stage name isn't her real name? In fact, it's more of a title – as if she were married to a British lord.

Those are the only discreet and subtle hints I am willing to offer, except perhaps to mention that her fans are known to be Little Monsters. And she would make a very good poker player.

Yes, *her*!

From across the room I watched closely as the Dalai Lama and his visitor brought their hands to their hearts and bowed in greeting, before sitting down to face each other on separate sofas across a coffee table. At the head of the table, Tenzin oversaw the pouring of cups of coffee and offering of cookies from a tray in front of him. Then he settled into an armchair, with that particular manner of seasoned diplomats, so discreet a presence that it was almost as if he disappeared completely into the background.

Outside, the swirling gloom of fog darkened, cloaking my windowsill seat in deep shadow. Just as I preferred it. Like most cats, I like to observe without being observed. To make up my own mind about visitors, before they so much as suspect I am even there.

This particular visitor was to share the stage with the Dalai Lama at a conference on mental wellbeing. Her visit was to help prepare for the event. At His Holiness's prompting, she explained that while she had started out on her career wanting to succeed as a singer, along the way her purpose had broadened. She no longer sought only to entertain: she wanted to touch people's lives. To make an impact. In particular, having been abused when she was young, her aim was to help others who had endured the same trauma. She described how memories of her own abuse had been so distressing that they had continued to rack her with physical pain for a long time afterwards.

Listening attentively to her story, the Dalai Lama's face was filled with compassion. "Mind and body are one," he responded after a while. "Harm to one is harm to both."

His visitor paused, regarding him closely. "It took me a long time to work that out," she admitted. "I didn't understand what was happening, not for years. I thought I was going mad!"

His Holiness leaned over, taking both her hands reassuringly in his own. Gazing deep into her eyes he asked, "How did you find your way through?"

She mused for a while before saying, "With the help of doctors. Therapists. I have learned a lot." Then after a further pause, "Perhaps the biggest thing for me was the invention of an ideal version of me."

The Dalai Lama spoke her stage name out loud.

"Exactly. I thought of all the qualities I most wanted, and

decided that she would have them. Then I tried to imagine being her. When my fans responded to her, they were responding to my ideal self. Over time, it became easier and easier to accept that I was becoming who I most wanted to be."

"The imagined became real?"

"Yes."

His Holiness was nodding slowly. "Good psychology. We use it, very much, in Tibetan Buddhism."

"You do?" His visitor seemed surprised.

"You might say, it is one of the foundation teachings of the Buddha," he confirmed. "Thoughts lead to words. Words lead to actions. It all begins here," the Dalai Lama was tapping his head. "And here," he touched his heart. "As we think, so we become. In any situation, wherever we find ourselves, we are still free to think what we wish. Most of all, free to choose how we think of ourselves. When you decide to live according to the best version of yourself that you can imagine ..." He smiled, "How wise!"

"Thank you!" Even from the gloom of the windowsill, it seemed to me that His Holiness's compliment brought color to the cheeks of his visitor, before she said, "So much easier to say than to do, of course. Sometimes I fail."

"Changing mental habits ..." the Dalai Lama sat forward in his chair, "Difficult. Sometimes not always possible. So," he shrugged, "we accept. We accept, but keep trying."

"Self-acceptance," she responded.

"Most important." Leaning back in his chair, His Holiness chuckled. "We cannot help others fully, if we ourselves are suffering. Therefore, we must have compassion for ourselves first."

She nodded, her expression earnest.

"Show ourselves ..." a twinkle appeared in his eyes, "the same kindness that we would to a very dear friend."

No matter who came into this room, whatever their background, it was never long before they discovered their most benevolent instincts reflected by His Holiness. In his allencompassing presence they felt understood, appreciated, wholly accepted. Could there be a greater gift?

Continuing to follow the conversation, after a while I decided that it was high time I took His Holiness's advice to heart. Hopping off my cushion on the sill, I made my way unobserved across the room and around the furniture, before launching myself onto the sofa next to the famous pop star.

Initially startled, her expression quickly changed to one of delight. "Oh, how gorgeous!" she exclaimed, reaching out to stroke me. "So she *is* real!"

I angled my head upwards, the better to feel the scratch of her long fingernails on my chin. Female humans have their uses.

"I've always wondered if she really existed," she explained. "Or was she just an idea that someone had come up with."

"Well, now you know," said Tenzin. He had surfaced from the depths of his armchair ready, I knew from past experience, to swoop me away at the first sign of an allergic reaction.

But His Holiness's visitor showed none. Instead, while continuing to massage my neck, she murmured, "Seeing is believing."

From the sofa opposite, the Dalai Lama observed, "Yes, yes. And it works the other way too. Believing is seeing."

The visitor's forehead wrinkled. "If you don't see, how can you believe?" she asked. "Don't you have to see first?"

His Holiness gestured towards her and, once again, used her stage name. "Did you always see her, or did you first have to believe she may be possible?"

"Oh, I get it," she wagged a finger playfully. "The idea comes first. Then the reality."

"Exactly."

"As we think, so we become," she quoted back what he'd said earlier.

Enough of the chitchat and neck rub, I thought, stepping onto the coffee table and heading towards my ultimate destination – the milk jug.

I observed the questioning glances exchanged between Tenzin and the Dalai Lama. Between the Dalai Lama and his guest. At which point the pop star herself picked up the jug, placed her empty cup on the tray and poured milk into her saucer. They all watched in silence as I bent to lap with noisy gusto.

"Some beings," Tenzin observed, "are very skillful at manifesting the reality they wish."

They all burst out laughing.

THAT MORNING'S GUEST LEFT A SHORT WHILE LATER, BUT NOT before posing for an official photograph with His Holiness and an unofficial selfie with His Holiness's Cat. After watching the retreating figure of his visitor, hands folded at his heart, the Dalai Lama crossed the room, lifted me up and walked to the window. From downstairs, there came once again the sound of car doors. Then the growl of an engine as the vehicle started.

"I know you don't like the monsoon, and having to stay indoors," His Holiness said. "But it will be over very soon. You will enjoy the weather then, my little Snow Lion. The best of the year."

While I am a cat of many names, my very favorite is His Holiness's own special one for me: in Tibet, the mythical Snow Lion is a being of great courage and joy.

Red tail-lights disappeared into the mist, as the visitor's vehicle chugged cautiously across the courtyard.

And at that moment it didn't matter that the weather was bleak or that I couldn't go outside. As always, when being held by the Dalai Lama I was enveloped in the profound wellbeing that emerged from the presence of his oceanic benevolence. My purr rose in appreciation, and within a short while I had lost all sense of where my body and mind ended and His Holiness's began. There was only the glow of loving kindness, gentle and pervading far beyond the two of us, an energy to bring joy to all who had the hearts to feel it.

AFTER HIS HOLINESS HAD RETURNED TO HIS DESK I WAS SITting on the sill once again, paws tucked under me. Through a break in the mist, I observed another visitor making his way slowly across the Namgyal courtyard. Someone with whom I'd struck up the warmest of friendships in recent months, but who I knew for a fact had never met the Dalai Lama. From the way he kept looking over at our building, he was evidently on his way to visit now.

What was the purpose of his unexpected call? And was the orderly behind him really carrying what I thought he was?

CHAPTER ONE

ONE WEEK EARLIER

AS KITTENS, WE FEEL IT OFTEN. ALL IT TAKES IS A WINDBLOWN feather, an unexpected delicacy, or the alluring rush of water and instantly we are caught up in it. Wonderment. Enchantment. Being fully absorbed in the here and now.

By the time we reach senior status, way beyond the point of being impressed by such trivia, we have become knowing and indifferent. If we have been deeply hurt, and the scar tissue of our wounds has grown thick, we may be especially impervious to life's simple joys.

But we have lost something, have we not? The ability to be enraptured by the world around us. To give ourselves totally to the moment, without reserve. To see things as if for the first time.

All of which begs the answer to some intriguing questions.

Is it possible to recover the unaffected zest for life which once came so naturally? To become un-blasé? Can you and I, dear reader, awaken the kitten within?

Although I had no idea at the time, one tranquil morning as I dozed on top of the filing cabinet in the office of His Holiness's two Executive Assistants, the day was about to bring an unexpected answer to this question. And it was delivered with a drama I would have done my utmost to avoid.

Tenzin, the consummate diplomat, was sitting at his computer, tapping out an email to the Chancellor of Germany. In jacket and tie, with a slight tang of carbolic about him from the soap with which he always washed his perfectly manicured hands, he always looked as though he had just stepped out of a meeting with a world leader, Secretary of State or some other VIP – which, in the age of online meetings, he often had.

At the desk opposite sat His Holiness's Translator, Oliver. A large, jolly Englishman, with the clearest blue eyes sparkling behind his spectacles. Although Oliver is a Buddhist monk, he is also the son of a Church of England vicar, and possesses a radiant intelligence and goodness of heart that make him spiritually multilingual. With Tenzin, an irredeemable Anglophile, he shares a love of English breakfast tea, the BBC World Service – and an ardent enthusiasm for cricket.

Currently working on the foreword to a new book about the bardo realms, Oliver was unusually preoccupied that morning. As was Tenzin. There was none of the usual joking and chitchat. No time that day to analyze the Indian cricket team's latest win over the home team in Perth, Australia. It was all screen staring and keyboard clicking, with barely a word to each other and none at all to me.

Bored and incurious about their activity, human behavior being inexplicable to rational felines, I must have dozed off for a while. Next thing I knew, as the time approached 11 am, Oliver left the office. He returned a short while later, holding under his arm the most alarming object in the whole of Namgyal Monastery: the cat carrier.

Where it was kept and precisely how it manifested, I neither knew nor cared. But I was shaken by the way it had made such a sudden and utterly unexpected appearance. The casual, almost jaunty way that Oliver was swinging it from under his arm onto his desk. How Tenzin was simultaneously standing and turning to where I lay, unsuspectingly. With ruthless efficiency, he had me in his carbolic-fingered grip. Oliver was holding the carrier door open.

In a trice, I was securely locked inside the infernal apparatus.

"Just your annual check-up, HHC." Oliver leaned in to glimpse me through the cruel bars, as if their ambush was of little consequence.

I yowled miserably.

I continued to complain all the way to the vet clinic, but there are none so deaf as those who do not wish to hear. Once inside the chamber of horrors that is the consulting room, a new vet who described himself as a locum was pulling open my jaws and tugging at my eyelids, prodding my abdomen and subjecting me to that most grievous of all indignities – lifting my luxurious fluffy tail and inserting a cold thermometer.

"These need a trim," he observed dispassionately, splaying my claws wide.

Oliver gave his immediate assent.

As the locum systematically cut every one of my talons – a liberty which Oliver well knew I would most certainly not have tolerated at home, but which I was helpless to avoid while pinned down on the butcher's block – he continued with his clinical observations. "Their nails tend to wear less as they age. Has she become more sedentary these days?"

"HHC?" Oliver held his head to one side as he considered the question.

"How old is she?" he persisted, before Oliver had even answered.

"At least six." Oliver was calculating from the time that he'd started working with His Holiness. "Eight, maybe?" he hazarded.

When he finally ended the wretched clipping, the vet stepped over to a computer screen. "First presented for vaccinations here ten years ago," he announced.

"Ten?" Oliver was surprised.

"She's getting on," said the locum. "And with older cats, you need to watch out for their kidneys. If you're not doing this already, I'd recommend cat biscuits for seniors. They have a good dose of protein and vitamin E. Also lower phosphorous to reduce kidney strain."

Older cats? Getting on?! In mere minutes, I had been reduced from a perfectly content global celebrity to some frail geriatric with likely medical conditions. Who was this monstrous sadist in the white coat?

"Is she drinking more than in the past, would you say?" he persisted.

"Not noticeably."

"Keep an eye on it. Kidney issues are common as cats age. I think we'd better run some blood tests." He had inserted a needle into my leg before I'd even registered. "Not a bad idea when monitoring elderly cats."

Elderly?

"Seems that you've become quite middle-aged, HHC." Oliver tried making light of things as the locum retreated to his screen. Oliver was lifting the open cat carrier and guiding me back into it. On this occasion, I required no encouragement.

"Hmm," the vet was updating his records. It was while tapping on the keyboard, face reflected in the ghostly white of the screen, that he almost absently uttered the sentence that would haunt me for a long time to come. Responding to what Oliver had just said, the words were so shocking, yet they were uttered so casually as though just commonplace. "You know, thirteen is a good age for a cat to reach. For a cat with her hip problems, she's already had a good life."

I didn't hear anything after that. I paid no attention on the journey back to Namgyal. I didn't meow once. Oliver may have thought that I was simply relieved to be going home. In truth, I was shaken to the core by what the vet had said.

Evidently, most of my life was already behind me and my best years on earth had already played out. Was there really nothing to look forward to, apart from kidney failure and cat biscuits for seniors? Was the only thing ahead of me inexorable decline, sickness and death?

As soon as we were home and I was set free from the accursed carrier, I stormed from the building in high dudgeon. I didn't care how damp and foggy it was – I had to get out. Somewhere. Anywhere. After crossing Namgyal courtyard I was soon out the gates and heading along the road, tugged intuitively in a direction that had become habitual in recent months.

Next door to where we lived was a well-established garden, and at the center of its lawn a large and ancient cedar tree, beneath which was an inviting bench seat. I had passed many a happy hour in this garden – specifically, in the generous thicket of catnip which grew in one of the borders.

My destination that day was not the catnip, which was a sodden mess being the monsoon season. Nor the nursing home overlooking the garden, where I had become that most sought after of beings – the Therapy Cat. No, it was behind the nursing home veranda that I headed, across a kitchen garden profuse with vegetables, towards what had formerly been a large garden shed.

Even before I reached the shed, I could hear the soothing cadences of baroque music, despite the gray weather. I paused at the door for a while grooming myself, licking away the antiseptic scent of vet, my tongue sensing the strangely sharp edges of my freshly cut nails.

The man standing in the center of the room glanced over, observing my arrival but not allowing himself to be distracted by it, returning his attention to his easel. Which was exactly what I needed. Venturing inside, I soon reached my wicker chair, the one with the cushion, and made myself comfortable, before turning to study the artist at work.

THE FIRST TIME I'D VISITED, MONTHS EARLIER, HAD BEEN A most unexpected experience – just the kind to delight a cat as curious as I. There he had stood, with a canvas in front of him, adding bold sweeps of color, moving between easel and the bench behind him loaded with paints, palettes and brushes. A Bach divertimento issued from an ancient, paint-smeared sound system in the corner.

A large man with a shock of white hair and a subversive glint about his large, brown eyes, I knew exactly who he was – just as he knew me. We were, in fact, already good friends. On previous visits to the nursing home, in a room full of dozing residents, Christopher had always been the most eager to coax me over, declaring me to be "an angel". I reminded him of a cat he'd lived with for many years in the distant past.

He may have had blotchy skin and frayed cuffs, but he also seemed to have more life in him than most of the other residents. And something about him in particular intrigued me: brightly colored spots on his corduroy trousers, possessing a curious aroma.

It had been quite by chance the day when I had seen him walking along the path near the vegetable garden. Watching him undo the padlock on a shed door, then open it to reveal a place filled with light and color. Naturally, I had investigated.

What had struck me most, on that first visit to Christopher's studio, was finding myself in a veritable treasure-trove of sensorial delights – *and* being given tacit approval to explore the place to my heart's content. Then, just like today, Christopher glanced over and noted my presence, while continuing to work. I understood no unfriendliness in the absence of a greeting. He was not being unwelcoming. He was simply focused on other things, allowing me complete freedom to inspect the studio's every nook and cranny.

Stepping inside, I had taken my time to investigate every unfamiliar object and pungent scent in this intriguing place. Evidently, it had once been a rambling garden shed before having extra windows and a skylight installed, sisal carpeting laid wall-to-wall, and furnished with an assortment of unmatched items – two wicker chairs, a high table and a corner counter with a small fridge and kettle. Without question, the most enthralling aspect at ground level was the lengthy tunnel created by painted boards and canvases leaning against the three walls facing Christopher. An extended cavern into which a cat might vanish without trace.

I was immediately drawn to the scent of oil paint on canvas, that earthy, distinctive but not unpleasant aroma. Opening my mouth in full vomeronasal mode, I stood for a long while, nose to canvas, taking it in. Then I explored the tunnel of mysteries, dark panels interspersed with slits of light. The multitude of odors — paint, sisal, glue and the ancient imprints of soil enhancers and composting mulch. It was an Aladdin's cave of intrigue in which I immersed myself fully, coming out quite some time later.

Christopher was still painting, so I hopped onto one of the wicker chairs, soon to become *my* wicker chair, and followed his actions. I had never seen an artist in full flight before and he seemed engaged in a dance of sorts, moving to a dynamic that had nothing to do with the background Bach. Inspired by an energy to which I was oblivious; as I sat watching, he was utterly absorbed in his actions. The feeling I experienced reminded me of someone, but the vibrant novelty of this artist's studio with its colors and light and medley of aromas meant that I couldn't place who.

His frayed tweed jacket, the one he always wore in the residents' lounge, was thrown over the back of the other wicker chair. In one pocket, I noted a well-thumbed paperback. From my vantage point, as I surveyed the many canvases leaning against the walls, I saw one that was separate from all the rest. It was framed in gold and stood alone on the only shelf on the whitewashed wall opposite — a portrait of a vivacious, dark-haired woman.

After a long while, Christopher broke away abruptly, doubling over in a fit of coughing. Once he'd recovered, he carefully placed his brush on the bench and turned to me, opening his arms with an extravagant flourish:

"*The Owl looked up to the stars above,*

And sang to a small guitar,
'O lovely Pussy! O Pussy, my love,
What a beautiful Pussy you are,
You are, you are!
What a beautiful Pussy you are!'"

"*The Owl and the Pussycat*, my dear Minou!" he continued, the words tumbling from his mouth. "Written by Edward Lear. But you know that, I'm sure. How I've longed to recite those words to my own feline. Just a dream, Miss Puss. At least, that's what I thought. But here you are, so unexpectedly. From out of the ether. And not just any cat, but the most beautiful of beings with those gorgeous sapphire orbs."

He reached to stroke my neck, just as he did in the residents' lounge. I purred obligingly, wondering what to make of his extravagant words – not to mention, puzzled by the references to his dear Minou. A cat with whom he used to share his life, perhaps?

As a Mozart piano concerto rose to its grand finale, he was pottering in the corner, making himself a mug of tea. Once made, he settled into the wicker chair opposite the one I occupied, staring at the canvas on which he'd been working. He took a sip, before flashing me a glance.

"Oh, apologies, my dearest puss! Unaccustomed as I am to visitors, I've quite forgotten my manners." Putting his mug down, he heaved himself from his chair with some effort and broke into another paroxysm of coughing, before going to the counter and returning with an offering of milk inside a jam jar lid. He placed it before me, reverentially, before watching with deep fascination as I lowered my head to drink.

I continued until I'd lapped up every last drop.

"It's the simplest thing that gives joy, isn't it?" his eyes glistened with affection as he spoke. "Offering a treat to a passing puss." A mischievous glint appeared in his eyes as he said, "I do hope this may be sufficient inducement to persuade you to visit again."

So intriguing was his artist's studio and my freedom within it that no such inducement was needed. That cup of tea and lid of milk were to be the first of many, in what soon became a cherished routine.

WHEN THE DALAI LAMA HAD TO LEAVE DHARAMSHALA FOR several weeks, to oversee monastic exams in South India, I found myself spending many happy hours on the wicker chair, absorbed in this delightful new world of oil paints, Vivaldi, space and color, with Christopher the visual conjuror bringing forth sweeping landscapes and towering peaks, verdant arcadia and cascading waterfalls – or so he said. Because when I looked at the artworks he had finished, it was hard to guess.

"Abstraction," he once explained. "Not for the ignorant nor the faint-hearted. But *we* don't mind, do we? Nay, we thrive on it. All the world is a projection of mind, is it not, Mistress Babou?"

By now I had become used to the delightful if bewildering flow of words that he spoke, and the arcane terms of endearment he lavished on me. Unlike any other human I had encountered, I had come to learn that Christopher gave voice less to a sequence of thoughts than a general impression. A carnival of vibrant images and ideas, as hard for a cat to keep up with as the paint he so prolifically applied to canvases.

There was nothing abstract about the portrait of the woman, however. From time to time he'd break from what was on his easel, approach the framed image and pause, staring at it for the longest time. He might tilt his head to a different angle. Take a step or two one way or another, then review his work with a critical eye. Sometimes, very rarely, he might even reach with his brush and apply the tiniest speck of color, before standing back to survey the difference.

When we sat having tea in companionable silence, he was in the habit of leaning to where his jacket lay over the back of his chair, reaching inside the breast pocket and retrieving an envelope containing a handwritten letter, several pages long. I'd watch his eyes moving across every line, from beginning to end, with an intensity as though he were reading it for the very first time even though, from the depth of the page creases, it was evident that this was a letter which had been opened and closed countless times before.

He'd refold the letter with the greatest care, placing it back in the envelope and his jacket pocket, before leaning back in his chair and gazing contemplatively into the middle distance.

On one such occasion, I saw tears welling in his eyes. From the other chair, I reached out a front paw. The movement lifted him from his thoughts.

"Oh!" he leaned over to caress my neck. "What a sweet

thing you are, my dearest ocelot. All those years spent burdened by failure. And guilt. Such a waste!" He broke off for a prolonged spasm of coughing. "Still, we made it in the end, didn't we? Perhaps it was my karma to descend into Hades, for my own night sea journey. But here I am at the end of it all, at peace in the Himalayas with my very own Babou."

ONE SPECIAL DAWN, WHEN THE FIRST LIGHT SILHOUETTED the mountains with an irresistible clarity and promise, I left my first-floor windowsill very early and ventured outside to breathe the clean fragrances of pine and Himalayan oak. His Holiness was still away, the apartment empty, and I found myself walking in the direction of the garden, then Christopher's studio. Not that he would be there yet, would he?

But the door to his studio was open. And as I appeared, he turned to see me.

"Oh, *Exsultate Jubilate!* Pussy my love! You feel it too?"

I meowed.

"Of course you do. You are a creature of nature. Just as I seek an exemplar of pristine clarity and bliss, who should appear but the Sapphire Princess herself! We must make the most of this primordial dawn. Such a precious moment may never come again."

He was fixing a fresh canvas to his easel and loading a palette with paints – blues and yellows and white. Working rapidly, with a burst of ebullience he was dancing again, completely focused, absorbed, at one with the moment.

Watching closely, I realized for the first time since I'd started visiting where the strongly reminiscent feeling came from. A connection perhaps so obvious that it had eluded me until now. For when he painted, what I sensed felt to me like His Holiness in meditation. He was experiencing no distinction between self and other, subject and object. There was only what was happening here and now, a flow of joy.

Of course Christopher's mind was quite different from the Dalai Lama's – and who was I to guess at the inner experiences of the two? What I could discern, however, was the parallel shift that had occurred. A sense of sublime oneness, in both cases, so powerful that it seemed to radiate beyond their physical forms and permeate the very space around them – in which I happened to be sitting.

That dawn as he painted, Christopher paid me much more attention than usual, frequently glancing to where I sat. It was a different kind of attention than when he was being conversational. More as if I were his source, his inspiration. He looked at me as though in thrall to his muse.

He worked solidly for several hours before putting down his brush. The moment he did, he broke into the most prolonged bout of deep coughing I'd ever witnessed, having to steady himself by holding onto the bench as his whole body was racked with convulsions.

When he finally recovered, he had turned quite pale.

THE DAY THAT I SOUGHT REFUGE, FOLLOWING MY MOST

CONfronting of visits to the vet, I sat listening to Haydn and observing Christopher in his state of absorption. The same thing happened again – after the lengthiest period of concentration, Christopher suddenly buckled under the force of painful, heaving coughs.

On this occasion, there came the sound of footsteps hurrying on the path outside. Then the appearance of Marianne Ponter, nursing home manager, herself. A 50-something woman in formal jacket and elegantly coiffed dark hair, Marianne was soon hurrying to his side and helping him into an upright chair that Christopher had recently brought from the dining room.

As soon as he was seated and over the worst of the attack, she filled a glass of water and handed it to him. He thanked her, breathlessly. She rested a comforting hand on his shoulder.

"Goes with the territory," he told her, after a while.

"You're doing very well," she reassured him.

He gestured round the studio with the glass of water. "*This* has made all the difference," he said. "For which the only thing I have to offer you is my heartfelt gratitude. I wish it could be more. I wish that I hadn't completely run out of money. I'm painfully aware that I owe you 3 lakh ..." He gestured behind him.

On the small shelf next to the kettle was a stack of brown envelopes. Every two weeks, a fresh one was delivered. I'd been there when it happened, one of Mr. Naidoo's assistants from Accounts knocking on the shed door, envelope in hand. Christopher nodding in acknowledgement. The assistant walking wordlessly across the room and adding the envelope to the pile already there.

Unlike the envelope in his jacket pocket, I had never seen Christopher open a single brown one. They remained, untouched, where they were.

"You're not to worry about that," Marianne was decisive. "The Board has agreed for you to stay on compassionate grounds. That's settled."

"And I am enormously grateful to you for persuading them." Christopher contained an outburst of coughing, "I shouldn't be imposing for too much longer."

Compassionate grounds? I was disconcerted. Not much longer?

"All these years you've been a resident," Marianne moved the conversation on. "And only now you tell us you were an artist. We all thought you were a house painter!"

"I was," he nodded. "For many years. But before that, as a young man in England, I studied with some of the greats. There were exhibitions in Cork Street. Serious collectors. A couple of paintings shown at the Royal Academy."

"Heavens!"

"I still sometimes have a fantasy about that early promise developing to full and glorious flower. About my work becoming wildly sought after."

Marianne glanced about at all the paintings. "If that were to happen, all these would fetch you a fortune!"

"I know!" he glowed.

"More money than one would know what to do with!"

"Oh, *I* would know what to do with it!" he was ebullient.

"A benevolent fund for elderly artists. A place of sanctuary, just like the sanctuary you have given me."

"What a generous vision. The Christopher Ackland Benevolent Fund?"

He shook his head. "Oh, that's far too stuffy. More like The Sanctuary for Broke Old Bohemians."

Christopher pondered this with a smile, before his expression changed. "Truth is, sometimes it's not much fun being an artist. After my early success, it all became too much and I lost my nerve. Critics didn't like the direction I was taking, but I didn't know what else I could possibly do. Suddenly I was overwhelmed by the fear of failure. So I fled the country. It was cowardly, I know. At the time, I felt I had no choice but to disappear." His expression was strangely haunted. "I don't know why I'm telling you all this," he was shaking his head. "Haven't spoken about it for years. Anyway, I lived in Europe for a while, before finding my way to India. Eventually painting the homes of the New Delhi *nouveau riche*."

"Before arriving in the mountains?" Marianne prompted a happy resolution.

"When I heard about your place here, I *had* to come. Fancy being able to retire right next door to the Dalai Lama!"

She nodded, "Why the return to fine art?"

"Emphysema," Christopher smiled ruefully. Before adding after a pause, "There's nothing like a terminal diagnosis to make you realize the value of every single day."

There it was, beyond all doubt. Plainly stated. The coughing spasms weren't simply a temporary vexation, or the indignity of old age. They had a much more sinister significance.

"For the first time since I was a child, I've done what I love, without caring what anyone thinks." Christopher gestured towards his canvases, "Without worrying about buyers or critics or gallery owners. I've painted for joy."

She was nodding.

"Have a look around."

Marianne was hesitant, stepping towards the canvases ranged around the walls. "I'm no art expert," she confessed, looking from one to another.

"Don't have to be," he shrugged. "It's what you like that matters. This is my most recent," he gestured to three paintings laid out on the high bench. "It's a triptych of the Himalayas. I'm calling it *Blue Shadows*."

Marianne walked to the bench and took in the paintings. From where she was standing, they were upside down, the sky at the bottom of the canvases and the mountains at the top. Christopher flashed me a knowing look. Marianne didn't seem to realize.

Abstraction, dear reader.

"Very nice," she said, glancing about before spotting the portrait of the woman in the giltwood frame. "And who is this?" she asked, relieved to find something she recognized.

"Caroline. Love of my life. I left her behind too, more fool me. But I never forgot her. And after the doctor told me, you know, how long I've got, I decided that I mustn't die with regrets. So I managed to get hold of her address and wrote to apologize. She sent me back the most beautiful letter. And a small photograph," he tilted his chin towards the painting, "which I used to paint her."

Marianne was nodding. "Free spirit?"

"You can see that?" Christopher's face lit up.

"Right away. First thing that struck me." She turned, meeting his eyes with an appreciative smile. Before she caught sight of me, observing them both from my wicker chair.

"Ah yes," Christopher followed her gaze. "Every artist must have a studio cat. You know Kandinsky had his Vaske, and Picasso his Minou. Salvador Dali had an ocelot called Babou."

"An ocelot?"

"Species of wild cat. From the Americas."

Marianne raised her eyebrows. "I didn't know about that. Or about artists having a feline affinity."

"Established tradition, my dear. No sooner had you so kindly arranged for me to move in here than this little one appeared. She has the most amazing presence. Very tuned in. And the most extraordinary sense of timing."

Marianne looked at his indulgent expression for a while before saying quietly, "You do know who she is, don't you?"

"We've been introduced," he nodded. "On her rounds as our most esteemed Therapy Cat."

"Yes," she agreed. "She does that very nicely, in her voluntary capacity. But as well as being our Therapy Cat, do you know where she comes from?"

When he didn't answer, she took a step closer. "We don't want this generally known for reasons of her own safety," she said, looking at me. "She visits us from next door."

Then, as it took him a while to catch up with her, "This is the Dalai Lama's Cat."

"Good heavens!" Christopher was euphoric. "My sainted aunt!"

"It's true."

"I'm finding this hard …"

"I know."

"Such a privilege!"

"I'll say," agreed Marianne.

Christopher's rapture was complete. Staring at me, incredulously, it was a while before he could speak. "It's almost like receiving the blessing of His Holiness himself!"

As a cat who prefers playing the part of the observer rather than the observed, and finding myself the subject of sudden and enthusiastic attention, I felt that I had little alternative, dear reader. Hopping off the chair, I headed out the studio door at speed.

The two of them burst out laughing.

I HAD CONTINUED TO VISIT AND CHRISTOPHER HAD CONTINued to paint and talk and even sing very briefly. But the coughing bouts became more frequent and prolonged, and afterwards he'd remain bent over, clinging to the bench or chair for support, and it was the longest time before he could stand upright again.

My arrival always had a pleasing electrifying effect on him. If anything, more so with time. He waxed lyrical about the inspiring impact of my presence. Once he knew my identity, he wondered aloud if what he was experiencing was some kind of energy transfer; he was at the lowest physical ebb of his life but, paradoxically, he felt he was only now realising his artistic heights. He declared that the painting he had started on that dawn visit was his most accomplished ever. It was work he would have loved to have created all those years ago, in his darkest moments. But he'd had to complete his night sea journey to find his way here, so far from his place of departure. Was that, perhaps, the point?

He mused at some length about whether he should offer this, his greatest work, to the Dalai Lama, given how greatly he had been inspired by him, one way or another.

The tea breaks grew longer, always accompanied by treats for me. On one occasion, he'd pulled out the well-worn paperback from his jacket. It had a photograph of the Dalai Lama on the front, speaking into a yellow microphone, and the title *Mahamudra*.

"Your man has wise things to say about our minds – and our reality," he glanced over. "This book, more than any other, gave me back my sanity. If only I was capable of meditating."

My last visit to Christopher had been the most disconcerting. The studio had been empty. When he had appeared down the path from the nursing home, he was walking with a strange contraption on wheels, and had tubes running into his nostrils.

"Oxygen, Miss Pussy. O Pussy, my love." He sat down heavily, as soon as he reached the studio. "Such is the sharpness of my descent. You know, one of the few fears I have ever felt in life is the terror of drowning. But alas, that's almost certainly how I will go."

The present moment

Through a gap in the mist, I watched Christopher make his way to our building, progress slow and posture bowed. The orderly, a few steps behind him, was carrying what looked like the painting, now completed.

He wasn't using the oxygen tank, but between car and building he had to stop to rest. And it was the longest time after he disappeared from view before there was a knock on the door and an announcement, this time by Oliver, who ushered the visitor in before stepping into the background.

Christopher brought his hands together and bowed deeply to His Holiness. "I am so deeply grateful that you agreed to see me," his breathing was labored and he struggled to contain a cough. He was gazing at the Dalai Lama, as so many visitors do, with a strange mix of incredulity that he really was standing in the presence of one of the most famous people in the world, and at the same time succumbing to the irresistible tide of benevolent wellbeing in which he felt embraced.

I knew that he had also noticed me. He flashed a glance towards the windowsill on which I sat, whiskers tingling at this new situation in which we found ourselves. One in which I knew formality would prevent him from bursting out with *O lovely Pussy! O Pussy, my love* or other florid endearments.

But he had seen me, and I had seen him, and he had seen me seeing him, and our connection resumed.

"I would like to make you an offering, Your Holiness."

The Dalai Lama nodded. The usual protocol was for a visitor to present a white scarf or *khata* to His Holiness, which he would then place back over the neck of the guest, thereby returning their gift, augmented immeasurably by his whispered blessing.

Christopher had brought no white *khata* today, but from the corridor stepped the orderly I recognized from the nursing home. He was carrying the painting.

The Dalai Lama indicated that the orderly should place it on a table, in good light. It was quite unlike any art ever presented before in this room. The ultimate expression of abstraction, you might say, because it didn't seem to be *of* anything at all. At least, nothing specific. There were no mountains, forests or waterfalls. In yellows and whites and the faintest blues it was, rather, a panoramic impression of radiant light. Boundless space.

"It's called *Primordial Dawn* and I would like to give it to you, Your Holiness. Not least of all because you inspired me to paint it."

The Dalai Lama had been standing, palms together at his heart, studying the painting. With childlike wonder he stepped closer, staring at the thick lashings of paint on canvas. Leaning into it, he breathed the scent of the oils – just as I had, on my first visit to the studio. His was a multisensory appreciation. An awed discovery and concentration which filled the room with joy.

"This is magnificent!" he turned to Christopher eventually. "Quite extraordinary!"

Tears welled up in Christopher's eyes. Could there be any greater acclaim?

"Pristine consciousness," His Holiness confirmed.

Swallowing, Christopher nodded.

"I have never seen it done like this before. Visually. It is wonderful!" he said chuckling. Christopher couldn't help chuckling too.

"Why did you say that I am the inspiration?" he inquired.

"Well," Christopher shot a glance to where I was sitting on the sill. "A lot because of your book." He retrieved the paperback from his pocket.

With a curious expression, the Dalai Lama held his hand out in request, his mala beads dangling from his arm.

It was Christopher's turn to be surprised, as he handed it over. His Holiness flicked through its pages, taking in how extremely well-worn it was, inspecting the highlighting and margin notes, evidence that this was the most studied of books.

As he paused on one page, taking in a particular sentence, Christopher couldn't resist quoting it: *"If you wish to realize the meaning that is beyond intellect, with nothing to be done, root out your limited awareness and settle starkly into pure awareness. Plunge into the waters of this pristine lucidity, unsullied by any stain of conceptual thinking."*

"Good, good," smiled the Dalai Lama. "You have memorized these quotes, yes?"

Christopher nodded.

His Holiness fanned through pages, allowing them to fall open on another highlighted sentence. "Page 288?" he queried, eyes twinkling.

"*Without holding the mind either too tightly or too loosely, we have it soar off into its clear light state with clarity and sharpness and then let it glide in a relaxed manner without exercising mindfulness or alertness in any extensive, frenetic way,*" he recited.

"Excellent! This is like examination, yes? Like you are taking your monastic qualifications." Mischievously, the Dalai Lama let the book fall open again. "Page 121?"

"A favorite," replied Christopher. "*Just as any mass of clouds that appears in the sky both originates from and dissolves back into the sky, likewise all appearances of anything that exists both originate from and dissolve back into subtlest clear light mind.*"

Expression turning serious, the Dalai Lama closed the book and respectfully returned it to Christopher. Then he gestured towards the painting, "I can understand how you came to do this."

"I hope you will accept it," confirmed Christopher.

His Holiness paused. "Namgyal Monastery is not a gallery, a museum with elaborate security" he said, concerned about what he evidently perceived to be the very great financial value of the painting. "But on behalf of us all, I accept with our heartfelt thanks. It will make, I think, a good welcome for our visitors." He brought his palms together.

"I can't tell you how happy this makes me. You see, Your Holiness, I am a dying man. I don't have long to live. Knowing that you are willing to receive my painting is very meaningful to me."

For a long while, as the Dalai Lama held his gaze, it felt as though we were all caught in a vortex of overwhelming compassion. An experience of the radiant clarity Christopher had already expressed, in this moment being imbued with transcendental bliss.

His Holiness was gesturing towards the pocket in which Christopher had returned the book. "You already know the true nature of reality. When your time comes, meditate on this. You can look forward with confidence to the dawning of the clear light of death."

Following his words intently, Christopher's expression turned to one of disquiet. After a pause, he could no longer contain his anguish. "But I can't meditate!" he exclaimed, as if the Dalai Lama had just ordered him to do the impossible. "I know the concepts, the theory," he was apologetic. "It's just that I can't *experience* them."

The Dalai Lama looked thoughtful for a long while, before turning back to the painting and studying it. "When you painted this," he asked Christopher, "what were you thinking?"

Christopher was unprepared for the question. "I ... I don't really ... It's not like ... How to put this ..." He struggled for expression, before eventually saying, "When I'm painting, it's not like I'm thinking. Not in the normal way. I'm only focused on what I am painting."

"You focus on the object?" asked His Holiness.

"Yes."

"You are not wondering what color? Which brush?"

"That becomes instinctive," said Christopher. "It's hard to put into words. I ... I just ... I lose myself to it."

"You lose your ... self?" The Dalai Lama smiled quietly.

Emotion tugged at Christopher's lips, as his understanding began to dawn.

"You become non-dual with the object?" queried His Holiness.

Christopher swallowed heavily as he nodded.

His Holiness was describing a state of deep, meditative concentration, in which one's focus is so complete that there is no longer any sense of a meditator perceiving an object of meditation. There is instead only a singular experience of the object. A non-dualistic absorption in which self and time fall away.

It was a while before the Dalai Lama added, "I would like to request a commission. Only I can't pay for it," he chuckled.

"Of course, Your Holiness."

"Amitabha Buddha. You know him?"

Christopher was nodding. "The red-colored Buddha?'"

"The Buddha of Infinite Light and Life," the Dalai Lama confirmed, before turning to murmur something to Oliver, who was still standing at the door. Oliver left the room on some kind of errand.

"I would like you to paint his portrait. Full size," His Holiness gestured towards Christopher's canvas, *Primordial Dawn*.

"It would be the honor of my life," Christopher was both surprised and, at the same time, strangely exalted.

When Oliver reappeared with a sandalwood wrist mala, the Dalai Lama held it between his clasped hands and blew a breath of blessing on it, before offering it to his visitor. "My gift to you," he said. "To recite the mantra of Amitabha. Let me give you the mantra."

Three times, His Holiness recited the mantra: "*Om Amitabha hrih.*"

Three times, Christopher repeated it after him.

This is the sacred transmission by which mantras are offered from guru to disciple and by which a bond is made which will always connect the two – not only to one another, but to all the practitioners who have come before and will arise in the future. An energetic portal is opened, not only to Buddha Amitabha, but to the entire lineage of Amitabha practitioners.

"Now you have the mantra," the Dalai Lama confirmed. "One of our Geshes here at Namgyal, Geshe Wangpo, has a class every Tuesday night. Next Tuesday he is teaching a special class. I highly recommend that you go."

"Of course."

From the sidelines, Oliver approached the two, signaling that the audience must come to an end. Christopher bowed in prostration, hands at his heart. "Thank you, thank you, Your Holiness. I don't feel so afraid."

The Dalai Lama reached out, taking Christopher's large, blotchy hands between his own and gazing directly at him. "You have nothing to fear from death," he said with conviction. "A pure land awaits you."

Leaning forward so that the Dalai Lama's forehead was touching his visitor's, the two of them were held together in silent communion for the longest time.

Christopher stifled a sob as he stepped back. As he turned to leave, His Holiness asked, "When you paint, you are not always alone?"

Christopher couldn't help once again glancing in my direction, as he shook his head.

"Sometimes, this one is with you?" His Holiness gestured towards me.

"You *are* clairvoyant," said Christopher, somewhat tearfully.

"Just a simple monk," the Dalai Lama chuckled. "When she comes home, I have noticed the smell of oil paint," he said. "Now I have discovered where the smell comes from."

It was Christopher's turn to chortle. "She *is* an inspiration," he said.

A short while later they left the room, Oliver closing the door on the way out. Christopher broke into a fit of severe coughing.

⁂

THAT NIGHT I LAY AT THE END OF HIS HOLINESS'S BLANKET, purring gently while he sat up in bed reading. It was always one of my favorite moments of the day, just the two of us in the soft glow of his bedroom, a place of safety, warmth and reflection.

Eventually, the Dalai Lama stopped reading, placed the book carefully on his bedside table and looked down at me, as he always did before turning out the light.

"I hear your check-up at the vet last week was useful," he spoke softly.

It was the first time he'd referred to the visit – not, I was certain, because it had slipped his mind, but because he knew that I needed time to absorb what had happened. And, as so often with His Holiness, although the words he used were simple, the idea he expressed was profound. And almost the opposite of what you might expect. But I had already found for myself that it was startlingly true.

At the time, I most certainly hadn't thought of the vet's pronouncements as "useful". Who wants to be told by a man in a white coat that you have far fewer days ahead of you than behind? That the quality of your life is in irreversible decline? That the life you take for granted dangles from the most tenuous of threads?

But as I had discovered through Christopher, the value of life depends far less on its length than by what you do with it. On whether you value each precious day which it is your privilege to witness, or take it for granted. On your capacity to make the very most of whatever abilities you have to give joy to others, without fear or discouragement. *That* is what makes the difference between a meaningful life and one which passes by in an unexamined blur.

"It is a precious gift to realize life's impermanence," continued His Holiness. "Not to avoid or pretend otherwise, but to truly value it. Every single day, even the foggy ones. Then we can live with zest. Like little kittens," he reached down to tickle my neck.

Grabbing his fingers with a paw, I bit them playfully.

"And when we die," he murmured, lying back, hand reaching for the light switch. "It is like this." In an instant, we were in complete darkness.

"If we have had a happy and useful life, well then, tomorrow when we wake up, we will find happiness and purpose too."

CHAPTER TWO

YOU KNOW WHAT IT'S LIKE, DEAR READER, WHEN YOU STRIVE valiantly to do the right thing – and the universe, far from rewarding your noble efforts, dumps a cartload of manure on you instead?

You do? Well then, you'll know exactly how I felt when I woke from my late morning nap to find His Holiness away at an all-day meeting, the Executive Assistants' office deserted, and the fog temporarily lifted.

In the spirit of making the most of every single day, I knew what I must do. It was weeks since I'd called at The Himalaya Book Café. A visit was well overdue.

The world felt bleak and unpromising as I headed across the courtyard flagstones, shiny with the wet. Even though there was no mist at the time, I was feeling rather pleased with myself to be braving the elements in the interests of extracting the utmost from each passing hour. But I was still determined to avoid my lustrous cream coat being flecked with grimy pavement water.

Usually, when crossing the courtyard, I received a certain kind of attention. All the Namgyal monks knew exactly who I was and, on seeing me, would bow their heads reverentially or even bring their hands to their hearts in prostration. Visiting tourists were almost as excited to see me as they were to catch a glimpse of the Dalai Lama. There would be the inevitable selfies and posing with cameras, and even video calls to loved ones around the world, to show off about their encounter with His Holiness's Cat.

This morning there were no monks, and only a huddle of damp tourists in the far distance. But then, from nowhere, a huge, orange sphere hurtled directly towards me. I had no choice but to jump. For a cat as wonky on her pins as I, a vertical take-off is no easy matter. And my attempt was bungled. I was flinging myself upwards with maximum force. Floundering, midair. Sprawling sideways and inelegantly to the ground – most disastrously of all, directly into a puddle formed by a missing flagstone. I made a painful landing, before scampering away to the sound of a young boy cackling with laughter.

"Check out that cat!" he called to a friend on the other side of me.

I heard the loud thwack of shoe-on-ball contact, before the soccer ball came sweeping past me – not so close this time.

"It's a cripple!" laughed the other.

"Disabled!" shouted the first as I neared the gate, hindquarters smarting from pain and distressed by their thoughtless cruelty. I desperately hoped that the boys would pay attention to something else. Slipping behind the protection offered by market stalls ranged about the gates of Namgyal Monastery, I felt safe only once out of sight behind a crumbling, concrete planter box.

I inspected the gray-brown sludge streaked down both sides of me. My stained tummy and bedraggled tail. I had taken on the rancid whiff of the street. And as I attempted a perfunctory clean, I was struck by a recognition I did my very best to avoid – but which could sometimes appear with all the sudden ferocity of a fast-moving orange soccer ball – that the reason why the monks and tourists treated me the way they did had nothing to do with me. Not personally. They held me in high esteem only because of the person with whom I shared my life. Remove me from my privileged windowsill, place me outside on a dreary monsoonal day, and what was I? A cripple. A disabled cat. A clownish, grime-smeared figure of fun. Successful though I may be at overlooking this unpleasant truth most of the time, once it loomed into consciousness, the reality of it was undeniable.

I continued on my way. For the vendors and their customers down the street, a passing cat or dog was of no special interest. A holy cow would attract more attention and certainly more kindness. It was only after a walk of some minutes that The Himalaya Book Café came into view. Its corner doors were wide open and there was the familiar bustle of patrons sitting at outside tables. It was every bit the inviting haven I'd become so delightfully familiar with over the years. Or, should I now say, decade?

While the decor of the café and bookstore had its own allure, it was the beings within who drew me to this special place. A warm welcome was always assured, whether from Franc, who had arrived from San Francisco in a cloud of Kouros cologne years before and created the café. Or from his French Bulldog Marcel and Lhasa Apso Kyi Kyi, who shared the basket under the reception counter. A basket which, dear reader, I was sometimes known to share. Sam, the bookstore manager, and the most affable of bibliophiles, had a soft spot for cats. And it didn't hurt that Head Waiter Kusali, who presided over the place with discreet omniscience, always ensured that select morsels from that day's *plat du jour* were served to me ahead of my afternoon siesta on the top shelf of the magazine rack.

An almost daily visitor to the café was my favorite – *everyone's* favorite – Serena. Daughter of His Holiness's VIP Chef, the effusive Mrs. Trinci, and a good friend of Franc. Two years earlier, Serena had given birth to her first child, a little boy she and Sid had named Rishi. Given my closeness to the family, I had initially been curious to engage with the small, pink creature shawled in its white blanket. But as weeks then months went by, it became grimly obvious that a warm companionship was never going to happen between the baby and me. Serena continued treating me with deep affection – but I'd learned to keep my distance from young Rishi.

Making my final approach to the entrance of the café, I hadn't quite reached the doors when, suddenly, I was picked up and placed on one of the outdoor tables.

"Look what the cat dragged in!" The English voice was loud and female.

"Heavens!" A man with salt and pepper hair, 80s-style teardrop sunglasses and bad breath bent down.

"What does the President of the Swansea and Aberystwyth Cat Fanciers' Association have to say about this … specimen?"

"One doesn't want to get too close," his tone was haughty.

"The stench!" the other laughed mirthlessly.

"Indeed." He was wearing a lime green jacket with broad lapels, a mustard-colored handkerchief flowering in its breast pocket.

"Persian class, obviously. What we call a Colorpoint Longhair, otherwise known as Himalayan. Short, thick body, heavily boned. Masses of fur." I was assailed by halitosis as he studied me. "Condition is hard to tell. The coat isn't too matted but …."

"The state of it!"

"Probably a stray."

I'd had enough! Even though I was several feet off the floor and landing would be painful, I wasn't hanging around a moment longer to be insulted by appalling humans. I walked to the edge of the table.

"Hello!" It was the smug voice of the woman again.

"Interesting." The man suddenly grasped me by the scruff, and was pinning me down to the table. My hindquarters stung.

I meowed in pain. For the second time this morning I was being tormented by complete strangers. Had the whole world gone completely mad?

"Weakness in the hind legs," the man ignored my protest. "Probably congenital."

"That's why it's on the streets."

"The thing is worthless," he declared, letting go of my neck. "In any civilized country it would have been euthanized." Picking up a copy of that day's *Times of India* he pressed it against my body, using it to push me brusquely off the table, like the unsightly remnants of the previous diner's leftovers.

I fell to the ground with a jarring crunch.

"It should at least have been sterilized," he pushed me further away from the table with his shoe. "So the genes die out."

It was at the moment of my greatest humiliation that I heard a new voice above me, young and urgent. "This cat is not rubbish!" It was a female voice, with a strong accent I later discovered to be Colombian. "She is a cat of great highness!"

Lifted swiftly from the ground with the reverence of a treasured icon, I was hurried through the café doors in the strong arms of my unknown rescuer. A beautiful young woman with long, dark hair gathered in a pony tail and the smoothest, gold-colored skin, the look in her expressive brown eyes was one of fiery indignation. She was taking me directly past the reception counter to the bookshop, and the table around which Franc and Sam were sitting.

"This one is being bullied!" she said, her dark eyes filled with anguish.

"By whom?" Franc's face turned to thunder.

"Those ones outside," she jerked her head towards the couple now sitting at the table. "They treat her like rubbish."

"Look at you, HHC!" Sam was stroking my face with concern. "Did you fall in a pothole?"

Kusali manifested from nowhere with a damp cloth and thick towel, which he laid out on the table.

"Thank you, Natalia, for saving her!" said Franc, as she placed me on the towel.

Franc summoned Kusali and the two men conferred, heads together, as they stared in the direction of my tormenters, agreeing on some course of action.

"How can people bully a defenseless cat?" Natalia was already setting to work, gently wiping the worst of the stains off my coat.

"I didn't know you'd met Rinpoche," said Sam.

"Mr. Franc tells me about the special visitor, and to look out for her." Natalia regarded me with a reverence that couldn't be further from the ridicule I'd been subjected to outside. For the first time, I noticed that she was wearing a charcoal and white striped apron, that seemed to confer some kind of official status. It wasn't a uniform I had seen in the café before.

After a while, when my coat was cleaner and drier, she said, "Now I go to help Ricardo." She pointed to a man of a similar complexion and attire, who was standing next to a new, stainless-steel contraption in a rarely used corner of the restaurant.

"We're looking forward to it," smiled Sam, glancing at his

watch. "The others should be here soon."

IT TURNED OUT THAT DURING THE RAINY WEEKS SINCE MY last visit, the elderly espresso machine Franc had bought when he'd first opened the café had finally given up the ghost. Since starting the business, a lot had changed in the world – including people's passion for coffee. Nearly all Western visitors to McLeod Ganj came from towns and cities where a daily fix of barista-made coffee had become the norm. Plenty of the locals were adopting the habit. Coffee bars and kiosks were opening up all over the place. Franc had increasingly felt that The Himalaya Book Café was lagging behind.

Without further ado, he had researched top-of-the-range coffee machines and bought a nearly-new Italian one from a liquidation sale. At Serena's suggestion he had reconfigured the restaurant, creating a wall hatch at one end of the veranda. Henceforth, The Himalaya Book Café was to become a purveyor of McLeod Ganj's finest coffees – dine in or takeaway.

Once he had the coffee machine, Franc's immediate challenge was to find someone to operate it, which was where the two new staff members came in. Backpacking through SouthEast Asia, Ricardo and Natalia, both twenty-somethings from Manizales in the coffee-growing region of Colombia, had trained and worked as baristas, first in Bogota and more recently in Barcelona. Having arrived in Dharamshala only the week before, within hours of seeing Franc's online job advertisement they had met. Following reference checks and a successful audition at a friend's restaurant across town, they were hired.

And it just so happened that this morning was to be the moment of truth; they were about to put the new coffee machine through its paces. Franc and Sam had already gathered for the occasion, when there was a flurry at the door marking the arrival of their Honorary Taster-in-Chief, Aficionado-of-all-things-Italian and my Number One Fan, Mrs. Trinci. A few steps behind her came Serena – and I was greatly relieved to see no stroller in sight.

Serena's mother made quite an entrance in a sweeping sea-blue dress, her dark hair coiffed to perfection. As always, she was wearing gold costume jewelry, half a dozen bracelets clashing noisily about her right arm, as she blew kisses to friends across the café. Flamboyant and operatic, she was a less volcanic version of her former self since taking up meditation, under the personal tuition of the Dalai Lama. But she was no less colorful.

In her wake Serena, elegant in her late thirties, lustrous dark hair flowing down past her shoulders, looked exactly as her name suggested, in perfect counterpoint to her Momma.

"Look at you all!" beamed Mrs. Trinci, arms open, taking in where we sat on two long sofas, as if we were the most delightful group she could have wished to encounter. After she and Serena kissed Franc and Sam on both cheeks in the Italian way, she gestured to where Ricardo and Natalia stood at the coffee machine. "Isn't this wonderful!"

When she caught sight of where I was, standing on a grubby towel, her mascara-lashed eyes instantly filled with anguish. "My little *tesorina*! What happened to The Most Beautiful Creature That Ever Lived?"

"A puddle, I expect," said Serena.

Franc looked as if he was about to offer a more detailed explanation, then evidently thought better of it.

"Oh, *dolce mio*!" Mrs. Trinci bent down, smothering my head and neck with kisses, before straightening and summoning a waiter with an urgent expression. "This little one has been greatly distressed," she declared. Along with a demand for her panacea for all ills, "Bring her a treat!"

Mrs. Trinci and Serena sat facing the two men as the waiter reappeared from the kitchen with a small portion of clotted cream. As the center of attention, I thought how very different things were from when I had been the subject of a very different kind of focus on the table outside. And from a few minutes before that, when I had endured casual ridicule in the courtyard of Namgyal Monastery.

Was I truly The Most Beautiful Creature That Ever Lived – or a worthless specimen? A disabled cripple or a cat of great highness? Was it possible to be all of these things at the same time – and if so, how?

The humans were amused by the way I lapped the clotted cream with noisy relish, and laughed at how some of it became smudged onto my gray nose. Which didn't trouble me – that was for later.

Realizing that something was going on, Marcel appeared from under the counter, hurrying up the steps and nudging Franc's leg to request his own treat. Franc produced one from his pocket.

"No Kyi Kyi?" queried Mrs. Trinci.

Getting up to deliver Kyi Kyi a tidbit in her basket, Franc was frowning when he returned. "I'm worried about Kyi Kyi," he said. "She hasn't been herself lately."

Around the table there were anxious expressions. Marcel and Kyi Kyi had enjoyed very good health for as long as anyone could remember. Part of the family, here at The Himalaya Book Café, their wellbeing had always been taken for granted.

"Off her food?" asked Serena.

"That," Franc gnawed his lip. "And she's somehow lost her sparkle."

Mrs. Trinci's face was etched with concern.

It was Serena who caught sight of Heidi, browsing in the bookstore. She waved over, beckoning her. "Come and join us!" she called, as Heidi approached. "We're about to try out The Himalaya Book Café's very first barista-made coffees!"

Heidi Schmidt had arrived in McLeod Ganj two years before when Ludo, founder of The Downward Dog School of Yoga, had returned from a vacation in Germany with his gorgeous niece in tow. The future of their yoga school was assured, the silvering warrior had told his students, because Heidi was a qualified yoga teacher too.

After eighteen months studying at various ashrams around India, Heidi had returned to help Ludo. Her own classes proved popular, drawing a younger, different group to complement Ludo's regulars. Her enthusiasm for new approaches to personal growth would have been enough to guarantee her a warm welcome. It was also the way she held her blue-eyed beauty and poise with such unfeigned modesty that drew people to her.

"I'm no expert on coffee," she confessed, as she approached the table where the six of us were gathered.

"Doesn't matter," insisted Serena.

"I don't want to gatecrash."

"We're inviting you!"

Mrs. Trinci was already patting the sofa next to her, indicating where she should sit.

"I'm not even dressed properly," she protested, looking down at her yoga singlet and leggings, having recently finished a class.

"You're beautiful!" said Mrs. Trinci.

"It's only us," commented Sam. "Your students."

"And friends," added Serena. A sentiment echoed by the others.

As I observed from the table, where I was giving my face a post-prandial wash, my feline instincts told me that Heidi wasn't simply being polite. There was more to it.

"Come on," gestured Franc. "Sit down. We could do with your German sensibilities. I want to make sure we get our product right for all visitors. Round this table we have America," he pointed to himself and Sam. "Italy," to Mrs. Trinci. He raised his eyebrows quizzically at Serena.

"Italy slash India by way of England," she gestured to herself.

"Deutschland?" he urged Heidi.

Heidi brushed back a fallen lock of hair, before sidling onto the sofa next to Mrs. Trinci.

Ricardo arrived a short while later, announcing that the coffee machine was now primed for action. Early thirties and with the same glistening dark eyes and shoulder-length hair as Natalia, something in his stubble beard and casual manner conveyed a Latin chic.

He rattled off a list of coffee options, including items I'd never heard of. Mrs. Trinci and Serena ordered espressos, while Sam opted for a flat white, Franc a long macchiato topped up, and Heidi, with apologies, a chai latte. Ricardo noted their orders, his eyes lingering for a moment on Heidi – the only one not to order a coffee.

After he'd gone, I settled between Serena and Mrs. Trinci, listening as the conversation turned to coffee. How tastes differed from one country or age group to another. How different countries in the "bean belt" around the world produced different flavors, according to their terroir.

Mrs. Trinci was passionate in advocating espresso. Serena argued that this was an acquired taste. Franc weighed in against the syrup sweeteners used so commonly in the USA. Whenever this gang got together, they talked over one another as old friends do, free from restraint.

At one point Franc turned to Heidi, who had so far been pretty quiet, and asked what she thought.

"I'm not much use to you. I'm sorry, I hardly ever drink coffee." No longer the commanding presence she usually assumed at the front of the yoga class; she stared down at the table, a different version of Heidi than we were used to.

"Avoiding stimulants?" queried Serena, also wanting to draw her into the conversation.

Heidi shrugged, "That's never worried me."

"More a tea drinker?" suggested Sam.

Heidi was shaking her head, "Not much."

"Neither one thing nor the other," Sam tried making light of it.

Franc, flashing a look of concern at Serena, gave Sam a discreet nudge. "Well, I'm glad you ordered the chai latte," he told her. "I expect we'll get plenty of orders for it, so we need to check it out too."

But Heidi wasn't thinking about the chai latte, evidently struck by what Sam had just said.

"That's exactly it," her lips quivered as she glanced at Sam. "At school, what I really wanted was to be a ballerina. I attended the academy," she glanced about the table, not looking at anyone in particular. "I also liked gymnastics and there was talk of me representing the club. I couldn't decide which to choose: the academy or the gym. The academy decided for me. When I wouldn't commit 100% to their rehearsal schedule, they kicked me out. I was disappointed. So miserable that my gym performance was affected." She leaned forward, hugging herself with both arms. "Then the club didn't pick me either. So I lost out both ways." She was looking back at Sam. "Like you said, neither one thing nor the other."

"But you went on to become the most amazing yoga teacher!" Serena was the first to counter this bleak narrative, as Sam shifted uncomfortably in his seat.

"'Did I really?" Heidi looked up at her with an anguished expression.

"Of course you did!" Serena said with conviction, accompanied by emphatic endorsements around the table.

Mrs. Trinci instinctively went into maternal mode, stroking Heidi's arm and murmuring, "Si, si."

"Why do you think your classes just keep getting bigger and bigger?" demanded Sam.

For his part, Franc declared, "You're the best thing that happened to Downward Dog."

If the others were startled by Heidi's unexpected confession of self-doubt – and judging by their expressions, they most certainly were – they were about to discover its apparent cause.

Shaking her head, after the longest of pauses Heidi responded to Franc quietly, "I don't know. I don't think Uncle Ludo thinks much of me."

"I'm sure he does!" rebutted Serena.

"Why wouldn't he?" Franc was surprised. "The studio has never been so popular."

"Because he's old school," said Heidi. "He'd rather have seven serious students than thirty 'dabblers'. My classes are for all comers."

"Just as well," said Sam. "Not everyone can dive through our own arms for vinyasas."

"But it's like you said," Heidi met his eyes again. "Neither one thing nor the other."

"I know where Ludo's coming from," said Franc. "He *is* old school. Discipline. Focus. Do the hard yards. And I can hear him using the word 'dabblers'!" He affected a mock-German accent. "But commitment doesn't happen overnight. A teacher needs to carry people with them. And that's what you do so well."

Heidi was unconvinced. "I came here with all kinds of ideas about what I could do. Like the sound therapy last week."

"It was wonderful!" Mrs. Trinci's eyelids fluttered.

"The first time she's ever stepped inside the studio," observed Serena.

"I haven't felt so relaxed in years!" Mrs. Trinci feigned a beatifically relaxed pose.

"I don't think Uncle Ludo was impressed. What was the physical or spiritual purpose?"

"That's being very purist," said Sam.

"But he has a point," countered Heidi. "When I think of all he's done with the studio, you know, I just don't feel worthy of him. I've always had this feeling that there's something wrong with me. Why I couldn't decide whether I wanted to be a ballerina or a gymnast. A yoga teacher or someone who should be running relaxation sessions. It's like this … constant theme. The reason I came to your shop today was to see if I could find a book that would help me stop feeling like such a mediocrity."

Across the table, Franc wasn't having any of it. "The idea you think that there's something wrong with you would be laughable if it wasn't so sad, Heidi. The truth is that you have everything right with you – except for one thing."

She looked at him questioningly.

"You lack self-acceptance." Franc spoke clearly, but his face glowed with compassion. "You have made up negative stories about yourself, like the ballerina or the gymnast, and repeated them so often that you've gone beyond thinking of them as just ideas. They have become facts about yourself. Truths."

She was gazing at him intently.

"Fortunately," his expression turned gently humorous, "you're in good company, because a lot of us have done the same thing." Responding to her expression of surprise he said, "Still do it. The conditioning's hard to get rid of."

Around the table, others were nodding.

"I had a father who told me from a young age that I'd never amount to anything," Franc confessed. "Meantime, my nuclear physicist big sister was the apple of Daddy's eye. For years and years, I also believed there must be something wrong with me. I must have had some basic defect, or why else was I such a low achiever, unworthy of my father's affection?"

Heidi looked startled.

"Me too!" Sam could hardly contain himself. "Remember how depressed I was when I first arrived? Day after day I'd sit over there," he gestured towards a window banquette. "I was made redundant from a book chain in the USA," he explained to Heidi. "I knew I was a hopeless geek. At school, my class-mates were brutal about it. So when I was fired from my job, I fled to India – only to discover that I had brought my inner geek with me. So then I was unemployed *and* living in a foreign country with no social connections."

"Who happened to find himself in the right place at exactly the right time, only he didn't recognize it." Franc's expression was wry. "This place used to be called Franc's Café. I'd always wanted to turn it into a book café, but I needed a specialist in Mind Body Spirit books. Which this one ..." he elbowed Sam, "just happened to be. But do you think he would take the job?" Franc was shaking his head with droll disapproval. "I had to practically force him to run the shop for me."

"He did," confirmed Sam.

"How did you do that?" asked Heidi.

"I took a leaf out of Geshe Wangpo's book. You know, the heavy-duty lama at Namgyal?" Pulling himself upright and adopting a stern demeanor, Franc struck the table with his fist as he mimicked, "Confidence is necessary. Much confidence! You can sit there reading *The Tibetan Book of Dying* all day, or you can open your own bookshop. What's it to be?"

"I felt like I was getting in completely over my head," said Sam. "I mean, I'd only ever been an assistant in a massive bookstore. Now, Franc's wanting me to manage the whole thing. Orders. Displays. Accounting."

"It's what I call 'The Shitty Committee'," said Serena.

The others turned, startled by the unexpected remark.

"You know, the voices inside you that say, 'No you can't!' 'You've never done it before!' 'You're not capable enough.' Like a circle of old crones saying, 'Nah! Nah! Nah!'"

The others were chuckling.

"We've all got them," agreed Franc.

"The Shitty Committee!" exclaimed Heidi. "I like this idea!"

"So what do you do about them?" asked Sam. "The Shitty Committee?"

"Tell them to butt out!" Serena was emphatic.

They all laughed.

"Pay attention to The Shitty Committee," Serena looked at Heidi, "and you'll never do anything. You'll never be good enough."

"Si, si!" Mrs. Trinci was itching to speak. "This is how I felt when I was asked to cook for His Holiness."

"Not you too?" reacted Franc, astonished.

"When you say 'not one thing or other'," she clutched Heidi's arm. "That was me. I was a caterer. Not a Michelin star chef. I didn't know anything about Tibetan food. I used to get so stressed out because of this Shitty Committee." As she said it in her strong Italian accent, the others started chuckling again.

"I felt like ..." she was glancing at Serena. "*Impostera*."

"Imposter," Serena translated for her.

"Like this. Imposter," she agreed.

"The imposter syndrome," chimed Franc. "Always half-expecting to be caught out."

Mrs. Trinci nodded. "I think this is why I had the heart attack."

For a few moments everyone round the table digested the stories they had just shared, with mutual recognition. I, too, might have shared how self-doubt could appear from out of nowhere, with the speed of a bright orange soccer ball. Or courtesy of a so-called expert with halitosis, declaring you to be a worthless specimen.

"It's the same for everyone?" Heidi checked, after a few moments.

"Pretty much," nodded Serena, before turning to Sam. "Which author talks about 'the trance of unworthiness'?"

"Tara Brach," he replied immediately, gesturing towards the book store. "Third shelf along. *Radical Acceptance*. We always keep a few copies. Tara Brach is a psychologist and Buddhist teacher. It's a great book. I remember she tells the story about this regal white tiger called Mohani ..."

My ears pricked up.

"... who lived for many years in a zoo cage that was twelve feet by twelve. Iron bars and a concrete floor. She constantly paced about her cramped quarters. Eventually, the staff managed to create a natural habitat for her that was several acres big with hills, trees, a pond and plenty of vegetation. But the really tragic part is that when she was released into it, she found a corner just twelve feet by twelve and paced around till it was worn bare of grass. She saw out the rest of her days in that tiny area, even though she could roam free."

There were sorrowful expressions around the table.

"Even when we're free, we limit ourselves by our own thinking," Serena mused. "*We* are the ones who hold ourselves back from fulfilment, even when we have freedom."

There was a pensive silence and some nodding around the table before Heidi asked, "So, how do we kick the habit?"

One by one, as everyone looked up, they turned towards Franc.

This was an interesting acknowledgement. In the early days of this establishment, as Café Franc, the owner and maître d' had been much too full of self-importance for anyone to consider asking him a question about Buddhism. With a golden Om dangling from one ear, countless blessing strings around his wrist, and an aura of general smugness, he had all the external trappings of the Dharma without any wisdom. This was the same man who, on my first meeting, had been about to hurl me out the door of the café, after I'd been pursued by his slavering beast Marcel.

How times had changed! Geshe Wangpo had overseen the personal transformation. The Franc of today showed no outward sign of being a Buddhist. But over the years, meditation and study had made him calm, kind and wise. The sort of person whose friends came to ask him questions like how to cultivate greater self-acceptance.

Franc looked around the table from one pair of eyes to another, making sure to include me. "There are two levels, I guess. At an ordinary, everyday level, when we get clear about the fact that we're beating up on ourselves, we have to ask: Why am I doing this? Why am I my own harshest critic? I wouldn't treat a good friend this way. Not even a stranger. So why am I being so ridiculously harsh on myself?

"Once we fully accept that we need to stop, that we're doing ourselves no favor, then we need to use mindfulness to guard our own mind. Like spying on our own thoughts the whole time, so that we can catch ourselves when we slip back into self-destructive thinking."

"That's the hard part," said Serena. "Shutting down The Shitty Committee. Even when you really want to."

"Mind training. Taking control of our mind. It's very much

like physical training – like yoga," nodded Franc, meeting Heidi's gaze. "Even when you know the exact outcome that you want, it takes time. You can't just decide *I want to do this*," he nodded at Sam, "like, dive through my arms in a gliding vinyasa and expect to be able to just do it. Just like training the body, mind training takes time. We must keep applying the practices, bit by bit, until we find we've moved on from where we were."

There was a pause while everyone digested this, before Heidi reminded him: "You said there are two levels?"

"Ah, yes!" Franc leaned back in his chair with a contemplative expression. "The conventional and the ultimate. What I was just talking about was the conventional level. Mind training."

"And the ultimate?"

"At an ultimate level," he smiled ruefully, "we have to ask: What exactly is this 'me' that I'm so despairing of? Where can I find him – or her? Why do I sometimes feel so great about me, and other times I'm convinced this 'I' is deeply flawed. How can I have such contradictory ideas about me, myself and I?"

He paused, allowing his questions to sink in.

"Don't know about you," he continued, "but even when I was at my lowest, I still sometimes had some good moments. Times when I felt pretty happy about myself. It wasn't all doom and gloom."

"Si, si!" agreed Mrs. Trinci, with an unexpected enthusiasm that broke the earnest tone. Everyone chuckled.

"It's true!" She grew suddenly larger and more voluble as

she was struck by a memory. "When the President of France said my crème brûlée was the very best he'd tasted east of the Bosphorus, why of course I felt special. Even though I was stressed to a frazzle!"

"And when I quoted that line from the Abhidharmakośa that even Geshe Wangpo was struggling to remember," confessed Sam. "That gave me a buzz."

"Exactly," said Franc. "Sometimes up. Sometimes down. Sometimes we feel good about ourselves. Other times, not so much. At an *ultimate* level," he looked back to Heidi, "this idea of a 'me' we obsess about, is nothing more than that – an idea." He shrugged. "A story I make up about myself. Which, by the way, is a story that can easily change depending on who I've just spent time with, how much I've had to drink, or any number of things. And it's quite a different idea from the one that other people have about me. So, why get hung up about a passing idea?"

Heidi's eyes widened as she considered this radical notion. "You're saying that *I* am only a temporary idea?" There was the trace of a smile about her face.

He nodded. "Ultimately," he nodded, "a mere concept."

"This is quite ..." she shook herself, as though having just emerged from a swimming pool.

"Liberating?" Franc responded with a smile. "Yes. When we stop taking ourselves so darned seriously the whole time. When we let go of endless introspection and focus on the here and now, we find much more to be happy about."

"Anyway," Sam was urging her, "don't believe in all that

negative stuff about not being one thing or another. Any quality can be portrayed in negative or positive ways."

"Such as being adaptable," suggested Serena, prompting a smile from Heidi. "Creative."

"Thinking outside the box," proposed Sam, as Heidi's smile got bigger.

"Breath of fresh air," Mrs. Trinci took Heidi's right hand between her own and squeezed it encouragingly.

"Willing to try new things," agreed Franc. "And how many people can really say that?"

Heidi looked round the table from one to another, meeting their eyes with an expression of gratitude. "You guys! What can I say? You're better than therapy!"

"Practice-based psychology. Isn't that how the Dalai Lama says it?" asked Mrs. Trinci.

Hearing his name, I offered a chirrup-like meow.

As they chuckled, Serena reached over to stroke me. "Just as HHC confirms."

"What I like," said Franc, "is how the Dharma can help us wherever we are on our journey. You don't have to be an elite practitioner like some of those up the hill," he gestured towards Namgyal Monastery. "Even ordinary people like us, we also need the tools for transformation."

Something in what he'd just said seemed to resonate very strongly with Heidi. For a long while she stared into the mid-distance, struck by what he had said.

RICARDO AND NATALIA WERE ARRIVING IN AN ANIMATED procession, Natalia carrying a tray laden with cups of various sizes in bright-eyed anticipation, halting by the table so that Ricardo could place each order in front of his customers with a somewhat nervous formality.

Silence descended for a while as they all took mindful sips, savoring their drinks with the inscrutability of a panel of TV judges.

Mrs. Trinci was the first to speak. "The beans?" she challenged Ricardo. "Robusta or Arabica?"

"I prefer Arabica," he said. "Lighter and fruitier."

"Quite right!" she confirmed. "*Bellissimo!*"

"Beautifully smooth," affirmed Serena, glancing at where Natalia was looking at Ricardo with pride. "For a moment I felt I was back in Firenze!"

"I wondered how much milk you were going to add," Franc nodded towards his coffee.

"Macchiato is 'stained' in Italian," replied Ricardo. "Just a dash."

"But you did something else?" he asked. "it seemed to take the edge off."

"Hot milk with a touch of foam for extra body."

"Well, you get my thumbs up!" Franc toasted.

"Mine too," said Sam, showing us his mug. "I noticed the motif."

"We all did!" agreed Mrs. Trinci.

The top of Sam's coffee had been etched with the silhouette of a mountain peak.

"Actually, that was Natalia!" said Ricardo, as she glowed beside him.

"Nice touch," Sam told her. "I think you've given us a logo! We've been wondering what to put on the awning above the hatch."

Heidi was the only one who hadn't said anything yet. All eyes turned to her.

"I'm used to it sweeter. Much sweeter," she said. "Back home it's syrupy. But this," she looked up, meeting his expectant eyes, "is like a different drink!"

"A lot of places base their chai on syrups," said Ricardo. "I like to control the sweetness, so I use my own spice recipe."

"It's lighter and somehow ... cleaner," Heidi was smiling.

"I use almond milk for chai." There was an earnestness about Ricardo's expression. "The drink is popular with vegans, which was what started me down that track."

He talked about his time in Barcelona. How he'd known people who'd come to study art and music who preferred chai. The tourists who chose it over coffee. It was a subject that seemed to captivate him.

Under the table, I noticed Natalia surreptitiously pressing her foot against his, signaling that they should leave.

"I also think almond milk goes better with the spices," he was continuing. "Especially with a milk frother. It gives the drink a brightness ..."

He would have continued but Natalia was prompting him again, this time more insistently, crunching her shoe down on his, all the while maintaining her smile. "We will leave you to enjoy," she said. "Or would you like to order another round?"

What was all that about, I wondered, being the only one able to see what was going on beneath the table as well as above it. Chai latte seemed a strange subject of fascination for a barista.

⬤

Leaving the humans to more tasting, I retired to my usual spot on the top shelf of the magazine rack. All the excitement of the morning had left me quite weary, and it wasn't long before I had relaxed into a late morning doze.

But my contented slumbers were interrupted in the most disagreeable way. An ominous shadow was suddenly looming over me. And the smell, more than anything, caused me to stir. Halitosis: an aroma as unpleasant as its recent association. The President of the Swansea and Aberystwyth Cat Fanciers' Association was leaning in my direction, his face just inches away.

"It'll make a wonderful photo for the next magazine!" The woman was standing nearby, ready to take a picture.

"A celebrity snap like this – straight to the front cover, I should say!" chuckled the man, discharging a fresh wave of bad breath in my direction.

"You'll need to wake her up," prompted the woman. "We want to see the eyes."

Reaching towards me, the President was about to prod, when Kusali swooped from nowhere, pushing the visitor's extended arm away forcefully.

"She is not to be touched!" His glaring eyes and regal demeanor made for an intimidating mix.

"What?" the man was taken by surprise.

Unperturbed, Kusali was standing directly between the camera and me. "Rinpoche is not to be touched," he repeated.

"How dare you!" The wife's indignation was instant. "Reg – tell him!"

The lime green jacket with the mustard-colored handkerchief quivered, as the man puffed out his chest. "Do you know who I am?"

"That's not …"

"*I* am the President …" he was pungently explosive, "of the Swansea and Aberystwyth Cat Fanciers' Association."

He could have been the President of the United States for all Kusali cared. The wrathful silence of the Head Waiter's presence seemed augmented by the visitor's foot stomping.

Kusali was pointing towards a discreet sign on the wall. A camera inside a red circle with a line crossed through it. It had been put there three years ago, after a group of overexcited Korean schoolchildren had disturbed my afternoon slumbers. And while the 'no photography' rule was rarely enforced, the sign was maintained especially for vexatious visitors like the President of the Swansea and Aberystwyth Cat Fanciers' Association. And his wife.

The two of them had no choice but to leave. Not that they did so without much self-important bluster, with threats to write to management, harsh ratings on travel apps, and how they'd tell anyone they met who cared to listen about the grievous way in which they had been treated.

I kept my eyes open only long enough to witness their affronted retreat from the café, sans photograph. Between the time of my inauspicious arrival and my afternoon nap, the visitors had evidently discovered my living arrangements. As a result, in the course of less than an hour, they had dramatically recalibrated my value from that of worthless stray, deserving nothing less than euthanasia, to highly desirable cover model.

"At an *ultimate* level," I recalled Franc saying, "We have to ask: What exactly is this 'me' that I'm so despairing of? Where can I find it? Why do I sometimes feel so great about it, while at other times I'm convinced this 'I' is deeply flawed. How can I have such contradictory ideas about me, myself and I?"

The same thing evidently applied to perceptions of others. The dramatic change of heart on the part of the President and his wife had nothing to do with me. *I* hadn't changed in the short time I'd been at The Himalaya Book Café – apart from being marginally less grime-smeared than before.

No, their different attitude was entirely because of a new idea they had about me. A mere thought. I was the same thick-bodied, heavily boned specimen with inferior genes that I had been before. My new-found charisma was coming from their minds alone.

And once it had taken hold, the charisma proved compelling. Outside the café door, they sat once again at a table – this time apparently in waiting. Like any other visitor, my arrival must inevitably be followed by a departure – or so seemed to be their logic. Their photo op inside the establishment had been thwarted. But wait till they had their hands on me after I emerged, without the protection of the intimidating Kusali!

Which was exactly why, when Serena and Mrs. Trinci left after the coffee tasting, full of warm commendations to Ricardo and Natalia, Kusali ensured that they took me with them. With Serena leading the way, Mrs. Trinci clutched me to her ample bosom, the two women walking directly across the road to Serena's four-wheel drive, a luxury European vehicle her husband Sid had bought, to ensure the safe passage of his new son, Rishi.

I was aware of two pairs of eyes following us from outside the café, with rising resentment. I made a mental note to steer clear of The Himalaya Book Café for a while. Most tourists came and went from Dharamshala within a few days. I had no wish to encounter those dreadful people again.

AS SERENA PUT THE CAR INTO GEAR AND SET OFF UP THE HILL, she was talking animatedly about something new she'd seen earlier that day, when visiting Namgyal Monastery to prepare for the Dalai Lama's next VIP lunch. It had been displayed on the wall of the main reception room. After a while, I realized that the object of her enthusiasm was none other than Christopher's painting, *Primordial Dawn*.

"You hear people talk about being drawn into a painting," Serena was telling her mother. "I've never really had that feeling until I saw this one. It's just amazing, the way you're kind of transported to a sensation of space and light and beauty. There's nothing actually there, no object, no focal point. It's more like entering a higher state, simply by looking at it."

"I will go and see," Mrs. Trinci assured her. "When I'm stocktaking tomorrow."

"Tenzin tells me that Christopher Ackland, who painted it, is in the nursing home."

"One of Marianne's?"

Serena nodded. "She turned a garden shed into a studio for him. I'm going to suggest Sid visits him. The walls of his new office are very bare. The place needs cheering up. A painting like that would be just the thing."

Mrs. Trinci considered this for a moment before saying, with a wistful tone, "The whole house would be cheered up if this little one started visiting again." As she stroked me, the bracelets on her arm clinked together.

I looked up at her pensive expression.

"My little *tesorina*, I do so wish that you and Rishi could be friends."

I wished so too, every bit as much as Mrs. Trinci. But if I had learned anything this morning, it was that there is no accounting for the ideas that other people have about you, because those ideas are a projection of their minds, not yours. Whatever they may consider you to be, good or bad, is an opinion over which you have very little control. Indeed, your opinion of your own self, which can vacillate wildly over the course of even a morning, is merely an idea. One as fleeting as a Himalayan breeze, and ultimately as impossible to pin down.

To reclaim the lightheartedness we take for granted when

we are very young, it seems we must let go of the blizzard of thoughts and elaborations that consume us. If we wish to recapture the playful openness of kittens, the less thinking we do about ourselves the better.

We may very well tug back the curtain on intriguing new vistas. Explore and discover and work things out. But for the rest, in our familiar, everyday routine, how much more delightful the world seems when the mind is free from agitation. How much greater our contentment when our focus is on what we perceive in this moment, instead of the voices in our heads – including the carping negativity of The Shitty Committee.

Here and now, in the warm comfort of the car, amid the reassuring clink of Mrs. Trinci's bracelets, the lightness of Serena's laughter and faint trace of her perfume, what more was needed? My contentment was complete.

A WEEK OR SO LATER, IN THE EXECUTIVE ASSISTANTS' OFFICE, Tenzin was going through that day's media coverage, when he burst out laughing. Which was unlike Tenzin. A muted chuckle was more his style.

Opposite, Oliver looked up.

Tenzin was shaking his head. "You've got to see this," he giggled.

Oliver had soon joined him at his computer screen. I blinked open my eyes to find both men looking from the screen to me.

"It's not HHC is it?" asked Tenzin.

"Nothing close," snorted Oliver. "And I don't think it's even McLeod Ganj!"

The article, from that day's UK media, was the front page of the Swansea and Aberystwyth Cat Fanciers' Association magazine. It featured a photograph of the odious President and his wife, kneeling next to a wall on which the Dalai Lama's Cat was sitting.

Only it wasn't me. Even I could see that from the top of the filing cabinet. The cat in the picture was a Persian of sorts, with blue eyes and luxuriant whiskers. There the resemblance ended.

"*The highlight of our visit to Dharamshala was a personal audience with His Holiness's Cat.*" Tenzin read the caption out loud. "You've reached a new level of celebrity, HHC!" He half-turned to me, "We now have people faking having met you."

Back at his desk, Oliver smiled and shook his head, "Such a curious thing to tell tales about."

"Meeting HHC?" confirmed Tenzin.

"Meeting any celebrity really," he shrugged. "As if a fleeting encounter with a famous being somehow makes you more attractive."

"This one obviously thinks it makes him more attractive." Tenzin glanced from his screen to my clear blue gaze. "What do you reckon, HHC?"

I wish I could admit to some deep insight. Alas, I was actually thinking that it was just as well computers didn't communicate odor. For if they did, dear reader, Tenzin and Oliver would be holding their noses right now.

Chapter Three

Clairvoyance. Telepathy. Magical powers. These are ideas that make one's ears prick up, are they not, dear reader? One's whiskers positively tingle!

Many are the pilgrims who make their way to Dharamshala, drawn by the stories they have heard about the mystical goings-on in Tibetan Buddhism. Is it really true, they wonder, that a red-robed yogi could know everything there is to know about them at a single glance? That such a person might possess *siddhis* or paranormal abilities, like speed walking, levitating or even moving through walls? That these are not simply mythical tales from the distant past, but present-day realities?

On the first-floor windowsill of His Holiness's room, I have had the good fortune to eavesdrop on all manner of conversations about exactly these subjects for quite some years. And to meet a number of the yogis and yoginis I have just described. I always make sure, of course, to leave a swatch of cream-colored fur on their garments to remind them of the great bliss they felt in my presence, when they return to whatever cave, monastery or mountainside *gompa* they came from.

If you think it is vain of me to suggest that I am a source of great bliss, allow me to correct you. The truth is that such a yogi or yogini experiences reality in a perpetual state of bliss. Cat or no cat. Cave or castle. Life's great vicissitudes are of little consequence to such beings for one simple reason: they have trained their minds to the point where their experience of reality is one of profound and enduring wellbeing. Whatever their apparent circumstances, the reality they perceive is that of abiding contentment. And if we are lucky enough to spend time in their presence, some of this perception may rub off on us too.

How is all this possible, you may be wondering? How are people capable of such exalted states – let alone defy the laws of science?

Lounging on the filing cabinet of the Executive Assistants' office one morning, I saw Oliver glance up from the passage he was translating from Tibetan into English. His blue eyes sparkled as he was struck by what he'd just read.

"*One of the core truths taught by Buddha,*" he quoted out loud, having confirmed that Tenzin was open to interruption, "*is that our minds don't simply perceive reality. They create it.*" I heard the quiver of excitement in his voice as he spoke. "I know I've been studying the Dharma for years and this is a core teaching. Even so," he was shaking his head, "sometimes

I am still struck by the most basic elements."

Opposite, Tenzin pushed back in his desk chair. "So simply expressed," he said.

"And yet so profound in meaning!"

"So contrary to our usual assumptions."

Oliver was nodding. "In theory, I have no doubt about the way that my mind creates my reality. When I meditate, it's like holding up a mirror to my inner world. All those preoccupations, mental patterns, recurring ideas. Watching them arise day after day, it's quite obvious how the things I think about, the way I think about them, and my whole idea of what's normal is coming from me. How I build my own world, my mandala, with my thoughts."

Tenzin was nodding.

"But as soon as I get up off my cushion and go outside, that's not how it seems at all. But like it says ..." he was reading again, "*Far from it being the case that there is an independent world out there that has nothing to do with us, and all that we living beings can do is to make the best of it, more accurately, our reality is utterly subjective. It is, in fact, a projection. So ...*" he paused for dramatic effect, to emphasize what he was about to say, "*what if we were to train our minds to project an altogether different reality?*"

Tenzin was nodding in agreement. And as he intertwined his fingers and stretched out towards his computer screen, from the top of the filing cabinet I caught a faint, antiseptic whiff.

"The logic makes perfect sense, doesn't it?"

"Mind training," confirmed Tenzin.

Oliver held his eyes for a moment, before looking pensive. "The problem with Western culture is that this kind of training is so foreign to us."

Tenzin pondered on this for a moment, before tilting his head. "Not *entirely* foreign," he said.

"How so?" queried Oliver.

"*Physical* training," prompted Tenzin.

"Oh yes," he agreed, with a rueful smile. "Our obsession with the physical."

"People will go to the greatest lengths to be the best cricketer. Football player. Olympic athlete."

"Dedicate their lives to it."

"Remember that fellow – the triathlon man?" Tenzin's face lit up with incredulity, as he recollected the meeting.

"Who slept in an oxygen-depleted capsule every night." The Ironman visitor had evidently made quite an impression on Oliver too.

"Got up at 3 am to ride his bicycle in a sauna," Tenzin chuckled while shaking his head. "The same time His Holiness rises to meditate. You have to be impressed by the determination. The singleminded focus."

"Westerners have been doing that for millennia," said Oliver. "Since the time of the first Olympic Games in 800 BC, we've been putting our elite physical performers quite literally on pedestals and decorating them with laurels, if they are able to run faster or jump higher."

"Meantime our lot have been bowing at the feet of elite mental performers," observed Tenzin. "And offering them garlands. *Rishis* and *maharishis*. *Sadhus* and *sadhvis*. Masters of consciousness who have reshaped their minds. *They* have been our traditional heroes."

Oliver looked contemplative for a while before musing, "I know which kind of development interests me more. When we die, we leave our bodies behind. Mind, being formless, continues."

Looking up at Tenzin he added, "What's more, the fruits of the contemplative life are quite fascinating."

"*Siddhis?*" suggested Tenzin. Then as Oliver nodded, "They have always had a strong hold on the Indian imagination. As much as great physical attainments have been revered in the West – like breaking the four-minute mile. Walking to the North Pole. Climbing Mount Everest."

"I only wish that people in the West understood that the great practitioners, the *siddhis* of the Buddhist tradition, are not born that way."

"You mean, they're more like the triathlon athletes of the East?" suggested Tenzin. "They focus on the goal of inner development, go into rigorous mind training and ..."

"Get the results they do," interjected Oliver. "In the West, if people believe abilities like clairvoyance and telepathy exist at all, they see them as gifts you are born with."

"Rather than the product of mind training?"

"Exactly. Few people understand that mind training is like physical training," continued Oliver. "Like going to the gym. The practices work. If you put in the hours under proper guidance, you get the results."

Tenzin was following him closely. "And as the mind settles, veils of obscuration fall away. Rather than active thoughts, we experience the true nature of mind."

"The *Divine Ground of Being*, as Aldous Huxley put it." Oliver glanced back at the pages he was working on. "*The more we become acquainted with such a mind, the more we project a very different reality. One that arises from oceanic wellbeing and interconnectedness.*"

From the top of the filing cabinet, I reached out my front paws with an indulgent quiver, before yawning.

Both men looked at me contemplatively.

"I sometimes wonder about the mind of this little one," said Oliver. "And other animals."

"Non-verbal," said Tenzin. "Less conceptual thinking than us."

"The very state we seek to attain when meditating."

"In which *siddhis* quite naturally arise."

"You think HHC is telepathic?" asked Oliver playfully.

Tenzin's eyes narrowed as he regarded me. "Remember when we had to take her for her check-up last month? How carefully we had to avoid the subject, until the very last moment?"

I certainly hadn't forgotten. How the two of them had been working with a particular intensity, apparently absorbed by whatever had been on their screens.

"I didn't doubt that if we'd so much as *thought* about going to the vet, she would have vanished," said Tenzin.

Oliver was nodding. "In my mind, I avoided the whole

subject of the cat carrier for that very reason."

"Whether it's telepathy or non-verbal communication, I don't know," shrugged Tenzin, after a pause. "But they pick up on things, cats."

Oliver looked up at me with the regard that was due to a *siddha* who was quite capable of mind-reading, albeit one who inhabited a fluffy coat. "They certainly do," he agreed.

THE ROAD BEYOND THE GATES OF NAMGYAL MONASTERY WENT, in one direction, down the hill to The Himalaya Book Café and, in the other, past the garden with the lone cedar tree overlooked by the nursing home. Further along that same road was one of my favorite places to visit, where the environs became more suburban. It was a beautiful home at the end of a curved driveway, both distinctive in appearance and filled with the nooks and crannies that we cats love to explore.

Number 21 Tara Crescent was the family home of Serena, Sid – short for Siddhartha – and their two-year-old, Rishi. Sid's daughter Zahra from a previous marriage, with whom I'd shared the closest connection from the first time we'd met, was currently far away studying psychology at Oxford University.

I had been around since the beginning of Serena and Sid's life together. Witnessed the two of them at the same classes at The Downward Dog School of Yoga. Watched their courtship unfold from the gatepost of Sid's former home at 108 Bougainvillea Street, a grand but somewhat institutional building not far from the yoga studio. Serena's astonishment that the quiet and handsome man she'd found herself drawn to was no less than the Maharajah of Himachal Pradesh – something he had done his utmost to conceal, being discreet by nature. Sid's anxiety about how Zahra would feel towards Serena – her mother having died in a tragic car accident years before. Serena's struggle to conceive after they married and her worries that, in her late thirties, she may have left it too late.

Through all the dramas they had been supported not only by the Dalai Lama, who Serena had known since she was a little girl playing in the kitchen downstairs, but by another more ongoing presence.

Yogi Tarchin wasn't a monk, but he was revered as a meditator, *siddha* and inspiring teacher. Rinpoche, as he was generally known – a Tibetan title meaning "precious one" – had the warmest brown eyes and an ageless face, his gray moustache and goatee giving him the appearance of the quintessential sage. More than anything, the first thing you noticed about Yogi Tarchin was a radiant sense of lightness. Of joy. He conveyed the indefinable but powerful sensation that, even though he was as much flesh and blood as any other being, in another way he was hardly there at all.

Sid and Serena had maintained the Trinci family tradition of sponsoring Yogi Tarchin when he went on retreats. And I'd heard Serena telling Mrs. Trinci that he'd just returned from a threemonth retreat in a mountain cave. They had been thrilled when he'd accepted their invitation to stay in the guest cottage they'd built in their garden, to accommodate long-term visitors.

Welcome to join them in the main house whenever he

liked, Serena said his visits so far had been fleeting and arbitrary. Only after some days had gone by would they come to recognize a particular purpose behind these apparently random appearances. For my own part, I was most eager to be in his presence again – it was at least a year since we'd last met.

From the end of the driveway, Sid and Serena's home looked as inviting as ever. A raised, rambling bungalow with white walls and a spacious, wrap-around veranda, its most distinctive feature was a crenellated tower that rose up two stories, shrouded with ivy. Near its top was a room with wide picture windows on all four sides. I had sat in that viewing chamber on countless occasions, taking in the spectacular vistas and communing with the sun, the moon and the ice-peaked Himalayas ranged far above and behind the house.

I padded towards the house, past the established garden of terraced lawns leading to pine forests and beds of bougainvillea, bursting with crimson and purple flowers. I had watched their home evolve since Sid had first bought it. The addition of the bedroom wing. The guest cottage. Most recently, another extension with a separate entrance, where Sid had established his office. There was always some slight modification happening – just the thing to entertain feline curiosity – and the house had become like a starfish with three arms meeting at the center.

Up the stone steps I went, pausing to sniff at some astringent, vegetative matter a visitor had brought on the soles of their shoes. Through the open French doors and across a wide, handwoven carpet of elaborate design, in the direction of voices.

They were seated about the dining room table for what seemed like a business meeting. Six people in dark formal attire, including Sid at the head. With his back towards me, in a loose burgundy shirt, ochre pants and sandalled feet, Rinpoche occupied a chair further down the table, although in his unique way he seemed to inhabit an altogether separate reality.

Was this one of his apparently random visits, I wondered, or had he been invited by Sid? I had hoped to find him alone, perhaps in his cottage, able to enjoy the ethereal lightness of his being. As I sat in the entrance, watching the proceedings, it seemed odd to find him here in this gathering. The others around the table, four men and two women, were discussing manufacturing and distribution challenges with some solemnity.

After a while it became clear that they were the directors of the spice pack organization, which Serena had established years earlier with Sid's support. It had started out as a small-scale operation, where tourists returning home from Dharamshala would order pre-packed spice combinations, so they could prepare meals like those they'd enjoyed at The Himalaya Book Café. Profits from the operation were used to train unemployed youngsters from the local community in IT skills, to help them get jobs.

In the early days, Serena had managed everything. Profits had been used to buy computers. Sam delivered the IT training free of charge. But the charity had become so successful, it now employed twenty full-time staff, dealing with major spice producers in India and distributors throughout the world.

Hundreds of teenagers benefited each year – and as each year passed, the charity received dramatically increased numbers of pleas for help.

Around the table as the directors wrestled with the challenges they faced, Yogi Tarchin dropped his hand down the side of his chair and beckoned me with his fingers. He hadn't had to turn around to know of my arrival. He had sensed it.

I needed no further encouragement. Making my way to where he was sitting, I rubbed up against his extended hands and felt his fingertips run through my coat and curl their way up my raised tail. He didn't need to look down – nor I up – to communicate our mutual delight at being in each other's presence once again. Such a gesture would have been superfluous.

Weaving through his legs, headbutting his shins and purring with contentment, after greeting him I circled the table to an upholstered bench that ran the length of the wall opposite, and hopped up to better view the proceedings – as well as Yogi Tarchin himself. Beside me was a polished occasional table, loaded with silver-framed photographs of family highlights.

My arrival went apparently unnoticed by everyone round the table, except for Yogi Tarchin. Unused to being ignored in this household – albeit by mere visitors – I tested the extent of their preoccupation by launching into a vigorous grooming session. First by washing my ears and face while in a seated posture. Then lying down to give the fluffy expanse of my belly a good going-over. Still receiving no acknowledgement of any kind, I rearranged myself, as if on a yoga mat, to perform a very particular asana, one rear paw extended vertically, the other horizontal on the seat, the better to access an intimate part of my anatomy for that most delicate of ablutions – playing the cello. My efforts were to no avail, dear reader. Sid glanced over briefly, his face distracted. Yogi Tarchin was visibly amused. No-one else even seemed to notice.

Tired after the walk and grooming, and bored by the conversation about digital metrics, I settled down, looking past those gathered round the table to where Yogi Tarchin was observing the proceedings. His presence was so subtle that everyone else in the room seemed to have forgotten he was there.

I WOKE TO THE SOUND OF RAISED VOICES AS THE DIRECTORS bade their chairman farewell. Sid was at the door, seeing them off, before returning to the table. Although he was trying to conceal it, this afternoon's meeting had left him burdened.

Sid was a tall, elegant man, quite unselfconsciously regal in bearing. But right now his face looked drawn, his shoulders hunched.

"That was a particularly tedious meeting. I'm sorry you had to witness it," he said, dropping heavily into the chair he had occupied, at the head of the table.

"I came uninvited," Yogi Tarchin responded, his tone as free as Sid's sounded weighed down.

"Any observations?" Sid looked over to him. Although it seemed unlikely that someone who had recently returned from a three-month solitary meditation retreat would have much to say about complicated commercial details, Sid knew far better than to underestimate Yogi Tarchin.

And as was so often the case, Rinpoche's response came from an unexpected direction. "Just one question," he said.

"Yes?"

"Why are you doing this?"

"You mean, chairing the business?" Sid was taken aback.

Rinpoche shrugged, "Any of it?"

"Well it … it was Serena's idea to begin with. Raising funds to help get kids job ready. Improving their prospects, at the same time as creating distribution channels …"

"Very meritorious," interjected Rinpoche.

Sid paused, considering the question more deeply before replying again. "Serena and I both feel it's part of our Dharma practice."

Rinpoche's eyes glinted.

"The perfection of generosity," Sid explained.

"And you are helping many people. The kids. Their families. Those in countries far away. No question." There was a "but" in Yogi Tarchin's tone. A qualification he had yet to express.

Sid was following him closely.

"The purpose of the Dharma is mind transformation, yes?"

"Of course."

"And it seems that this has become a business much like the others you run, of which there are many."

"Since Rishi was born, I've taken over Serena's responsibilities."

"I understand," Yogi Tarchin regarded him warmly. "If it's

transformation we seek, the feeling of giving must be authentic. It must touch our heart." He raised his left palm to his chest and held it there.

Sid pondered this for a long while before asking evenly, "You're saying we should let go of the charity? Allow others to take it forward?"

"What I'm saying is that the perfection of generosity doesn't depend on helping thousands of people. Or even hundreds. It's not about changing the world," Yogi Tarchin's gaze was luminescent. "But changing our hearts. Empowering our loving kindness, our *bodhicitta*, until the point that it becomes spontaneous and heartfelt."

As Sid pondered this, the heaviness of whatever he'd felt burdened down by seemed to lift. Rinpoche's reminder of key principles was having a liberating effect. "Perhaps the whole reason we began this has somehow been left behind," he said.

"To be authentic, to create real change, it helps to cultivate kindness among those with whom we already have a karmic connection, a special bond," said Rinpoche. As he did, he moved his gaze from Sid's eyes to the table next to where I was seated, the one with the photographs in their silver frames. His focus settled on one photo in particular, near the back of the table. A picture of Sid and another man dressed in finery, in front of an arched doorway. Between them what appeared to be a beautiful, bejeweled princess – or was it his bride?

Contemplating what Rinpoche had just said, Sid wasn't following his teacher's gaze. He wasn't even looking at Rinpoche's face, but somewhere else, far away.

Rinpoche tried again.

"Once we can cultivate a heartfelt wish for the wellbeing of people with whom we already enjoy bonds of loving kindness," he gestured directly at the photograph, "it becomes much easier to widen the circle of our benevolence in a genuine way."

Rinpoche was making it as obvious as possible. Short of coming around the table, picking up the photograph and handing it to Sid, or saying the names of the people in it out loud, his message couldn't have been clearer.

But Sid looked only briefly at the table where Rinpoche was pointing, before his gaze fell away into the mid-distance again.

Yogi Tarchin's expression came the closest I could imagine to a look of frustration. I held his eyes intently, before blinking slowly. He understood. I would get this.

Moments later, he was standing and bringing his hands together at his heart.

Sid was immediately on his feet, reciprocating the gesture, surprised by how abruptly his teacher was leaving the room. But what reason was there to stay? He had delivered his message, although Sid had only partly understood it.

FOR A WHILE AFTER HE LEFT, SID SAT BACK IN HIS CHAIR, DEEP in contemplation. Then as he was gathering together various documents tabled at the meeting, there came the sound of footsteps and wheels on the veranda and, moments later, Serena appeared pushing the stroller.

Rishi caught sight of his father and waved his arms, gurgling happily, in the same instant that Serena caught sight of me.

"Oh, I see," she nodded towards me, sharply turning the pram so that it faced the other way.

Already standing, I was about to hop from the bench.

"No, no. Stay!" she commanded, calling out for Maria, Rishi's nanny, as she guided the stroller to the other side of the room.

Returning a few moments later, minus the stroller, she was relieved to see me still there.

"Close call," she leaned down to kiss Sid. In a sky-blue dress and with an uplifting citrus fragrance, she was as warm and vivacious as ever. "He didn't see her," she continued, as they both looked at me. "And since she hardly visits anymore, I didn't want to frighten her off."

Sid was nodding. "We actually had two Rinpoches at the meeting," he said.

"Really?" Swinging her purse off her shoulder, she put it on the table, pulled out a chair and sat next to him. "How did it go?"

"We worked through the agenda," Sid's tone was even. "The usual. Demand outstrips supply."

Serena was nodding.

"The most interesting point of the afternoon was the least expected. From Rinpoche. The other one."

Serena looked curious.

"After everyone left, he asked why we, actually *I*, am doing this."

Serena's brow furrowed. "Chairing the organization?"

"Any of it," said Sid. "To begin with, I told him about getting the kids job ready, while promoting local spice producers. But he wanted the deeper reason. So I told him it was part of our Dharma practice."

"Generosity," agreed Serena.

"Yes, which was when he came out with his comment that the perfection of generosity doesn't mean we have to affect thousands of people, or even hundreds. We don't have to save the world."

He held Serena's eyes with an expression of significance. "What he was saying was that the perfection of generosity is about personal transformation. And the best place to start is among those to whom we already feel close. With whom we have a karmic connection. We begin with them, cultivating our loving kindness, and then work to transfer that same feeling to people we don't know so well."

My moment had come. An opportunity to communicate the message Rinpoche had already attempted. With a good deal less subtlety than the other Rinpoche, I got up and performed a brief sun salutation.

Serena was nodding. "This is the same advice Lama Tsong Khapa gave on practicing *tonglen*. The importance of authentic feeling."

"That's what he was saying."

They both looked over to where I stepped further along the banquette, then sniffed the occasional table which was pungent with wood polish, before hopping up onto it. As they watched in silence, I stepped among the framed photos with all my feline sensibilities, taking care not to disturb a single one. Except for the photograph to which Yogi Tarchin had so unmistakably attempted to draw Sid's attention. That one I made sure to flip, so that it fell with a clatter on the highly waxed surface.

Then I hopped off the table and onto the carpet.

Serena was immediately coming round the table. "Rinpoche, that´ s not the sort of place I'd expect you to go!" she exclaimed.

Indeed! Nor was it.

"I wonder what …" she mused aloud. Then as she reached the table, noticing which picture had fallen, she picked it up and gestured with it.

"You at Arhaan and Binita's wedding," she said.

Sid was following her curiously.

"Which reminds me – I keep meaning to ask you, but always forget. Have you heard what's happened to Binita?"

Sid shook his head, "Arhaan's funeral was the last time …"

"There's been some kind of financial shock. Just like you predicted." Serena's face was portentous.

Sid lowered his gaze to look solemnly at the carpet.

"Binita and the girls have lost the house. They're living in some horrible dump in Delhi."

"Where did you hear this?" asked Sid after a while, gaze still fixed on the floor.

"Emily Cartwright."

"She and Binita went to the same school."

Serena was returning the picture on the table. "She hasn't been in touch?"

Sid shook his head. "Maybe that's who Yogi Tarchin meant."

"If he knew what Arhaan had been saying about you …" Serena was shaking her head reproachfully.

"This is Rinpoche," Sid met her eyes. "Of course he knows. And," as he recollected the conversation, "he did seem to be gesturing towards the table, but I wasn't following that closely. I was trying to figure out what he meant."

I walked towards the open door.

"Rinpoche!" Serena called after me.

I turned, fixing her with my sapphire stare.

"Won't you stay for a treat?"

Usually I was open to edible inducements of all kinds. But this afternoon I had already made the reconnection with Yogi Tarchin that I had wanted. And undertaken my unexpected assignment.

Turning back to the veranda, I ventured into the late Himalayan afternoon, taking in the scent of pine blowing from the nearby forest. Twilight shimmering through the warm monsoonal mists. My work today was done.

ONE OF MY FAVORITE TIMES OF DAY IS LATE IN THE AFTER-noon, when Tenzin and Oliver arrive in His Holiness's office. Their purpose is simple: to review where things are at and to prepare for the day to come. The kind of meeting that happens,

I imagine, in a million other places around the world. But it's the *way* they come together that draws me to them, and why I usually get off my windowsill and hop up on the chair next to the Dalai Lama.

The three men share a genuine appreciation for each other, mutual supporters in a heartfelt cause. More than that, the openness they share has a benevolent quality to it, a spontaneity so that even though they have had a thousand such meetings in the past, every time they gather there is the sense of fresh possibilities.

That afternoon as usual, Tenzin arrived with a tray of green tea. Oliver was carrying the thick manuscript he had been translating. Having updated one another on the day's events and discussed plans for the rest of the week, the Dalai Lama sat back in his chair and glanced from Oliver's face, fair-haired, blue-eyed and humorous, to Tenzin's Tibetan features, perceptive, kindly, his short-cut hair graying at the temples.

"And what about you?" he asked the two of them, with heartfelt regard. "You have had some useful discussions, yes?"

As was sometimes the case with His Holiness, it was unclear whether this was a general inquiry or if he was merely prompting them to express what he already sensed.

Oliver, being less reserved by nature, was the first to respond. "Tenzin made an excellent point this morning about mind training, which could be helpful with certain audiences," he said, touching the manuscript. "I was reading him some of this earlier, when he commented that even though training the mind may be a foreign concept for many, training the body is something we Westerners take for granted."

His Holiness immediately began to chuckle. "Remember in Washington DC," he gestured to Tenzin. "Opening the hotel curtains first thing in the morning. There's this," he imitated a jogging motion. "Every few seconds, another one or two running past the hotel."

"All day long!" Tenzin shared the humor.

"Even 8 pm. 9 pm. 10 pm. Like this!" The Dalai Lama was pretending to run again. "Constant training. Day and night. Training the body. Same in Los Angeles. Sydney too."

"In the East, the traditional heroes are those who train their minds," offered Tenzin. "In the West, it's those who train their bodies. Olympic athletes. Sports stars."

His Holiness pondered this for a while before nodding. "True," he intoned, in that warm baritone of his. "But even ordinary people who will never be a sports star, or an Olympic athlete. However, even they understand the value of training the body – to better deal with whatever happens physically. To keep in good shape. What about training the mind – to better deal with whatever happens mentally? For emotional wellbeing. There is not so much understanding of this."

"And as a result," continued Oliver, "less understanding about the natural qualities of the mind. The things we are all capable of doing, but need to train if we wish to experience."

The Dalai Lama nodded. "The Buddha gave a discourse on the fruits of the contemplative life in the *Samaññaphala Sutta*. The higher fruits, insight and supranormal powers. He explained it in detail."

"In the West, if people do believe in clairvoyance or mind-reading at all, they think these are abilities you either have or you don't."

His Holiness shrugged. "They arise quite naturally from a quieter mind. With too much coarse conceptual thinking, there is no room to notice subtle phenomena."

Beside him, I was recollecting that afternoon at Sid's dining room table. How Yogi Tarchin had tried to draw Sid's attention to the photograph of Arhaan and Binita in a way that seemed obvious. How Sid, deep in thought, had missed the cue. We are beyond being helped, even by other more realized beings, unless we are in a receptive mental state.

"Without cultivating some level of mental quiescence, it's hard to cognise what is right in front of us – just as we can't see in a snowstorm," continued the Dalai Lama. "But with some level of training the true conventional nature of mind becomes apparent. Its luminescent clarity. The feeling of abiding peace within."

"The mind of clear knowing," confirmed Oliver. "The *tathagatagarbha*?"

His Holiness nodded, smiling. "To me, it is wonderful that we can all make this discovery for ourselves. How we are all the possessors of this pristine mind."

As he spoke, the Dalai Lama was also communicating what he was saying at a more subtle level. Inviting us to share in his own experience of consciousness. And although we were still three humans and a cat sitting in a room together, in a different way we shared in the dawning of a different reality, one which quickly gave way to a feeling of boundless tranquility. The knowledge that our usual preoccupations, habits of thought or concerns were like mere froth on the ocean surface. At a deeper level, the consciousness we all shared was the same: radiant, boundless and utterly blissful.

"At an ultimate level, all of us *semchens* have Buddha nature."

In that delightful glow of energy, it was hard to know if His Holiness was saying the words out loud, or speaking directly to our hearts. "It is unborn, because it has no beginning. And unceasing, because it can never be destroyed. Our purpose is to realize it. To actualize our ultimate nature as beings of pure great love and pure great compassion."

Chapter Four

It may strike at any moment and through any of our senses. The glimpse of an object maybe, or a particular view that halts us in our tracks for reasons we don't fully understand. The waft of a fragrance that instantly transports us to an earlier time and place, with an emotional heft that catches us unawares.

In my own case, it was sound.

For the past two weeks workmen had occupied the First Aid Room, further along the corridor and on the other side from the Executive Assistant's office. It was a room I had been familiar with since my earliest days at Namgyal. Small, white and clinical, equipped with a bed, two upright chairs, and a large cupboard filled with medical supplies. Because it was so rarely used, Tenzin sometimes went there to eat his sandwich lunch, while listening to the BBC World Service. We had spent many restful and educational hours thus engaged, there being nothing more delightful to a cat than a slight change of scene, while remaining on familiar ground.

More recently, I'd steered well clear of the gruff voices and sturdy boots of workmen coming and going – their visits accompanied by much banging and reverberations along the passage.

But one morning I emerged from His Holiness's quarters to find that they had gone. Calm had once again returned to our floor. It was as I approached the First Aid Room door, to sniff whatever new and intriguing scents may be present, that I heard it. And instantly had to get closer.

I clawed at the door and meowed loudly. Moments later, the sound of a key being turned in a lock and the door drawn ajar.

"HHC!" Oliver's face loomed above me. Without glasses.

Requiring no invitation, I was already making my way inside around his bare ankles.

The sound was much louder here – and utterly delightful.

Oliver locked the door behind us.

Since I'd last visited, the First Aid Room had more than doubled in size, a door in the wall leading into a new chamber occupied by a modern handbasin, toilet and – the source of my unexpected joy – a shower. Removing the towel from around his waist, Oliver stepped inside the cubicle. I headed to the mat directly beside the frosted panel and gazed up, transfixed.

Running water of all kinds is a source of unceasing fascination for we cats. But it was the way that particular water ran that was both mesmerizing and unexpectedly reminiscent of a much earlier time. A time before I was rescued by the Dalai Lama, and even prior to my being on the streets of New Delhi. A dimension of which I was unaware I had any knowledge, any recollection, having been so very young at the time. This was, after all, long before my siblings and I had been stolen from our home by two urchins looking to make a fast rupee.

Could it be that, without knowing, I had been carrying with me the imprint of a running shower, from my very first weeks as a kitten? Had I been born to a home where I had been exposed to the delightful gush of flowing water? Or was this sound an evocation to the feline collective subconscious, as might be proposed by the good Dr. Jung?

Something certainly triggered in my mind that morning. Some wonderful and inexplicable cognitive lurch I'd never experienced, which made me feel connected to a different reality, that had evidently been there but never suspected, a mere turn of a faucet away.

As the water fell, Oliver hummed. It seemed to be shifting his mood too. It wasn't just the constant rain of water, but the delightful trickle made by rivulets down the tiles and frosted panes. The flow as water swirled into the drain. The dreamy dance of *prana*.

I sat enthralled, all the time he was in the shower. And the moment he stepped out, I stepped in. He didn't say anything, but watched as I sniffed the tiles and lapped at small puddles, happy to feel the wet on the pads of my feet and the fur of my tail. While he toweled himself dry and changed into his robes,

I paused contemplatively in this new and pristine sanctum, reveling in having discovered it in my own home.

"You approve, HHC?" asked Oliver after a while, his question entirely rhetorical. Although I was familiar with His Holiness's bathroom, it was occupied by a bath – a different object entirely and one in which I had no special interest.

Dressed in his robes and wiping down the basin and other surfaces so that they bore no sign of his having been here, Oliver said, "You'll be pleased to know that showers are to be a regular thing. I have permission to have one whenever I cycle to work. Like today."

He looked down, meeting my gaze. "This needs to go," he patted his tummy.

I sidled up to his legs, curling my tail around them.

"A lot more cycling, I expect," he said, his blue eyes thoughtful behind his spectacles.

LATER THAT WEEK, I PAID A VISIT TO THE HIMALAYA BOOK Café. With the worst of the monsoon weather in retreat, and the coast well and truly clear of so-called cat fanciers, I made my way unhindered across the courtyard, out the gates, and down the road to the café. In addition to lunch service being in full swing, a short line had formed outside the new coffee hutch. By the look of things, Natalia and Ricardo were in full swing too.

On my way to the magazine rack, I passed the two dogs dozing in their basket under the reception counter. As I paused,

Marcel got to his feet as always, all the better to sniff me. Kyi Kyi, a gentler soul with whom I shared the bond of being a rescue pet, usually came up to me, wagging warmly. This morning, however, she stayed where she was, snout buried in the blanket, her only acknowledgement of my arrival was a brief opening of her eyes.

Seeing the two dogs comfortably snuggled and doted on by all the café regulars, it would have been easy to assume that the French Bulldog and Lhasa Apso had always led the most pampered of lives. However, in the case of Kyi Kyi this was far from true.

I still vividly remember the day I had arrived in the Executive Assistants' office to find her in a wicker basket next to the radiator. I had been instantly jealous to discover an interloper in this inner sanctum and a dog what's more – albeit an unusually skinny one, whose coat was in very poor condition. Indignation was followed by a certain remorse, when I heard what brought her here. Her owners, a family in Dharamshala, had moved away, leaving her in the kitchen of their former home. Her pitiful night-time whimpering had alerted a neighbor to her fate. After two nights, he'd broken into the house to discover her at the end of a heavy chain without food or water, almost dead.

Poor Kyi Kyi had suffered greatly at the beginning of her life. It was only thanks to Chogyal, one of His Holiness's Executive Assistants at that time, who knew both the neighbor who had rescued her, as well as Franc, her willing adopter, that she'd come to enjoy her current circumstances.

Now she was suffering again. I paused for a moment, wishing I had the same power as the Dalai Lama, the ability to communicate what so many beings sensed in his presence, that boundless and abiding experience of wellbeing. I regarded her closely, blinking slowly. Her tail twitched once as she held my gaze. Then she shoved her snout further into the blanket, closing her eyes again. As Marcel and I watched, no language was needed to explain what was happening. We both knew.

From the magazine rack that afternoon I observed the usual bustle of the café – a deliberately East-West hybrid of white tablecloths and cane chairs, the walls bedecked with embroidered Tibetan wall-hangings or *thangkas*. Tourists would discover this tranquil haven, away from the hyperstimulation of India, and sink gratefully into their chairs to order food and wine, unwinding in an environment that, while exotically Himalayan, also felt like home. Then they'd venture up the few steps to Sam's store, to stock up on books and magazines.

During the post-lunch lull, I opened my eyes to see an attractive young woman being served a chai latte by Ricardo, in one of the more private banquettes. It took me a moment to realize who it was – Heidi! Wearing make-up. This was something she never did when teaching yoga. And looking much more animated than the last time I'd seen her.

When I woke from a comfortable doze, the two of them were still talking spiritedly, Ricardo now sitting opposite on the banquette. From time to time, Heidi would slip a surreptitious glance in the direction of the coffee machine, where Natalia was servicing the mid-afternoon line. Ricardo, I noticed, didn't look over towards Natalia once.

Only after quite some time had passed did Ricardo stand to wish Heidi a fond farewell, before returning to the coffee machine. The moment he got there, Natalia stepped aside, tugging her barista's apron from around her neck and tossing it on the counter. A brief and fiery exchange followed. Then she stormed from the café at high speed.

In recent months, Franc had adopted a habit that was most absorbing. Glancing about his domain, after checking that Kusali had everything under control in the café, Sam in the bookstore, and now Natalia and Ricardo at the coffee station, he'd open the door near the magazine rack which led to a staircase. I'd hear his footfall on the stairs and, within moments, Marcel and Kyi Kyi would scramble from their basket to hurry after him.

Above The Himalaya Book Café was an apartment which had had various uses over the years – as a temporary home when Sam had first opened the bookstore, and as an office when Serena set up her spice pack business. Both having long since moved out, I was naturally curious about why Franc was visiting so often – usually for about half an hour at a time.

One day I decided to find out for myself. Even on the first flight of stairs, I became aware of music coming from above. On the second flight, it was louder still. Not the kind of background music played downstairs in the café. Up here it was slower, more serene.

Finding the upstairs door ajar I squeezed in, making my way to what used to be a lounge room. Franc was lying motionless, spreadeagled on the carpet, listening to music being streamed through a speaker in his phone. It sounded classical, beginning with a cello melody that was both poignant and lyrical, progressing through variations, gathering in scale and volume, before driving towards a magnificent orchestral surge. On either side of their master, on two flat tartan cushions that used to furnish chairs in the room, Marcel and Kyi Kyi also lay motionless. So I settled down too, in the shuttered semi-darkness, listening to music.

After it ended there was complete silence. For the longest time, Franc and the two dogs lay as if still resonating to the music, still moved by the heartfelt emotions it expressed, allowing its impact to continue to wash over them, drawing back little by little, like waves ebbing from a beach.

Finally, Franc propped himself up on an elbow before sitting.

"Oh, you've joined us Rinpoche," he said, seeing me sprawled by the window. "I wondered how long it would take."

At that moment, I realized it had not been by chance that the doors, both upstairs and down, had been left ajar. They had been Franc's invitation to me.

ONCE STARTED, THIS WAS A ROUTINE I WAS ONLY TOO HAPPY to continue. Usually, the music was meditative in nature and Franc had his favorites, which I'd heard him talk about before.

Whether it was *May It Be* by the 2Cellos, Barber's *Adagio* or Mozart's *Laudate Dominum*, there was an uplifting transcendence to the music, a sense of being transported to a different reality.

On other occasions, I found Franc not lying on the floor but standing in the middle of the room, waving his arms, while the room pulsated with much livelier music. It took me a while to work out that, in his imagination, he was conducting an orchestra. Keeping the time, cueing in instruments, indicating changes of tone through graphic facial expressions.

This was no spiritual exercise, at least not in the strictest sense. But it was a special one for Franc – and his two devoted canines. I already knew how big a part classical music had played in his early life. Growing up in San Francisco, he had learned the piano – I had heard him perform on the café's own upright on several occasions. It was a study that had opened the door to a much wider experience of music than he might otherwise have enjoyed. His later training as a meditator meant that now, later in life, while lying on a carpet in a soft-lit room, he was able to focus without distraction, his attention enabling an immediacy to what he experienced. Being fully present to every moment, every nuance, open to every expression of the composer and performers, meant that the music communicated more powerfully than ever before, with a clarity and intensity for which there were no words.

ON THIS PARTICULAR DAY WHEN FRANC APPEARED

MID-AFternoon at the door to the stairs, checking on the café, bookstore and baristas, Marcel emerged from the basket and trotted towards him. Halfway to the steps he paused, looking back to the basket under the counter. Kyi Kyi hadn't moved.

Franc paused too, following his gaze, before returning to the counter, lifting the little Lhasa Apso in his arms and holding her to him. He gently carried her upstairs.

The session was different that afternoon. Marcel settled on his cushion to Franc's left. But as Franc sank slowly back onto the carpet, he held Kyi Kyi to him, so that she was lying on his chest, close to his heart.

I saw him mouth the words *Spiegel im Spiegel,* as he chose that title from his list. The single piano notes that sounded evoked such purity and light that they could only refer to the small, vulnerable being on his chest. There was such delicacy and tenderness in those exquisite cadences as they were joined by the slow bows of a cello in a lower register, supporting them with gentle, sonorous strength.

It was a piece as utterly captivating as it was moving. The musical description of an unassuming but deeply felt love. And at the very end, the piano notes tiptoeing away, higher and higher, felt like an understanding that, however sweet the music they had made together, the two must go their separate ways, at least for the moment.

After the music had finished we rested in silence, sharing in a recognition of what was happening and the way we felt, all that we had shared over the years as dear friends, and the sublime but devastating poignancy of our time together.

Returning home, I was using my usual outdoor route to the apartment I shared with the Dalai Lama, one which avoided the inside staircase and security, when I heard a distinctive voice coming from the kitchen. Mrs. Trinci.

"Four hundred million!" she was exclaiming. "You told me about the apartment block. I knew this. But four hundred million rupees!"

"And worth less than half what he paid for it," Serena's tone was frosty. "As Arhaan knew full well at the time."

Slipping through the open kitchen window, onto a counter, a stool and the floor, I had just made my appearance when there came a different noise: the repetitive banging of a small fist on a counter and the voice of two-year-old Rishi.

Seeing me hone into view, Mrs. Trinci was quick to respond. "Oh, my little *tesorina!*" she crooned, her voice sweet and eyelids crinkling. "Come, come my darling," she gestured that I should join her on her side of the counter. Oblivious to my presence, from overhead Rishi continued thumping and repeating a tuneless rhyme.

"Let me find a tasty soupçon for The Most Beautiful Creature." Mrs. Trinci opened the cupboard of small dishes, including the ramekins in which she usually presented me with treats.

"What was Sid to do?" Serena continued from the other side of the counter, out of sight to me too. "Binita was a dear friend of Shanti's. The four of them had been so close at university.

101

Arhaan was absolutely desperate. Sid was worried he was going to do something stupid."

"No!" Mrs. Trinci's eyes flashed across the counter.

Serena sipped from her coffee before saying, "Well, he would definitely have gone bankrupt, leaving a trail of creditors across the country. No one would have done business with him again."

I KNEW OF THE TIME SERENA WAS REFERRING TO, HAVING once heard Sid tell her the story. It had been during their early days together, when Sid was still a widower living at 108 Bougainvillea Street. Wanting Serena to know exactly who she was getting involved with, after Sid had confessed to being the Maharajah of Himachal Pradesh, a fact he'd done his best to conceal, he had shared some of the dramas of his personal life. Losing his wife Shanti, who was killed in a fatal car accident, had been the most defining moment of his adult life, leaving him alone with his much loved daughter, Zahra.

Arhaan's had been a very different and ongoing saga. Always the extrovert and joker, he and Sid were polar opposites in temperament, but had been in the same class growing up. Meanwhile, Shanti had been close friends with Binita, the two girls sharing a love of swimming, vying with each other year after year in the annual school championships. When Sid began dating Shanti, it was all but inevitable there'd be a time when she, Binita and Sid would encounter Arhaan. And from the moment he set his eyes on Binita, a woman of dazzling beauty, Arhaan had been determined to make her his wife.

The two men had left university, married for love – unusual for members of a higher caste in a land of arranged marriages – and embarked on separate careers in business. Arhaan had become a property developer and flashy man about town, daring in the deals he struck, living in ever-bigger mansions and driving showy cars. Scoffing at Sid's conservatism, he extended himself well beyond his means. When a sharp downturn in the property market left him ruinously exposed, it was Sid to whom he had turned, begging for help. He couldn't survive without a bailout, he told his friend. If Sid were able to loan him two million dollars, he could find a way out of disaster and be forever in his debt.

Loyal Sid, a man who never flaunted status or money, had come to the rescue, buying an apartment building from Arhaan for twice its market value.

"From that day forward, things were never the same," Serena continued. "Sid said he didn't want constant gratitude from Arhaan – that would have been awkward for them both. But what he didn't expect was the feeling he got from his friend. It was almost as if Arhaan resented him. He seemed to have the view that Sid had made his wealth easily through family connections, or good fortune, rather than by being a prudent businessman.

"After Shanti was killed, Sid saw less of Arhaan and Binita. And when the two of us got together, even less."

"What happened to Arhaan's business?" Mrs. Trinci interjected. "Did he come good?"

Interested as I was in Serena's story, my more immediate focus was on the ramekin Mrs. Trinci was holding in her hand. Empty. I stared at it, willing her to fill it with a delectable treat.

"He reinvented himself. That's the word Sid used. He got out of property and into stock markets. He became involved listing companies, both here and overseas. He still had the trappings of a wealthy man. Even more so."

"He paid Sid back?"

Serena shook her head. "Sid never mentioned the subject again. Nor did Arhaan, even after he bought a house in London for very much more than he owed Sid. Sid told me that he kept hearing stories about Arhaan getting into debt over his head again. Business contacts in Delhi told him that Arhaan's wheeling and dealing was getting out of control. Then two years ago, he and Binita suddenly turned up here, in Dharamshala. Remember me telling you about that strange visit?"

"I do! Si!"

"So awkward! Out of the blue, he was telling Sid how he'd never forgotten how much he had done for him, how he'd always wanted to repay him, and how he now had this opportunity, through Silicon Valley insiders, to buy cryptocurrency that was going to multiply twentyfold within the year. And he was offering Sid a portion of his own entitlement worth two million dollars."

Mrs. Trinci's frowned. "Sid has to pay him?" she was trying to get this straight. "Again?"

"Yes."

"Two million dollars?"

"Yes," Serena had to compete with Rishi, who was now squeezing a fluffy toy that played jingly music and cackled loudly. "The idea being that the two million would soon be worth twenty."

"Why didn't Arhaan just give him back his two million dollars? Or offer to invest it for him?"

"Just what I asked Sid."

"I hope Sid didn't …!"

"No," replied Serena, before trying to shoosh Rishi.

In the short pause that followed, I meowed. Loudly.

"Oh si, si!" Mrs. Trinci opened the fridge door and bent to peer inside.

"Sid told Arhaan that he didn't understand cryptocurrency, and he never invested in things that he didn't understand."

Mrs. Trinci, somewhat distracted, agreed.

"But Arhaan asked Sid again. The following month. Said he wouldn't be doing his duty to him, as a friend, if he didn't insist Sid take up the offer. I remember Sid coming off the call. He looked disturbed – and you know, it takes a lot to rattle Sid."

Mrs. Trinci had retrieved a large, sealed bowl from inside the fridge and placed it on the counter. "Rattle?"

"Suspected there was a lot more going on than Arhaan was saying. He was worried that Arhaan had overextended himself again. Only this time it was a much bigger deal, with powerful people involved around the world.

"That was the last time they spoke. Two weeks later, Arhaan

died of a heart attack. After the funeral, we hardly heard from Binita again, although Sid contacted her several times with offers of support. Then out of the blue, Emily Cartwright tells me that Binita and her three daughters are living in some squalid dump in New Delhi. Turns out that, just like Sid predicted, they lost everything!"

"Oh my!" Mrs. Trinci wailed. "These are the ones Sid is going to visit?"

"He went yesterday."

Food on the counter, ramekin next to it, Mrs. Trinci was not focusing. At least, not on me. I meowed again. As it happened, Rishi chose that very moment to start bleating. More time passed while Serena found him a drink from a bag she'd brought with her, while Mrs. Trinci did her best to distract him, singing an Italian nursery rhyme while wiggling her bottom from side to side.

"Very difficult visit," continued Serena, when Rishi was more settled.

"They were embarrassed about where they live?"

"That was part of it," said Serena. "But it was much worse. And very personal. You see, what none of us knew is that, for weeks before his death, Arhaan had been blaming Sid for what was happening."

"No!" Mrs. Trinci looked horrified.

"He'd told Binita it was all Sid's fault."

"But ..."

"That Sid had pulled out of the biggest deal of his life at the last minute, destroying everything."

Mrs. Trinci was shocked. "And Binita believed him?"

"At the time she did. But with everything that's come out about Arhaan since his death, she's had to learn some uncomfortable truths. Sid had a chance to set the record straight."

I meowed once more, my plea clearly audible. Engrossed in the story, Mrs. Trinci didn't even register.

"Sid came home last night," Serena was preoccupied too. "He's really worried for them. The three girls followed in Binita's footsteps, training as beauty therapists. As much for their own benefit as anything. Sid said they're very pretty, like their mother. Binita never worked and the girls probably thought they wouldn't have to either. Now they're struggling to survive. The younger two are twins and they took on some fake modelling assignment. They were almost caught up in a sex trafficking operation."

"Mamma mia!"

It had become clear that I wasn't going to be able to compete with Serena's riveting tale, or Rishi's commanding presence. If I wanted attention, I was going to have to take action. Stepping behind Mrs. Trinci, I did something I had never done before. At least, not to her. She may have been my all-time greatest gastronomic benefactor, but right now there was no benefaction to be had. Which was why, with gentle but firm deliberation, I sank my teeth into the heel of her left foot.

She shrieked, jolting her leg away.

I delivered my most plaintive, blue-eyed gaze.

Serena's head peered over the counter. "The little wretch!"

she chuckled.

Mrs. Trinci had returned her foot to its former position, and bent down to stroke my neck. "Forgive me, my *dolce gattina*," her voice was filled with apology. "I have not been paying attention."

Within a few moments, she was holding the bowl on the counter, spooning a serve into the ramekin, and placing it on the floor. I was soon lapping up deliciously thick goulash gravy.

"I can tell Sid's working on a plan to help them. He's always devising strategies. Pulling ideas together."

"This Binita is very lucky to have him as a friend. Most other people would have given up on the family a long time ago."

"She came from a modest background. Her parents were old-fashioned and unworldly. She and the girls trusted Arhaan implicitly. He let them all down completely. Some of the stories she was telling Sid made me shudder," Serena spoke with feeling.

"You wonder how people can carry on in such situations. How they find the fortitude to keep going."

"Hmm," Serena was contemplative. "Binita and Sid talked about that. Binita told him how nothing in her life was what she'd hoped for. How helpless and desperate she felt most of the time. Then, Sid said she came out with the most unexpected thing. When she was much younger, she and Shanti used to be keen swimmers, quite competitive at school. Swimming wasn't something she'd ever been pushed into or decided by her parents. She'd chosen it for herself.

"She told Sid that the only thing that had kept her sane has been swimming. Apparently, she goes to the local public pool to swims laps, up and down for at least an hour a day."

"You used to swim as a girl, remember?" said Mrs. Trinci.

"Of course. And I can remember what Binita described to Sid, the feeling of being immersed in a different medium, just breath and water, lap after lap. Being in the zone."

There was a pause before Mrs. Trinci said, "Doing something that gives us joy every day takes us to a different place. That's so important, no?"

"It is, Momma," replied Serena.

"Like this little one." Seeing that I had finished my snack, and momentarily forgetting herself, Mrs. Trinci leaned down to pick me up. "Giving her a hug," she said.

At that very same moment, Rishi caught sight of me. Instantly, he let out a bloodcurdling shriek.

"Oh, *merda!*" Mrs. Trinci was carrying me out of view. Through the kitchen, along the corridor, up the stairs to security. "So, so sorry, my precious one," she crooned. Her eyes, heavy with mascara, filled with anguish. "I don't know why he does this."

Nor, dear reader, do I. As the large unsmiling security man radioed his colleagues, so that the door could be opened just far enough to allow the passage of a furry body, and I made my solitary way inside, all I knew was that since the arrival of young Rishi, with his inexplicable horror of cats, life had become more complicated.

ON THE END OF THE DALAI LAMA'S BED THAT NIGHT, I HAD one of those dreams that feels curiously jumbled. In my dream, Franc was lying on the carpet of an empty room, his chest rising and falling, and on it his beloved Kyi Kyi. She may be gravely ill, but during this special time of complete immersion in music, sublime and mutually felt, there was only the sensation of profound connection and abiding peace.

I dreamed of Binita swimming for mile after mile, not in a swimming pool but in the wide blue ocean, arms and legs working in steady rhythm. On land, her world was falling apart; but here in the caress of the water she was able to find refuge, for a while at least. A place of healing from which she would return with the strength she needed to face another burdensome day.

I dreamed of Christopher, standing at his easel, oxygen line running to his face, applying sweeps of color to the canvas, stroke after stroke. He was physically present in his old jacket and paint-spattered corduroy pants, but in some more important and transcendental way, absorbed in a different reality.

When I woke in the early morning to join His Holiness in meditation, the theme that wove its way through my dreams could hardly have been clearer, given that it spoke of an intuition I had not only felt myself, but had already acted on. In a life the Dalai Lama often used to say was flavored with *dukkha*, or dissatisfaction, both trivial and profound, how wonderful it is when we are able to find an activity that lifts us out of ourselves?

Where may we find such a gift?

If we are lucky, we can retrieve it from our kittenhood. We may be returned by some chance encounter, some slender thread, to a golden world where we once gave ourselves without reserve in more innocent times. To an activity in which we may engage with an open heart, not for any material gain or advantage, but simply for the joy of the thing itself.

While this may seem a trivial matter, a pursuit of no great consequence, it is anything but. For until we become practiced meditators, it is in precisely such moments that non-duality may best be found. And it is only when we fully lose ourselves that we may experience a much wider and more glorious reality.

In future weeks, I would discover how the glory of that reality may be amplified beyond measure.

AND SO THE FOLLOWING MORNING, WHEN OLIVER ARRIVED to work, pink-faced and perspiring in his cycling clothes, I was there to meet him. Ready to follow him to the bathroom. Poised beside the shower door as he stepped in. Reveling in the flow of warm water, as soon as he opened the faucets. Transported once again, to a different age and place that I didn't fully understand, but that made me feel mysteriously enraptured. No longer the Dalai Lama's Cat. Not even feline. Just pure joy!

CHAPTER FIVE

It had been the first afternoon in a long time when the weather was sufficiently calm and dry for an assistant to not only open the windows of His Holiness's room, but leave them open. Mountain air streamed into our living quarters, along with soft afternoon sunlight. After weeks of feeling closed off from the natural world and the life-giving presence of the forested mountains, the infusion of *prana* was delightful.

On the sill, paws tucked under, I felt suffused with contentment as I overlooked the courtyard below, where the familiar circadian rhythm was playing out: shadows lengthening, twilight deepening and, as darkness fell, orange squares appearing along the monastery walls.

It wasn't long before the temple lights came on and monks were making their way across the cobbled pavers and up the steps, leaving their sandals outside and entering through the great red doors. Through the gates of Namgyal Monastery, people from McLeod Ganj were arriving, bags slung over their shoulders, blankets draped over their arms, speaking with the quiet but avid anticipation which always preceded a class given by one of Namgyal's most inspiring teachers – Geshe Wangpo.

Some of these students were dear friends of mine. Sid and Serena from along the road. Sam and Franc from The Himalaya Book Café, along with Sam's girlfriend Bronnie. Ludo and several of the long-standing yoga group, including Merrilee, Ewing and Suki.

Car headlights slowly swept across the flagstones, as an ancient white station wagon rolled into the square. Generally, the only vehicles permitted through the monastery gates were those transporting the Dalai Lama or one of his VIP visitors. Who could this be?

I watched the car proceed across the courtyard, pedestrians stepping aside, as it made directly for the temple. Once it had maneuvered as closely as possible to the building, it came to a halt. The headlights were turned off. From the driver's side, a man in an orderly's uniform stepped out at the same time as a nurse climbed from the back. Rounding the car, they opened the passenger door facing the temple and leaned inside.

At first, I saw only a mop of white hair and heard a groan of discomfort. But as their patient took several steps from the car, I recognized the tweed jacket and familiar stooped silhouette. The less familiar oxygen tank which the nurse was carrying beside him, as the two assistants helped him up the steps and into the temple. Evidently, Christopher had taken

His Holiness's advice to heart. And as he had decided to attend Geshe Wangpo's teachings, despite the many challenges that attending the class might bring, I decided that I would too.

A frisson of excitement always accompanied my arrival at the Namgyal temple. Most students would elaborately step aside, to allow me access to wherever I wished to go, some bringing their hands to their heart as they did so, other more audacious or impulsive types reaching out to touch me – the closest they would get to touching the hem of the Dalai Lama. The temerity!

My usual spot in the temple, a place that might have been purpose-built for me, was a shelf at the back which afforded a great vantage point from which to survey proceedings. Stepping into the temple this evening, however, I saw Christopher on a chair in one of the back rows, oxygen tank at his feet and tube leading up to his nose. The aisle chair next to him was vacant – evidently for me.

Christopher had been looking ahead contemplatively, when he noticed the movement beside him and turned. "Oh, *Gaudeamus Igitur*, Pussy my love!" he exclaimed under his breath, stroking me. "I didn't think I would know a soul here and then along comes my favorite *semchen*!"

I leaned over to headbutt him. As I did, I noticed that his trousers bore spatters of red paint. Evidently, he had been working on His Holiness's commission.

Namgyal temple at night, with its sea of flickering butter lamps lighting up the golden faces of Buddha statues, and drifting incense, was a living, breathing sanctuary, a place of both wonder and peace. I had observed this many times in the past, and saw it again tonight on Christopher's face. As tradition dictated, the Namgyal monks who attended sat on cushions in the rows closest to the teaching throne, with non-monastics further back on cushions or upright chairs, as they preferred. As the moment of Geshe Wangpo's arrival drew close, and the last students snuck through the doors and quickly settled, any murmured conversation came to an end. The atmosphere, redolent with expectation, was so still that you could hear the soft clunk of the dowels at the bottom of the *thangkas* blowing against the walls in the night breeze.

Then the moment arrived and in he came, his round, muscular presence supremely powerful as well as heartwarming. Sweeping to the front, he prostrated three times before the assembled Buddhas, before taking his place on the teaching throne and gazing out across his assembled audience with that inimitable combination of vigor, mischief and compassion.

"Tonight, I talk about the death process," he said, after the traditional affirmations had been chanted – taking refuge, *bodhicitta* and the *lam rim*. "The Buddha once said that contemplating one's own death is the greatest meditation. He invited us to think about it not as a distant prospect, not as something that one day we'll need to deal with, but as an event that is definitely happening. Perhaps much sooner than we think. So why this emphasis on impermanence and death?"

As always, his students sat captivated by his presence. Looking up at Christopher, I could see he was instantly engrossed, Geshe Wangpo talking about the reality he now lived with. A subject that many other people did their utmost to avoid.

"When we imagine our death as an imminent prospect," Geshe-la continued, "as something unavoidable and certain, only then do we recognize the true value of being alive. The incredible preciousness of our waking hours. The awesome privilege of being healthy and free to choose how to spend our time.

"Our life as a human being with some leisure and good fortune is not to be squandered. It's an opportunity that's rare and priceless. When we truly know this, we are profoundly grateful for the potential that each day brings."

Absorbed by the teachings, Christopher was nodding with conviction.

"We quite naturally prioritize what is meaningful and important, rather than waste energy on things of passing value. Also, we learn not to take for granted the chance to say 'I love you' or 'I forgive you' or 'I am sorry', for it is a chance we may never have again. This is important."

Geshe Wangpo didn't raise his voice because he didn't need to, the significance of what he was saying being communicated by more than just words – but as a palpable sensation.

Christopher carried physical proof of what Geshe-la was saying inside his jacket pocket. The oft-read letter he'd received from Caroline, in response to his own apology after decades of silence. The unexpected absolution he had been granted, only after receiving his terminal diagnosis. Nevertheless, that had helped unburden him from the weight of untold emotions, igniting the artistic flame that had come back to life with such unexpected glory.

"You don't have to be a Buddhist to understand these things," said Geshe-la. "Anyone can see the value of living in accordance with this truth. Of appreciating what is precious and making the most of what we have.

"There is also, however, an additional set of reasons why meditating on death is important to us Tibetan Buddhists. Quite simply, the death process offers an opportunity of a lifetime. Here we must have faith, not in the great gurus of the past or even their teachings, although they have the same view. But faith in meditators who are able to attain states of subtle consciousness, which most of us beginners cannot access."

Geshe Wangpo liked to use inclusive words like "us beginners", although there was no doubt that he was much less of a beginner than most of his audience. As for the advanced meditators he referred to, I was reminded of the conversation between Tenzin and Oliver that I'd overheard from the filing cabinet. How the *yogis* and *yoginis* of the East had their equivalents in the Iron Man triathletes of the West. In both cases, ordinary beings whose dedication to training enabled them to attain accomplishments that were extraordinary – well beyond the capabilities of most beings.

"The advanced meditators of our tradition are capable of doing things which we cannot," said Geshe-la. "Those who have achieved calm abiding – *samatha* – who can settle their minds on an object of meditation for as long they wish, without effort. These people are also capable of working with the subtle energies in our bodies, energies which cause the arising of great bliss.

"A consequence of working at this very subtle level can be that the heartbeat slows, until it stops completely. Normal breathing is suspended. Eight visions arise, patterning the death experience. By the way, these are visions you may sometimes glimpse very briefly as you fall asleep, as your consciousness withdraws from the sense doors.

"They are always the same visions, and they are a description of the death process. Becoming familiar with them, knowing what to expect, is very useful. Quite possibly, the most useful training of our life. Because when we know about the opportunity that awaits us when we die, we can make the most of it. We have a once-in-a-lifetime chance to end the cycle of birth, ageing, sickness and death. Instead we may attain nirvana, even enlightenment itself."

Geshe Wangpo went on to describe the death process. How, as the body begins shutting down, a person feels a sense of heaviness and sinking, with appearances becoming hazy, like a mirage. In the second stage, there may be a sensation of thirst, together with the gradual loss of bodily sensation. It may seem as though smoke has entered the room – so evident is this that hospice workers sometimes report their patients asking if there is a fire nearby. Stage three sees the body lose its warmth, the sense doors close down – the dying person has no more experience of sights, sounds, sensations or odors. Perhaps only the subtle residual sense of taste. By stage four, the last stage before physical death, even the sense of taste is lost. All that might be perceived is a subtle flicker of life force, like a single candle flame blowing in the wind. Before that disappears too.

At such a time, Geshe-la explained, a person is declared dead by doctors. With no heart, lung or brain activity, it is assumed that they no longer possess consciousness. But from a Tibetan Buddhist perspective, this isn't the end of the story. For while one's physical processes have closed down, subtle consciousness still remains in the body, and will go through its own four stages of dissolution, each stage accompanied by an inner appearance in the mind of the dying person, culminating in the most important experience of all.

First, an appearance of white like moonlight. Then the experience of radiant red, like a glowing sky at sunset. An all-consuming blackness comes next, during which a period of complete unconsciousness is likely. But this is by no means the end. It is followed by the most subtle and special of all encounters – a panoramic vision of tranquil clarity and peacefulness, the kind of deep *samatha* to which we aspire in meditation.

"Even if you think you can't meditate," there was a tremor of excitement in his voice as he spoke. "Even if your concentration is poor, your mind scattered, and you think you're getting nowhere. Even then, if you have some familiarity with this chosen object of meditation, you will find that it quite naturally arises at the end of the death process. A boundless luminosity, a spacious lucidity. This is the Buddha nature we all possess. The light within. Known in Sanskrit as our *tathagatagarbha*. It is the mind of clear knowing, the basis on which enlightenment is possible. Isn't it wonderful to know that the dawning of this, our most subtle consciousness, awaits us when we die?"

THE ATMOSPHERE IN THE TEMPLE HAD A PARTICULAR ENERGY to it, which often happened when an inspiring lama sat on the teaching throne. There was an oceanic tranquility, and yet a vibrancy at the same time, as the impact of what he was saying resonated among his students.

Looking up, I saw Christopher's lower lip tremble and his eyes gleaming, as he absorbed Geshe-la's teachings. The expression of conviction on his face suggested that Geshe Wangpo's teaching accorded with all that he was familiar with in his book titled *Mahamudra*.

Even though Geshe-la's question had been rhetorical, such was the engagement of his audience that one man, a Western tourist, couldn't help raising his arm to ask, "If we are all going to experience the clear light of mind when we die, why do we need to meditate before then?" His tone wasn't impolite, but genuinely curious.

A ripple of laughter followed, before Geshe Wangpo responded with a sincere expression, "That's a good question. A very important question.

"When we train in a subject, any subject, we notice things that those who are untrained don't notice. A doctor can observe symptoms of illness in a person, which someone with no medical training has no capacity to see. A bush guide can immediately detect signs that a lion is nearby, whereas a city dweller has no idea until it's too late. The same, too, with mind. Without training, the clear light of death may appear and we won't cognize it, or recognize it, for what it is. An extraordinary opportunity has arisen and yet most beings have no idea what's happening, let alone what they may do with it."

Geshe Wangpo paused for a while, sitting forward on his cushion and closing his eyes, commanding the attention of everyone in the room, underlining the importance of what he was about to say. "The greatest tragedy," he spoke in a low voice, but one that reverberated throughout the temple, "is when the clear light of death is experienced not as our true nature, not as the subtle oceanic consciousness from which all else arises, but instead as a feeling of personal annihilation. Yet this is the most common response.

"We have lost our body, our anchor to physical reality. We have lost our sense perceptions and the habitual mental activity with which we are so familiar. And typically, our instinctive reaction is 'What about *me*?! Where did *I* go? *I* want to exist!' It is this impulse, this wish to manifest in a way that is so familiar to us, a way we believe to be separate and independent, that propels us into our next lifetime.

"Instead of identifying with the clear light as our own true nature, who we really are, it is we who unknowingly propel ourselves into rebirth, because of the ingrained habit of our self-cherishing mind. This," he nodded towards the man who had asked the question, "is an important reason why we meditate. To experience our own Buddha nature. To rehearse our death."

The visitor brought his hands together at his heart and bowed to Geshe Wangpo.

His question had the effect of opening the floodgates to many other questions. Geshe Wangpo had always favored interactive sessions over dry monologues and now more than a dozen arms shot up in the air.

"If the wish for self-existence is what propels us into our next life ..." began Ewing Klipspringer who, like so many others, had come to McLeod Ganj to find redemption, "why are some of us born human, and others as animals, etc.?"

"Because of whatever karma ripens in your mind at the time you seek self-existence," replied Geshe-la.

"So, if we are to be reborn," Ewing followed up, "how can we make sure it will be good karma for a positive rebirth?"

"Generally, karmas arise from those mental habits that are strongest, closest, most frequent and most familiar to us. If we are habitually angry, self-centered and cause harm to others, such thoughts can only yield negative karmic outcomes. Conversely, a mind that is peaceful, gentle and benevolent will only produce positive outcomes. Another reason for mind training in this life."

"How do we know when people have actually died, if it is not only about heart and brain activity?" asked a female tourist from Europe.

"As long as their subtle consciousness remains, there will be a slight warmth here," Geshe-la pressed the center of his chest. "At the heart. When that goes, subtle consciousness has also left."

"Does this mean we shouldn't move people immediately after they die?"

"Unless they have some meditative experience," he reassured her, "chances are that their subtle consciousness will leave the body very soon after conventional death."

"Not like *tukdam*?" prompted one of the Western monks from Namgyal Monastery.

"*Tukdam*, Tibetan for 'clear light', is what happens after the dissolution of body and conceptual consciousness, when meditators are able to remain in the clear light of death. It is an incredibly blissful experience, free from agitation. Highly advanced meditators are able to remain in this state for days, sometimes weeks. During this time, their bodies are as fresh and radiant as though they were only asleep, even though they are dead from a medical perspective. You can find many accounts of this happening, even recently. On Tibet.net just look up 'Tukdam'."

A forest of hands reached into the air, as soon as Geshe Wangpo stopped speaking. For the first time, Christopher's was one of them. Ignoring all the questioners directly in front of him, Geshe Wangpo zeroed in on Christopher, gesturing towards him in a way that seemed to signal permission to speak, but with a certain regard too.

Once chosen, Christopher raised himself to his feet with some difficulty, to better face the teacher. "Forgive me if I haven't got this right – I am still learning," he said, voice deep but wavering, and distinctively British.

Many faces were turning to look at the elderly man with the tweed jacket and oxygen lines running into his nose.

"My name is Christopher Ackland. As I understand it, our

mind projects our reality. As much as we may wish to experience nirvana or even enlightenment, our karma and delusions may propel us to experience life as an animal or, if we are very fortunate, a precious human rebirth."

Geshe-la was nodding.

"I don't mean to sound ungrateful. But what if we don't want another human rebirth?"

Scattered chuckling sounded from around the room.

Reassured, Christopher continued with greater confidence. "I'm done with loneliness. With financial struggle. With having my hopes raised and dashed. But I also know that I'm not pure enough of heart and mind to experience nirvana, much less the mind of a Buddha. So I suppose my question is whether there is another option; is it only samsara *or* nirvana?" After a moment he added with a smile, "This question is one of urgent relevance to me."

Had he been at a community or other such meeting, as Christopher lowered himself carefully back into his chair, he would have done so to a round of fervent applause. Not only out of sympathy, but because he spoken to the heart of many of those present. He had gone directly to a question that they had been wondering about too, and articulated it with resounding clarity. A surge of supportive energy streamed in his direction.

Geshe Wangpo was nodding as he gazed about the room, acknowledging the appeal and importance of Christopher's question. The compassion everyone shared for his plight – which would, in turn, become our own.

"You are right that our mind projects our reality. Nirvana

and Buddhahood are not easy to attain. Yet samsara has many sufferings. What to do?" Geshe Wangpo reframed the question for those who may not have heard.

"As it happens, an enlightened being, through great compassion, has manifested a pure land for those who wish to be free from samsara. This pure land is a state we can access, or project, even when our minds are still tainted by karma. A state in which we can abide until we have purified all negativity and perfected all virtues. This pure land is called Sukhavati, the place of happiness. And the Buddha of Infinite Light and Life who manifests it for our benefit is Amitabha Buddha."

At the mere mention of his name, Christopher's eyes filled with tears. Amitabha! The same Buddha whose portrait His Holiness had commissioned from him. The portrait on which he was already working.

Others in the temple were also moved. Several rows ahead, I noticed Sid bow his head in reverence at the mention of Amitabha. Franc exchanged a glance with Ludo.

"If we wish to cultivate the practice of Amitabha as a *yidam*, as a manifestation of an enlightened mind, this must be based on a good understanding of *sunyata*, or *Mahamudra*."

A well-thumbed book on just this subject was in Christopher's jacket pocket right now.

"We must also learn his mantra. It is nice and short: *Om Amitabha hrih.* Geshe-la gave his class the transmission of the Amitabha mantra, having them repeat it three times, just as the Dalai Lama had when Christopher had visited.

"Based on an understanding of *sunyata*, and through

familiarity with the appearance and name of Amitabha, at the time of death," Geshe Wangpo looked directly at Christopher, "it is possible to escape samsara and attain Sukhavati."

Closing his eyes and bowing his head, he brought his palms together under his chin, murmuring something softly in Tibetan. For a moment, everyone in the temple focused on what he was doing, understanding its purpose without the need to be told. Geshe Wangpo was offering Christopher his blessing.

USUALLY, AFTER GESHE WANGPO'S TUESDAY NIGHT CLASSES, people would leave Namgyal temple in a quiet but steady flow, monks returning to their living quarters, visitors crossing the courtyard and leaving through the gates.

That evening, however, there was a different mood. People who were coming out of the temple seemed reluctant to leave. It was as though that evening's teaching had engaged them so deeply that they weren't yet ready to go. A particular focus of attention as they emerged was Christopher, who had made his way slowly out of the temple helped by several students.

Wary about being caught in the footfall, I waited for most of them to leave before hopping from my seat and making my way through the great temple doors. From the top of the steps, I observed a group of students gather around Christopher, grateful and solicitous, as he waited for the nursing home car to take him home.

"What a wonderful question!" Merrilee was congratulating

him. "You asked exactly what I wanted to know, but I've never been quite sure how to put it."

"To get Geshe Wangpo to talk about *yidams,*" Franc's expression conveyed the consequence of what had happened. "That really is something. He's very old school, you know. He doesn't usually even mention Kriya tantra."

"I've never heard him mention Sukhavati, except with students he knows well," confirmed Serena.

At the center of the group, despite his worn jacket, oxygen lines and dependence on a stick, Christopher possessed a magnetic appeal.

"I ... I have to confess that right at this moment, I feel like a damned fool," his bass voice commanded attention. "I have lived next door for the past eight years," he turned in the direction of the nursing home. "Most of them, in reasonable health. Not once have I come to a class before tonight. And it's been ... a revelation! I wonder how much further along the path I could have travelled, if I'd come here before."

There was a pause before Sid, in his own quiet but elevated tones said, "But you arrived in a spiritually evolved state, like our friends are saying," he gestured around the group. "You connected with Geshe Wangpo in an exceptional way."

Emotion rose on Christopher's face as he held Sid's gaze. He seemed about to speak. But as he opened his mouth, he bent forward and started coughing heavily, gasping for breath. The students rallied around him, including one who was a nurse, as violent spasms racked his body. They were holding onto him as headlights appeared through the monastery gates. The car that was to take him home crept cautiously towards the group.

By the time the car had halted, Christopher was standing upright again, his breathing labored but returning to normal. An orderly from the nursing home had opened the rear door of the vehicle and was approaching him.

"If I may, before you go," Sid's eyes met Christopher's again. "My wife and I are great admirers of the painting you gave His Holiness."

"*Primordial Dawn*," said Serena. "He put it in his reception room, for all his visitors to enjoy."

"Really?" Christopher was astonished.

Sid nodded. "We wonder if you have any work for sale."

"I have a whole studio of paintings," said Christopher, in a tone that suggested the idea of selling them hadn't entered his mind.

"May we please visit?" asked Serena.

Christopher was allowing himself to be guided towards the car by the orderly, settling slowly into the back seat in such a way that the line to the oxygen tank remained connected.

"You'd better make it soon," he glanced up from the car.

"Tomorrow afternoon?" asked Sid.

Then Franc was asking, "May I come too?"

"I'd love to see your work!" Merrilee was effusive.

Several others joined the chorus.

"Good heavens!" Christopher was beaming. "Enough for a gallery opening! But *you'd* have to provide the champagne and canapes."

Next afternoon I walked through the garden to the nursing home, arriving to find Christopher with a walking stick in his left hand and paintbrush in his right. Working on a very large canvas, baroque music in the background, he was in his usual state of absorption. He glanced briefly as I hopped up on a chair, attention remaining on his work. There was no owl or pussycat, no literary allusions, no word salads of endearments. Christopher was in the zone.

Leaning heavily on his stick, applying careful strokes to the canvas, his expression was one of rapt intensity. Watching him closely, as we cats like to do, I saw that his lips were moving subtly and constantly, a repetitive quality to their motion. Supported by oxygen from the tank on the floor beside him, as had become the norm, even though his breathing was labored – at times he seemed on the brink of coughing – such was the power of his focus that it held all interruption at bay. And after the longest time staring, I worked out the pattern being formed by his lips: *Om Amitabha hrih.*

He was applying red paint with his brush. A lot of it, from the artist's palette nearby. Sitting side-on, I couldn't see the painting, but I could see him. And as I recalled his visit to the Dalai Lama, I thought his confession that he couldn't meditate was strange because, in reality, his single-pointed concentration was exceptional. It felt profound without being forced. Arising not through sheer willpower, but with an effortlessness that came through much practice. He was doing what he had done, on and off, for the whole of his life. It was second nature to him.

I don't know how long I sat observing. Aware of changes in tempo, as one piece of music followed another. Taking in the aroma of oil paint, pungent and earthy. Watching the artist in his state of sublime enthrallment. At least an hour after I arrived, I sensed a presence at the door behind me. Turning my head, I saw we had a visitor – Sid.

A minute or two later, Christopher noticed the figure at the door, Sid being far too polite to interrupt someone so obviously engaged in his endeavors. Resting his brush on the palette, Christopher turned to Sid and tried to say hello. But his body wouldn't allow it. Having held off from so much as a single splutter through all that time, as soon as he opened his mouth, just like the night before, he broke into the most violent convulsions, doubling over as he coughed and gasped for air.

Sid was instantly by his side, holding him so that he wouldn't fall over. Within moments, Serena was also there, picking up the oxygen line which had fallen to the floor, and helping to reattach it. Franc, Sam, Bronnie, Ewing and Merrilee were hovering in the doorway, holding an assortment of baskets and carry bags – evidently, they had been waiting behind Sid.

Eventually, after the worst of the flare-up was over, Sid guided Christopher to the upright chair so that he could rest. Serena poured him a glass of water which he gratefully accepted.

"We really didn't want ..." Serena began, hand still resting on Christopher's shoulder.

"No, no, no," Christopher was shaking his head. "It's the

..." his chest was heaving from the effort, "emphysema."

Both Sid and Serena looked over and saw me in my usual wicker chair.

"Rinpoche!" Serena greeted me.

"You know her too?" asked Christopher.

"She's a close family friend," smiled Serena. "My mother calls her The Most Beautiful Creature That Ever Lived."

"So she is." As he looked at me, Christopher's eyes were gleaming. Then he noticed the group in the doorway. "You all came?" He was surprised, but delighted. "I'm afraid I am not in much of a state to entertain."

"We brought our own entertainment," Merilee brandished a bottle of champagne.

"We know how to party!" proclaimed Ewing.

"Good Lord! You'd better come in quickly," Christopher grinned. "We can't have management finding out. They'll think I'm running a nightclub!"

The small group was soon inside the door, popping open the champagne, pouring glasses, taking the lids off shallow trays of finger snacks and offering them around.

"This is like a proper exhibition opening!" Christopher needed little persuasion from Merilee to accept a glass of bubbly. Eyes glistening he told them, "You know, I was quite sure those days were well behind me."

"It must be so cool to be a painter," Bronnie was gawping at all the canvases arranged against the walls. "What's it like, to create all this?" She swept her arm around the room.

Christopher chuckled, "You know, my dear, everyone is

a painter – it's just that most people don't realize it. We paint the whole world with our thoughts, you see."

"Spoken like a true yogi," said Franc.

"But it's true, no?" responded Christopher. "We apply broad swathes of color to this person and that object, without even realizing what we're doing. We do it unknowingly and all the time to everything and everybody, so that our entire experience of reality is like a painting, a creation of our own mind." Meeting Bronnie's gaze he repeated, "We're all painters!"

He told them they could look at any painting except what was on his easel, because that was incomplete. Sam, Bronnie, Ewing and Merrilee were soon viewing the paintings ranged about the walls in a clockwise fashion. Serena was discreetly shifting the easel with Christopher's current work so that it faced the wall. Sid stepped over to the high table where the triptych was laid out. Just like Marianne Ponter, I observed, he looked at the paintings the wrong way up. Unlike her, however, he immediately stepped round to the other side of the table and gazed at the three paintings. He looked utterly spellbound. Christopher, I noticed, was watching him closely.

Sid turned, regarding Christopher with a look of deep regard. "Have you ... named these?"

Christopher nodded. "*Blue Shadows*."

Sid continued staring at them. "Remarkable!" He gestured towards Serena, who joined him and was similarly captivated.

"Are they for sale?"

Christopher shrugged, "I suppose they can be."

"I'd like to make you an offer," said Sid. "A fair one. Would you accept 2 lakh?"

"Gracious!" exclaimed Christopher. "Are you quite sure. I mean, that's a very decent offer for an old cove like me."

"I have done my research," nodded Sid. "Royal Academy Summer Exhibition. Sales to Fillingdons. The Skea and Sommers-Cox Collections. In my opinion, uneducated though it may be, this work is not only equivalent. It surpasses your previous expression."

"You *have* been busy,' Christopher chuckled, with a wheeze that threatened to turn into a splutter – but fortunately didn't. "As it happens, that's my opinion too."

"I know exactly where these will go," Sid turned to Serena. "You know the main wall next to my office door? The light is perfect!"

She nodded brightly.

"So – we have a deal?" asked Sid.

When Christopher consented, the two men warmly shook hands.

Franc was the next to make an offer – a single, smaller painting of rhododendrons for the wall next to the new coffee hutch inside The Himalaya Book Café. "It will be our first proper, grown-up piece of art!" he enthused.

"An original Christopher Ackland!" agreed Serena.

Franc offered 1 lakh but Sid urged Christopher to settle for nothing less than 1.5, "A bargain even then!"

Christopher looked around at the neat pile of brown envelopes stacked on the narrow shelf beside the kettle. "Would you mind passing me one of those," he nodded towards them.

"The top one."

Serena duly obliged, and Christopher took some time to open it, retrieving the statement from inside and glancing at the bottom line.

"I don't suppose you could rise to 1.2 lakh, could you?" he asked Franc, with a gleam in his eye.

"Of course," agreed Franc.

"The figure of 3.2 lakh has special significance for me," he shook the statement, before handing it back with the envelope to Serena.

Merilee was doing the rounds with a fresh bottle of champagne. Ewing was handing round the finger food. Sam and Bronnie asked Christopher about a small painting of a cedar tree at the center of a garden – a scene we all recognized as it faced directly onto the road outside.

"One day, I expect we'll return to the States," said Bronnie. "I can't think of a more beautiful reminder of our time here in McLeod Ganj."

Christopher's glance settled on Bronnie's hand for a moment. "Are you two engaged?"

They nodded.

"Set a date?"

"Next spring!" beamed Bronnie.

Christopher nodded, "Well then. Let this be a wedding gift, from me to you."

The pair were astounded. "We can't just take this from you!" exclaimed Bronnie.

"Why not? The cedar tree and the bench beneath has been

one of my favorite vistas in the past few years. I'd like this painting to go to the home of someone who treasures the garden as I do."

"Oh, we do!" Sam told him.

"It's a special place for us too," Bronnie's eyes were brimming.

"Well, then?" Christopher regarded the pair benevolently. "Would you refuse the wishes of a dying man?"

AFTER THEY HAD TAKEN IN ALL OF THE PAINTINGS, ASKING about the striking portrait of Caroline and admiring Sid and Franc's new acquisitions, they settled on the carpet in front of Christopher, sipping champagne and passing around plates of food.

"You know," Christopher told them somewhat breathlessly, when there was a lull in conversation, "You all have no idea what you've just done for me." He was looking in particular towards Sid and Franc. "I've got no money at all. The only reason I'm allowed to stay here is because Marianne Ponter persuaded the nursing home board that I'm a charity case. Every two weeks a new statement arrives," he gestured towards the brown envelopes. "According to the most recent one, I owe my care-givers exactly the same amount that you two gentlemen have just agreed to pay me. So, I can discharge my financial obligations." He paused for a moment, with an expression of relief. "That's ... something I'd given up all hope of doing. I don't mind a pauper's grave" he mused. "But I never wanted to leave the nursing home out of pocket."

Sid and Franc were quick to assure Christopher how much they valued his work. Conversation turned to an exhibition of his other paintings – perhaps at The Himalaya Book Café?

But Christopher shushed them. "Very sweet of you to offer," he said. "But really. I'm very near the end of my life. Just one more job to finish," he pointed at the canvas facing the wall. "Then I'm done."

Everyone looked at him, startled by the unflinching candor of what he'd just said. Along with the curious contentment of his tone. I took the silence that followed as my cue. Getting up from the wicker chair, I walked the short distance to where he was sitting, before launching myself onto his lap, circling the spattered corduroy fabric several times, then settling down. I felt his hand on my neck, the slightly tremulous touch with which I'd become acquainted in recent weeks. I purred protectively.

"Your painting," Franc was looking at the back of the easel. "Can you tell us what it is?"

"My final work," smiled Christopher, "is a commission. In fact, the subject of Geshe Wangpo's wonderful teaching last night."

"A Dharma subject?" speculated Serena.

Christopher delivered an enigmatic smile.

"The death process?" queried Sam.

"We'd love to see it!" enthused Bronnie.

"My dear," he looked at her kindly. "It's unfinished. I never show my work until it's complete."

"How complete is it?" Sid displayed his skill as a negotiator.

Christopher's expression softened. "Almost," he confessed.

"It would be such an honor." Detecting a shift, Franc brought his hands to his heart.

They were all gazing at him with beseeching expressions.

Christopher looked from one face to the next, before sighing. "Oh well," he said after a while. "I suppose it's nearly done. As am I," he gestured that Serena could turn the canvas away from the wall.

On Christopher's lap, I was looking at his visitors, not the painting, as Serena rotated the easel. I knew the moment that they saw the painting, not only because the expressions on their faces had taken on a kind of exultant wonderment. But also because the whole atmosphere changed. There was an energetic shift of the kind that marked the arrival of the Dalai Lama in any room that he entered. The visceral charge felt as a physical sensation by those who found themselves in the presence of boundless purity and benevolence.

I turned to look at the vision that held them all transfixed. It was Amitabha Buddha – but not as he appeared in traditional *thangkas,* sitting on a multicolored lotus in the midst of his pure land. Christopher's whole canvas was devoted to Amitabha's face and torso, his vibrant red-colored body so vividly dynamic that he appeared in the midst of blissful, energetic light. There was a dramatic power to the image, as though Amitabha was actually there. Christopher had conveyed his qualities of infinite light and infinite love with compelling immediacy.

Sid's eyes were filled with tears. Serena had her hand over her mouth. Franc had instinctively brought his hands together at his heart in devotion. "Extraordinary," he was the first to speak.

"Quite unlike anything I've ever seen," agreed Serena, emotion tugging at her mouth.

Sid turned to Christopher, bowing his head before saying, "This is the most spectacular vision of Amitabha I have encountered." His words were filled with emotion. "May I ask who your most fortunate patron is? And how the work came to be commissioned?"

Christopher, somewhat overcome by the visible reaction of the audience to his work, pondered for a long while before saying, "Let me explain. You see, the past few months have been quite extraordinary. Beginning with my terminal diagnosis."

In short sentences, delivered between shallow inhalations, he told them what I'd overheard him recount to Marianne Ponter. How he'd taken up painting again – for the sheer joy of it. How, on an impulse he attributed to me, he had donated his painting *Primordial Dawn* to His Holiness.

"The reason for this joyful gathering," he beamed, "is because we met through Geshe Wangpo last night. The reason I went to the teaching was because the Dalai Lama told me to. And the only reason I spoke to His Holiness was because of this little one." As he continued to stroke me, I purred with appreciative gusto. "So, you could say that Amitabha Buddha arose through the influence of the Dalai Lama's Cat."

"A being whose influence should never be underestimated,"

Serena spoke to murmurs of assent, with a smile in her voice.

"What extraordinary gifts you have created for His Holiness," observed Sid.

"The gifts His Holiness has given me are far greater," Christopher replied.

In the silence that followed, it was evident that the group wanted him to elaborate.

"I never thought that I could meditate," he nodded. "For a long time, I've known the theory. I've had some understanding of concepts like the sublime reality of *Mahamudra*. But I mistakenly believed that I couldn't embody such wisdom, because I was unable to meditate on a cushion. What His Holiness made me realize is that when I paint, I am completely absorbed with the object of my work. My focus is total. Which is why he commissioned me to immerse myself in an object of the most profound virtue and power." Christopher gestured to the painting behind him.

"As I've been painting, it's all been coming together," his voice was filled with emotion. "The understanding and the doing. For the first time, I've come to recognize that my life hasn't been quite the wasted opportunity I believed it was until recently. Even the fallow years served a purpose." He nodded with conviction as he looked from one enthralled face to the next.

"Most of all," he told them, "I've completely lost all fear of dying. For who is it, exactly, that dies? I have come to know that there's nothing to be afraid of – and you shouldn't be afraid of death either. We end painting one reality. We begin painting the next. You know, I didn't think I'd ever feel this, but in the strangest of ways, I'm actually quite looking forward to seeing what comes next."

Chapter Six

The rainy days grew fewer and further apart. Gone were the heavy blankets of fog and instead, when they came, the early morning mists were as ethereal as drifting waves of incense. From the first-floor sill I observed the fading of the monsoon season, along with the quiet dawning of one of my favorite times of the year.

Autumn in the Himalayas is a season of delight – warm days, lush vibrancy and brilliant color everywhere you look. After the rains, plants are thriving and verdant, blossoming in vivid profusion. Birds trill and swoop through pine-clean air infused with the scent of a thousand flowers. The autumn sky, a sweep of vault-like clarity, reveals the ice-capped mountains in all their sublime transcendence. Although they have been there all the time shrouded from view, as the veils of cloud cover fall away from our familiar, protective guardians, they always appear startlingly closer than we remembered.

On such days, every sinew in a cat's body tells one to venture out. To explore. To make the most of whatever undiscovered marvels may await, after months of being cooped up.

It seems that humans feel the same way.

One afternoon, I was enticed by an alluring fragrance coming from the direction of the garden next door. It was the faint hint of catnip. When I got there, I was surprised to find Bronnie Wellensky laying a blanket on the lawn under the cedar tree. By her side, a wicker basket replete with drinks and cartons of food.

I had known Sam's girlfriend Bronnie for years, watching the two of them from the time that Bronnie had arrived to pin a flier to The Himalaya Book Café noticeboard, seeking part-time volunteers to offer kids computer training. Sam, the newly appointed and nervous bookstore manager, had been unable to resist the vivacious, can-do Canadian in her late twenties, who all but demanded he offer his services as a teacher.

Since then, the relationship between the two of them had unfolded, Bronnie's confident demeanor coaxing Sam out of his shell. The two of them had moved into an apartment above Mrs. Williams, an elderly woman who had seemed like the neighbor from hell. Along with the other café regulars, I had been privy to the ensuing drama.

"Hello Rinpoche!" Bronnie greeted me, snapping her fingers in the manner of someone more familiar with dogs. It was the kind of gesture that may have prompted umbrage among some felines, but I knew that Bronnie had a good heart.

More to the point, the moment I approached her, I sensed that something about her had changed.

I stepped towards her curiously, sniffing at her with intuitive recognition as I allowed her to scratch my neck. Then I made my way to that particular part of the flowerbed where the patch of catnip had grown thick and luxuriant in the monsoon rains.

Bronnie was smoothing out the blanket and retrieving a few items from the basket. It was the first time I'd seen her prepare a picnic, but an afternoon like this could hardly be more inviting, the magic of the day in vivid contrast to the overcast dreariness of the previous weeks.

It wasn't long before Sam arrived, mounting the steps from the pavement, flopping onto the blanket beside her and delivering a tender kiss.

"Isn't this just wonderful?" she gestured, hands open to the sky.

"Perfect!" Sam lay, head resting on the ground, staring up through the branches of the cedar. "I didn't know you were into picnics?"

"Family tradition, growing up," she said. "But this is the first in India. A special occasion for a special day."

She was looking at him, pointedly. Her dark hair, often disheveled as she hurried from one thing to the next, was brushed into a sleek curtain about her face. As I'd already observed, she had applied lipstick and a touch of eyeliner, and instead of her usual jeans was wearing a pretty dress.

Sam continued gazing into the tree. "It *is* a special day," he said. "And everyone wants to be outside, even at the café. The biophilia effect, it's called. Our instinctive love of other living beings – nature, animals, plants."

"Uh-huh." Sam, Bronnie knew, was being Sam. Prompted to account for the wonderfulness of the day, he was off in his head retrieving the relevant data.

"Eric Fromm the psychologist came up with that term, but of course it's always been with us. Aristotle believed that walking outside cleared the mind – *solvitur ambulando*. Some of the greats like St. Augustine, Einstein, Darwin and Tesla believed the same. Not many people know, but Beethoven even used to hug a tree in his garden. He was the original tree hugger."

"Really?" Bronnie was taking plates out of the wicker basket and laying them on the blanket.

"Are you aware that it's actually public health policy in Japan and South Korea to grow forests outside the major cities and encourage people to spend time in them. *Shinrin-yoku*, it's called. Forest bathing. The natural killer cells in our bodies are boosted dramatically when we spend time under the trees, breathing in the phytoncides they emit."

"I wasn't aware."

'Most folks are surprised," agreed Sam. "They don't realize that we actually physically change when we're in nature. Cortisol levels go down. Blood pressure decreases. Our immune system is boosted. It's even been shown that you heal more quickly if you're in a hospital room with a window looking onto a garden."

"Is that so?"

"And that's just some of the impacts on body. They've also done tests showing that time in nature improves our creativity."

"It does?"

"And our ability to focus."

"I wonder how they'd test that?" she mused, removing the lid from a box to reveal two generous portions of a feta and goat cheese tart, which she added to the bountiful display.

"It's really interesting," Sam had the answer. "What they do is take one group of people and ask them to walk around a city center for an hour. Another group wanders through the countryside. At the end, they give them all the same article to read, which contains a number of errors – typos, grammar, that kind of thing. They ask both groups to mark up the mistakes.

"The people who walk through the fields are much better at picking up errors. The theory is that their minds are less busy. Less thought pollution. They have more mental clarity, making it easier for them to focus."

"Well," Bronnie smiled. "Now would be a good time for *you* to focus."

"Oh?" queried Sam. "On what?"

"On here and now. This moment. On me!"

It was unlike Bronnie to draw attention to herself quite so deliberately. On the blanket, Sam turned, for the first time really noticing her. "You look really great, babe," he said.

"Thank you."

Glancing at the spread, he took in all that she'd arranged. "And that's my favorite tart."

"I know."

"Did you go all the way to Jean Claude's?"

"I did," she beamed. "For you."

Sitting up he kissed her, caressing her cheek. "So beautiful!" For a while he took in her bright smile and glowing presence, registering that something was happening, but not knowing what to make of it.

"What?" he murmured after a moment, as her radiant gaze towards him continued undiminished.

"What d'you mean, what?" she returned.

"What's happening?"

"That's for you to find out," she was playful.

"Okay." He looked at the basket, observing a bottle of wine. "You bought new glasses?"

"Picnic glasses."

"A drink?" he offered.

"Apple juice would be nice."

"Not a wine?"

"Better not," she said. Then after a pause, "In my condition."

"These acrylic glasses are great!" Sam enthused, not skipping a beat as he held one up by the stem. "Perfectly proportioned, but so much safer."

The two of them ate, Bronnie dropping heavy hints which continued to elude Sam. For an especially brainy person, he could be remarkably dim-witted. But he did know enough to realize that he was missing something.

When Bronnie lolled back on the blanket in the warmth of the idyllic afternoon, I roused myself from the catnip and crossed the lawn. If I were lucky, there could be a few remnants of goat cheese left on her plate.

Sam noted my appearance. Bronnie explained that we'd already seen each other.

After extensive sniffing, I found a single but delectable soupçon of cheese which I ate with fulsome relish.

Sam was lounging in the late afternoon warmth, his first serve finished and halfway through a glass of wine. He looked benevolent and bemused. Perhaps, I thought, I could help make him aware of what my mammalian instinct had alerted me to. Climbing onto Bronnie, I circled her stomach in the way that we cats do when preparing to sit.

"Look at that!" Sam exclaimed, glancing to where Bronnie met his eyes, beaming broadly. "Rinpoche is very particular about laps. Has she ever sat on yours?"

"Never," Bronnie's eyes were sparkling. "Until today."

As Sam still wasn't getting it, I began kneading her stomach with great deliberation. When even this pantomime failed to prompt a reaction, I lowered my head as though this was needed to detect the profound shift occurring within her.

For a long while Sam stared at this, his analytical brain no doubt taking in my vomeronasal response, computing that I was scrutinizing some kind of change – chemical, hormonal perhaps – and connecting this with other data inputs. The "special day" comment. Bronnie refusing wine. A reference she'd made to pink or blue. Eventually he asked, somewhat breathlessly, "Are you … pregnant?"

"Finally!" she cried, exultant, arms lifting above her head.

Sam was incredulous.

"*We're* pregnant!" she corrected him.

He leaned over to kiss her, at which point I hopped off. "I just can't believe …!

"I know," she was holding him to her. "Well – we have been trying."

"I thought it would take longer!" He was elated. "You hear of some people …"

"We've been lucky. We *are* lucky!"

"Lucky," he propped himself on his elbow, staring at her awestruck, "beyond anything I could have imagined."

A FEW MINUTES LATER, BRONNIE AND SAM WERE SITTING, radiant with their news, when a familiar figure appeared on the sidewalk. It was Serena dressed in her yoga gear, long dark hair tied in a ponytail. Behind her, Natalia and Ricardo were similarly attired.

Glancing over, as she caught sight of the two of them with their exhilarated expressions, she called out, "Look at you two lovebirds!"

As they waved back, Sam murmured to Bronnie, "Shall we tell them?"

"Why not?" she smiled. "They're like family."

"You're looking very cozy!" observed Serena.

"We have some news," Sam was beaming.

They halted.

"Just between us, for the time being," he told them. "We're pregnant!"

He was jubilant.

Immediately, all three passers-by were in the garden. Sam and Bronnie were on their feet, with much hugging and congratulations. Bronnie told them she'd only had the pregnancy confirmed that morning, so it was early days. Responding to their compliments about her appearance, she explained how the picnic was as much to celebrate with Sam, as it was about the glorious day, but how very slow he'd been on the uptake – the first telling of a tale which would no doubt undergo further embellishment with repeated telling in the months and years ahead.

"It's amazing how people find each other here in McLeod Ganj," said Serena, eyes twinkling. "Sid and me. You and Sam," she held Bronnie's hand. "I'll bet an outgoing Canadian like you never thought you'd end up with a geeky American?"

"Never!" Bronnie was laughing.

Ricardo and Natalia had their arms around Sam.

"You guys look like you're heading to yoga," said Bronnie. "But it's in that direction," pointing opposite to where they were walking.

"A different plan for this evening because it's so glorious," Serena told her. "Heidi's doing an outdoor class and meditation. Right across the road, on the lawn of the Old Sanitorium."

"Sounds great!" said Bronnie.

"It will be special," said Ricardo. "You are welcome to come."

"Thanks, but we're not exactly dressed for it," she said. "And Sam's on his second glass of wine."

Having remained unacknowledged all this time, it was only when I rubbed myself against Serena's legs that she leaned down to stroke me. "Rinpoche's at the center of things, as always."

Glancing down, Natalia was evidently more attuned to my wishes than most. "Do you think she wants yoga?" she asked.

I had overheard Franc telling her how I attended classes at The Downward Dog School of Yoga, overseeing the stretching and bending from a shelf at the back of the room. Sometimes I was even garlanded in flowers and known as "Swami". My new Colombian friend had remembered.

Serena got down on her haunches and looked at me uncertainly. "The Old Sanatorium is up quite a short but steep hill."

There was only the briefest of pauses before Natalia proposed, "I carry her, yes?"

WHICH WAS HOW, DEAR READER, FOR THE SECOND TIME IN A month, I found myself in the arms of my new South American fan, crossing the road and ascending a driveway so steep I'd never have attempted it without good reason.

"Such great news!" Serena smiled, turning to wave at Bronnie and Sam.

"They are a nice couple," agreed Ricardo.

"And Sam is very kind," said Natalia. "He helps me with reading."

"I've seen you on the sofa with Sam's recommendations," Serena said, gesturing a pile of books.

"When I came to India, I knew nothing about Buddhism. I am from a Catholic country, si?" explained Natalia. "Suddenly, all these people around me are Buddhists. I want to know how they think."

"You have a better idea now?" queried Serena.

Natalia nodded, "But I am still a little confused. I thought Buddha was a man. But I read about these women Buddhas."

Serena smiled. "The historical Buddha who lived two and a half thousand years ago, Shakyamuni Buddha, he was a man. But enlightenment is a state beyond being male or female. Enlightened beings can choose to appear in any form they wish. And since the time of the Buddha, many people have become enlightened. So ..." short of breath, Serena paused for a moment, hands on hips. "We have female Buddhas like Green Tara, White Tara, Prajnaparamita and many others. In Tibetan Buddhism, the feminine is associated with great wisdom."

Natalia, younger by two decades and not short of breath, was nodding. "That's cool," she said. "The female is ... valued."

"The divine feminine?" Serena glanced behind. Several class members were following them up the short hill. "Absolutely!"

"So these female Buddhas, they are *yidams*, right?"

Serena nodded. "If you wish. There are any number of *yidams*, male and female."

"What's the difference ..." Natalia persisted, "between a Buddha and a *yidam*?"

"A *yidam* is a Buddha with whom you cultivate a personal connection, heart and mind, to help you attain the same state as them. Different people are drawn to different *yidams*."

"So all Buddhists don't have the same *yidams*?" Natalia was surprised.

"No," Serena shook her head. "It's an individual thing. Some of us are drawn to certain *yidams* and others to different ones. There are dozens, maybe even hundreds of *yidams* across the different lineages. You might say that the *yidam* we choose is who we wish to become."

"The best version of ourselves?" confirmed Natalia.

In an instant, I was transported back to His Holiness's room on the day he received his famous pop star visitor. The one with the Little Monsters. How he had congratulated her on creating an ideal version of herself, then imaging it to be real. How believing is seeing.

"Exactly," said Serena. "We all wish for enlightenment. The paths we take towards it are as individual as we are."

The steep driveway flattened out and ahead was a lush green lawn, where students were already setting up yoga mats. A short distance away, a disused, colonial double-story building with a columned portico and wide veranda faced the lawn and what lay on the other side of it – the Himalayan mountains, serene, ice-capped, ever-mysterious. While the sanatorium building itself was in disrepair, with boarded windows, cracked plasterwork and part of the roof caved in, plants in the flower beds around continued to blossom with balsam and portulacas.

"Ultimately," said Serena, "all *yidams* are aspects of the same enlightened mind, like separate facets of a diamond. Different entry points to the same thing. The Buddhas are not like children – if you give one of them most of your attention, the others won't get jealous!"

They all laughed before Natalia said, "Thank you for explaining." Her voice was warm. "This is very interesting."

The Downward Dog School of Yoga had always taken in the mountains. The studio Ludo had constructed years before, at the suggestion of the Dalai Lama himself, had large sliding doors fronting onto the panoramic vista. Its walls were clad in mirrors, the better to draw the view inside.

All the same, it was one thing sitting indoors looking out at the mountains, and an altogether different experience being outside, feeling the breeze on your whiskers and the warm afternoon sun on your face. Everything about the *prana* of this special day felt like an invitation to be out in nature – an invitation to which many had responded.

Apart from all the yoga class regulars, walking up the hill with colorful rolls under their arms, there were many unfamiliar people too. Heidi had arrived earlier, with mats from the studio for newcomers. When demand exceeded supply, people had to make do with towels. A few hangers-on were there, not for the yoga class, but simply to observe from the sidelines. It was the largest attendance I'd ever seen and had quite a different quality to it. There was something celebratory in the air, an unspoken acknowledgement of the wonder of nature.

At the edge of the lawn a rockery was profuse with flowers, beside which people had cast off shoes, bags and various items of clothing. At one end, a smooth boulder offered the perfect spot from which a feline spectator might follow the proceedings.

And so I did, observing Heidi take her place facing the Old Sanatorium, offering the class the full benefit of the mountain vista behind her. I followed the easy poise with which she led her students through a variety of stretches, while briefly explaining their purpose. How she gave options which challenged more flexible practitioners, without leaving their creakier counterparts behind.

Ludo was in the group, not far from me. Several times I noted an expression of surprise on his face, deepening into one of concern. As a seasoned observer of his classes, I could guess the reason. A practitioner of Ashtanga, Ludo always followed the same sequence of asanas in their prescribed order. No freewheeling or improvisation. No shortcuts or new ideas. The pursuit of perfection required rigor and discipline.

Heidi's sequence of stretches seemed to have the same purpose but came in a different format. There were antidotes for computer users who spent all day hunched over their keyboards, lengthening body parts that were too often tense. Inversions to place people's heads, for a few minutes at least, lower than the rest of them, so that the flow of *prana* in their bodies was reversed, and blood flow to their brains enhanced. A brief period of vigorous lunging and arm movements was followed by systematic relaxation, after which Heidi invited everyone to relax in meditation posture.

Once they were seated and still, she asked them to attend, with singular focus, to each sense one at a time. Sound was the first: the surge and fall of the wind as it blew through the nearby forests. Bird calls. Passing traffic on the road down the hill. All sound was to be listened to, free of the inner monologue that would inevitably arise, unless one remained vigilant.

There was to be no judgment either – judgment inevitably led to further mental chatter. For the purposes of this meditation, sound was neither good nor bad. Pleasant nor unpleasant. It was simply sound.

Moving through the other senses – feeling, odor, sight – she encouraged the same deliberate tuning in to one door of perception at a time, in forensic detail. It was a honing of the senses, a narrowing of attention.

Then Heidi told us to observe whatever streamed through *all* of our senses – an instruction that felt so liberating, so free, that it was only then that we noticed how subtly she had led us away from narrative chatter to be fully present in this moment. We were simply here and now, facing the mountains, their icy caps and the rivers flowing from them reflecting the color of the setting sun – glistening gold peaks etched against a lapis-blue sky. Here, with the mountain breeze in our faces, the glow of sunset on our backs, the evening birdsong mellifluous in the trees around us, and the bewitching perfume of evening flowers.

"When we come into nature," Heidi's voice was slow and soothing as the sound of the wind in the branches, "we think of ourselves as visitors, separate from the trees and the mountains and the sun. We don't feel intimately connected to them. We believe that we are unrelated."

After a lengthy pause she challenged, "But how accurate is this idea? Consider our breath. How our life depends on it. Inhaling and exhaling – this defines us as being alive. With every breath we take, we inhale oxygen made by the trees, the plants, the grass. With every exhalation, we breathe out carbon dioxide, needed by these same plants to survive. So, we are not that separate from the trees and plants. In fact, we are in a relationship with them. We need them. They need us."

For a while the group sat with this insight, the truth of it resonating at a level deeper than usual, because of quieter minds.

Heidi took a different angle. "Our body is comprised of 90% water. Where does the water come from? Ultimately from the rivers, the oceans, the rain. We consume it, in one form or another, and for a while it becomes a part of who we are. Then we pass it out, just as we breathe out carbon dioxide. The water returns to nature, having included us in its flow.

"Once again, the rain and the rivers are not something disconnected from us. We are completely dependent on them. We are part of the water cycle."

Above us came the deep honking of geese. A flock of six graylags, in perfect formation, slowly crossed the sky from one horizon to the other.

"What of every cell in our body?" Heidi continued the analytical meditation. "They come from somewhere outside us. Ultimately, from the earth. Whether we are plant-based eaters or carnivores, the source of our nutrition is the soil itself, just as it is the support for every other living being. We process food and pass it out. None of us has a cell in our body we can call our own that belongs exclusively to us. That is uniquely ours. And no cell is older than seven years old, because our cells are always being recycled. We are constantly engaging with earth. Every solid part of us comes from soil."

She paused.

"And none of this could happen without the sun. If there was no light, no heat, there would be no trees or plants. No food or chance of survival. Without the sun, we would soon die."

If anyone had failed to make the connection before, there was no avoiding it now, with the sun about to slip behind the building, its final lengthening rays warming the necks of all who sat, poised and spellbound in that moment.

"So, far from being visitors to nature," said Heidi, "far from being separate from the trees and the earth and the sun, it is more truthful to say that we are part of all this. We don't go into nature; we emerge from it. We *are* manifestations of the earth, the air, the water and the sun.

"For a few moments, try to focus on this thought: I am nature. Nature is me."

Behind the group, the sun had dipped below the horizon so that the mountains in front reflected the glow it had left in its wake. Their lofty peaks were now an impossible cerise, with molten rivers of red flowing down their sides.

For the longest time, everyone remained completely still, more connected than ever to the extraordinary vista before us, non-dual not only with the transcendent, ever-shifting dance of light above, but with all that was below – the forests and the rivers that ran through them, the verdant plants and profusion of flowers, the sky, the clouds, the very earth itself. Each one of us recognizing that I am how I am because all this is how it is. Each a different aspect of the same reality.

PEOPLE LEFT THE CLASS THAT DAY WITH A QUIET REVERENCE. Rolling up mats and walking down the short hill, they were still living with the impact of what they had experienced, wanting to continue in this state of reverential connection.

Some of the yoga regulars helped by collecting up studio mats. Several had grass stains and at a tap next to the veranda, Sid was on his haunches, washing these off. Attracted by the sound of running water, I descended from the rockery to join him. Which was when I discovered that this evening's class hadn't been to everyone's liking.

"I just didn't understand what you were doing!" Ludo was whispering heatedly to Heidi on the veranda.

"Preparing the body before settling the mind," she replied. "As is traditional."

"That," Ludo wagged his finger, "wasn't preparing the body. Not properly. You left out some of the most important asanas."

"Time, uncle. We only had an hour! I wanted to give people a taste of both yoga and meditation."

"Doing neither, according to Guruji!"

At the tap, overhearing the same conversation, Sid was frowning.

I instantly remembered Heidi's conversation at The

Himalaya Book Café. How miserable she had been about exactly this criticism. How she had believed it revealed a deep, personal inadequacy, stemming back to her childhood.

Round the table her friends had tried their best to persuade her otherwise. How Serena had warned her not to give heed to The Shitty Committee. How Franc had invited her to ask exactly where this inadequate self was to be found – a line of inquiry not so far from the very same one through which she had guided her students with such sensitivity this evening.

How would she respond to Ludo?

Evidently, she had taken the advice of her friends to heart, because the next thing I heard her say was, "That may be *your* view, but with respect, other people think differently."

"The asanas are the asanas!" Ludo insisted. "We must respect the sequence. It's there for a reason. You can't just take things out or put things in!"

"Why not?"

"How can you get the results, if you don't create their causes?" He spoke with conviction. "How do you become an elite yogi? First the primary series. Then the intermediate. Finally the advanced."

"Uncle, most people will never manage even the primary series! You know that!"

"Step by step, all is coming," Ludo's reply was instinctive. "Discipline. Practice."

"Not everyone is cut out to be a yogi, let alone an elite one. Most people are struggling just to cope with everyday life. Should we leave them behind?"

"If they want to do something else, they can look for it."

"But we have the power to help, however far they evolve. Even if they never come to another class," she was gesturing towards where a group of students was disappearing down the hill. "If we made them aware of something special today, if we gave them happiness for just a short time, if we planted a seed ..."

"That's defeatist talk!" interjected Ludo. "Students of The Downward Dog School of Yoga set their sights on the summit. We won't stop until we get there."

"Perfection for the few," Heidi rebuffed him. "What about the suffering of the many?"

"We are not elitist. We welcome all comers."

"You're not being realistic!"

"*You* are the one who is not a realist!" He was vehement. "There is no contentment for a weak mind!"

Heidi fled down the steps from the veranda, eyes bright with tears. Seizing mats from beside the rockery, she was soon walking down the hill. Ludo followed in his own time, dignified and resolute.

Finishing wiping down the mats, Sid turned off the tap and looked at me sadly. "What to do, eh, Rinpoche? What would the Dalai Lama have to say about this?"

ONLY MINUTES LATER I ENCOUNTERED HIS HOLINESS, HAVING descended the steep, but thankfully brief, driveway and returned to our apartment. Taking my standard shortcut via the outside of the building, I'd usually slip through a reception room window kept open for my use. But today, further along the same narrow ledge, I noticed that another window was also open. And not one I'd ever known to be open before.

I must, of course, investigate.

What I found should not have surprised me. The large hinged windows of a rarely used balcony room were fully open and there, sitting on a cane chair, was the Dalai Lama.

"Ah, my little Snow Lion!" he chuckled, as I appeared. "You have been outside too?"

With a meow, I hopped from the ledge to the floor, and a short while later onto his lap.

"On days like this I would love to do the same as you," he said, stroking me. "To be free to explore the outside world. To walk in the forest. To lie on the grass and feel the sun on my body. But security, I think, would not like it.

"Sometimes there are limits on what is possible. We can't all do the same thing. But that's alright, not so? What we do may be different, one from another, but none of that matters, so long as we remember that all the joy we find in the world outside comes from mind itself."

I leaned against him, head to his chest, gazing past the maroon robes and open windows to where the mountain peaks were darkening against the crystal sky. Many times His Holiness had described the mind of a meditator who attains calm abiding as being like an autumn sky, possessing a boundless lucidity beyond description. And so it was this evening. The vast cloudless sky was perfect in its clarity, seeming completely without color.

In time, as the sun slipped further and further beneath the horizon, the first spray of silver flecks appeared in the sky, the mountain peaks glistening in icy luminescence. And still the beauty and peace of it continued. The profound, unstoppable wellbeing. All of it accompanied by my own soft purring, and the rhythmic lub-dub lub-dub lub-dub of the Dalai Lama's beating heart.

CHAPTER SEVEN

Where does wonderfulness come from, dear reader? And how about its opposite – awfulness? What is it that makes some things – or people – a source of untrammeled delight, but others truly beastly? And how is it that one can turn into the other, so very quickly and unexpectedly?

These are questions worth pondering, are they not? Especially when the level of beastliness you have to live with becomes insufferable. For a wise and mature-aged feline, seeking to live with greater zest, wouldn't it be good to have a reliable way of infusing one's life with a constant flow of one, while ensuring as little as possible of the other?

As I ventured out on a particular morning, little did I know that the answers to these very questions were about to be revealed – and in a way that was further from anything I could have imagined.

Bougainvillea Street was one of those typically wind- ing McLeod Ganj roads which pass through stretches of ram- shackle shops, cramped houses and barren patches of nothing in particular, before turning to reveal the bountiful flower boxes of an apartment block or the highly waxed wooden doors of some official building. It was up this street that The Downward Dog School of Yoga was to be found. And some- what closer to home, on the opposite side from the yoga studio, my ultimate destination for the day: the high, whitewashed walls and ornate gates of what had once been the home of the Maharajah of Himachal Pradesh.

Things had been happening at 108 Bougainvillea Street. In recent days I'd overheard snippets between Mrs. Trinci and Tenzin in the VIP kitchen, about major renovations to the bedrooms and plumbing. Serena had spent most of one morn- ing on the phone to landscape gardeners. Sweeping changes were afoot.

Even Franc and Sam were somehow involved. There had been impromptu meetings at the bookstore checkout with Serena, to discuss joint marketing. Quite what it all meant, I had no idea. But I intended to find out. And today was an important milestone, it seemed, because Sid and Serena were visiting to inspect building renovations that were well under- way. Accompanying them as their guest of honour would be Yogi Tarchin.

Sid's former home had always had a somewhat stately

appearance. Set amid rolling lawns, with a perimeter of soaring cedars for privacy, I recalled the building as a substantial double-story, with marble steps, a formal entrance hall and a curiously institutional feel – a place with neither the gleaming impersonality of an office foyer, nor the welcoming warmth of a private home.

It was here that Sid had lived with his daughter Zahra, before he'd met Serena. Then a widower, coming to terms with the loss of his late wife, Shanti, in a car accident, this had also been Sid's business headquarters.

In recent years, since Sid and Serena had moved into their own home with the tower, Sid had rented out Bougainvillea Street, and I had paid it little attention when passing by. However, if I sometimes paused to sniff at the elaborate wrought-iron gates and caught the distinctive whiff of a particular pair of canines, an involuntary shudder would pass through me. This place and I had history.

One of the greatest traumas of my life – or so I had believed for a time – was when I was spotted by these two rampaging beasts further down the street. Off their leashes, they had immediately given chase. I had darted into a spice shop for refuge. They had followed. Mayhem, a shrieking storekeeper and clouds of turmeric ensued, followed by a frantic pursuit. I had only just escaped those baying hell-beings and their slavering chops by scaling the gates of Sid's house – a feat made possible by the adrenaline pounding through my system. For hours I had sat, spice-smeared and miserable on the wall of Sid's former residence, until I was rescued by Serena on her way home from yoga.

I had come to think differently about what had happened – and my pursuers – when a similar pursuit, only weeks later, had ended with my back to Sid's wall and nowhere to climb. I'd had no choice but to puff up with the fury of a wrathful deity and bare my fangs at the two beasts, who came to a startled halt, unsure what to do next. Stinging one on the nose with a swift claw strike, when he had the temerity to shove his snout in my direction, the two had quickly backed off. From that moment on, I was no longer a terrified victim but instead Snow Lion the Subduer – the Vanquisher of Golden Retrievers!

Pausing at the gates of 108 Bougainvillea Street today, I found the place a hive of activity. Gates open, a huge truck was backed up, with deliverymen ferrying a succession of bathroom items into the building. The outside walls had been repainted and adorned with gleaming tiled frames, giving the place an unexpectedly opulent flavor. A van of signwriters pulled up and men began to take measurements for whatever sign was to be mounted near the entrance.

Meantime I stepped inside, to see the gardens had been transformed into a place ripe for exploration by an inquisitive puss. Gone were the staid rows of flowerbeds, and instead there was a luxuriance of foliage everywhere. Hibiscus hedges created new enclaves around leafy seating areas which hadn't existed before. Palm trees rose above cascading waterfalls, lush with tropical flowers. The perimeter of cedar trees still provided reassuring privacy – the only thing familiar about this new and lavish Arcadia.

After a while, the truck was finally emptied of bathroom fittings, the deliverymen piled in, and the vehicle lurched away amid a belch of dark smoke. With the short driveway empty, I crossed glistening stone pavers to the front veranda. The front doors were open and from inside came the sound of distant voices. Were Sid and Serena already here inspecting the premises? If so, had they brought Rishi with them? And what exactly was this place to become? It had the atmosphere of a boutique hotel, the kind that featured on glossy magazine covers. But neither Sid nor Serena had ever spoken a word about wanting to become hoteliers.

The front doors were flanked by large brass tubs of camellias in lavish pink flower. Each tub was set on a wheeled base, and had evidently been watered recently. The puddle which had formed beneath the drainage holes was exactly the kind that required further investigation.

I padded over to one tub and sniffed the water curiously. I took my time as I inhaled, detecting hints of loamy nutrients. There are few kinds of water more delightful to a cat than one replete with earthy elements. It was while I was taking a few tentative laps that I became aware of a noise nearby. One which was disconcerting: a repetitive babble, growing louder. Shielded out of sight by the tub, I peered round the space behind. Sure enough, Rishi was emerging from the front door, crawling along the ground.

Fortunately, he hadn't seen me. He continued happily with

his rhythmic chant. Wherever he was, Serena couldn't be far away. I'd wait till she was on the scene and had him in her arms before I revealed my presence.

At least, that was the plan.

Things suddenly changed with the arrival of a sinister presence. In the middle of the open gate, just a short distance away. It was a dog from one of the ramshackle houses down the street. A mean-spirited, wiry-haired creature I always avoided, having watched him snap aggressively at passers-by. Always on the scrounge for food. I had no idea why he was so transfixed by Rishi, until I saw what Rishi was holding in his hand. A piece of sandwich.

Rishi had seen the dog and wasn't in the least concerned. Continuing his tuneless singsong, he bounced along the veranda, waving the food up and down. The dog moved closer, zeroing in on the prize, calculating his chances of snatching the morsel and making off with it.

Rishi would be shocked by the unexpected raid. Aggrieved to lose his snack. But it might be much worse. As the dog continued his stealthy approach, dropping his shoulders to the ground, I realized that this could become very nasty. The dog could inflict serious injury on a being as small and soft as Rishi. And if Rishi were to show the least sign of resistance, it could turn into a violent attack.

What was it about 108 Bougainvillea Street and dogs? How come both my previous threatening encounters with canines had occurred at this address? Even though *I* wasn't the one being threatened this time, I felt impelled by an unexpected instinct. Rishi might be frightened of me for no good reason. But he was Serena's baby. He had no chance at all against a vicious street dog. Having slipped from the protection of his devoted parents for mere moments, Rishi was about to have the shock of his life.

I drew back on my haunches in preparation.

The dog was edging inexorably closer, belly on the ground, body curving left and right.

Rishi was still chanting, but his mood shifted. Staring at the approaching dog, the tone of his infant voice was changing. He was waving his arms less, finding it hard to make sense of why the dog's posture was so submissive – but its lips were starting to curl back in aggression.

Groveling before him, making clear its demand for food, it came within just a few feet of Rishi. At this point it revealed its true colors and snarled savagely. Rishi let out a shaken gurgle.

I leapt from my hiding place, taking both dog and Rishi unawares. Obsessed by Rishi's sandwich, the dog hadn't observed me in the shadows. Now I was flying towards it, reprising my role as vanquisher of canines. Front claws out, I was whipping through the air.

In that double time, every moment stretching as though elastic, to last very much longer than is usually the case. I saw Rishi's expression change from shock, as he finally recognized what the dog was after, to an instinctive drawing back of his arm to protect his food. His face filled with rapidly changing emotions of fear and horror. At which point I appeared right before his eyes, connecting a ninja-like strike directly to the dog's snout. It let out a startled whimper and sprang back. Just as a white van pulled into the gates, forcing it from the driveway.

After my balletic and entirely atypical kung fu, I landed a short distance away from Rishi, meeting his eyes directly. He stared at me, processing what had just happened. Would there be an operatic outpouring of delayed shock? An end-of-the-world meltdown, as he realized what had just happened?

To my surprise, after glancing to where the dog had disappeared behind the van and shoving the corner of his sandwich against his cheek, Rishi regarded me contemplatively. How much of what had just happened had he consciously taken in? Was he registering, on some level, that I had just saved him and his snack?

"La-la-laaa!" he proclaimed finally, hopping up and down on his bottom before turning towards the front door.

RISHI WAS PROCEEDING INSIDE AT THE SAME TIME AS THE voices became clearer. Sid was explaining something to Yogi Tarchin as the two came down the stairs. Serena was already standing in the middle of what had been remodeled as an upscale reception area, all gold and cream with red trims.

She interrupted whatever they were saying with a soft but urgent, "Look!" She was pointing towards where Rishi was bumping cheerfully along the floor – accompanied by me.

"Amazing!" Sid was delighted.

Yogi Tarchin nodded with a composed smile.

"How did *that* happen?" Serena's expression was ecstatic.

A uniformed woman arrived with a tray of drinks.

"Lemonade, Yogi Tarchin?" gestured Serena.

"Thank you," he smiled, picking up a glass.

Serena came to collect Rishi before the three adults crossed the room to the veranda, which was replete with plush new furniture. Overlooking the blooming gardens, it felt like we were in a rarefied sanctuary, cocooned and tranquil. Not that either the gardens or the house were on Serena's mind right now.

As I sat on a seagrass mat, a short distance from where Rishi was still toying with his food, she was staring at us, shaking her head. "This is so amazing!" she murmured. "Rishi has been terrified of HHC since the first time he saw her. Now today," she snapped her fingers, "he's totally fine with her. What's that all about?"

"Who knows?" Sid was following her gaze. "I'm just relieved."

Yogi Tarchin was watching the two of us. "All is mind," he said, after a pause. "Rishi's fear of HHC never came from HHC. She has no inherent qualities to be afraid of."

Oh, no? I delivered a sapphire-blue stare. Ask the savage street dog. Or the Golden Retrievers. They might tell you differently.

But as soon as their images passed through my mind, so did that of the President of the Swansea and Aberystwyth Cat Fanciers' Association, poking me away with his shoe like some unsavory detritus. Moments before Natalia carried me away, declaring me to be a cat of great highness.

Whatever qualities I possessed, it seemed, existed only in the minds of those who perceived me.

"It's the same with everything," said Yogi Tarchin, lifting his glass of lemonade. "Where does the deliciousness of lemonade come from?"

"Not from the lemonade," chuckled Sid. "However it may seem."

"Exactly! If that was so, everyone would love lemonade. But there are plenty of people who don't. Plenty who would find it too sweet, too tart, too concentrated or too watery. Which means the delightfulness of lemonade comes from the mind of the person perceiving it as delightful. And whatever happiness is produced by the mind only arises because of a previously created cause."

"Such as giving someone else a tasty drink?" asked Serena.

"Could be," agreed Yogi Tarchin. "There are so many possible causes shaping our experience of reality, moment by moment. What's important is to recognize the true cause of whatever pleasantness we experience, rather than the apparent causes – like lemonade – which are merely the conditions. What's *actually* happening is that we are enjoying the results of previously created karma."

The pause that followed was filled with the chatter of bulbuls in nearby bushes, and the distant drone of a lawnmower around the other side of the house.

"When we really understand that ..." said Serena after a while. "When we want to integrate it into our lives, it's really motivating to get out there and do positive things."

Yogi Tarchin regarded her earnest look with a playful expression.

She tilted her head to one side, inquiringly.

He chuckled with mischief.

"What?" she asked.

"You are right of course," he told her with a twinkle. "Doing positive things. Like what Sid and you are doing here. It is going to be wonderful – of benefit to your friends and to so many other beings!" He took in the gorgeous vista of gardens and house, before looking from one of them to the other. "But you can create powerful causes for positive experiences just by sitting here. I think of it as being intelligently lazy."

"You mean by meditating?" queried Serena.

"Invoking the Buddhas' blessings?" proposed Sid.

Yogi Tarchin leaned forward in his chair, raising his glass. "Celebrating!" he told them, with a smile. "Celebrating your own happiness, as well as that of others."

WHEN WE CELEBRATE SOMETHING, EXPLAINED YOGI TARCHIN, we create a surprisingly powerful cause to enjoy whatever is the object of celebration. If we celebrate a person being promoted to senior executive level, we create the cause to be elevated ourselves. In celebrating the success and happiness of others, we generate the karmic causes of our own future success and happiness.

As with so much Buddhist psychology, there is pragmatism

in this approach. Rejoicing in the successes of others helps us overcome jealousy. We are less likely to be resentful, when we understand how the triumphs of others offer a pathway to our own fulfillment. We may more wholeheartedly celebrate their successes, when we know the effects that we're creating for our own future. And if we can bring ourselves to celebrate the happiness of people we dislike, we not only overcome jealousy, but hatred too.

How powerful is the karma created by celebrating? According to Yogi Tarchin, very powerful. "As Buddhists, we aspire to attain enlightenment, Buddhahood itself, which can appear very distant and unattainable. But just by celebrating the actions of someone of a higher level than ourselves, we create half the amount of virtue that they have. And by rejoicing in the virtues of Buddhas or bodhisattvas, we can attain a tenth of the benefits they have gained, because their level of development is so much greater than ours.

"So you see, rejoicing is a very profitable business. It takes no physical or mental effort, but it's easy and brings wonderful results."

Listening intently, Sid and Serena looked delighted. "I'd like to celebrate your powers of concentration as a yogi!" Sid raised his glass of lemonade, toasting Yogi Tarchin.

"And I'd like to rejoice in your compassion and wisdom!" Serena chimed in.

"I am just a humble meditator," he protested. "Better that you rejoice in the virtues of all Buddhas and bodhisattvas of the three times and ten directions."

"As in our chant every morning," confirmed Sid.

"Which is why we do it," nodded Yogi Tarchin. "It's not just a ritual. Not only out of reverence. We are creating the causes to become Buddhas ourselves. In the meantime," he nodded towards them both, "I celebrate your success in creating this beautiful place."

"Well, Rinpoche, I don't think I can claim the credit for the idea," Sid met his gaze. "That was yours, when you visited on the day of our board meeting."

"Not that you picked up on it immediately," smiled Serena.

"True," he nodded. "Back then, I didn't even know that Binita was in trouble."

It was Serena whose gaze settled on me first. Then Sid's, followed by Yogi Tarchin's. And even Rishi's. One by one, all four humans were turning to look at me.

"Perhaps we should celebrate having HHC in our lives?" suggested Serena.

"Whenever she is around, unexpected things happen," observed Sid.

Rishi, sitting on the mat nearby, had been scrutinizing me closely. At that moment, he raised his arm and reached out to touch me.

My journey home took me past The Himalaya Book Café, the side with the new hutch serving coffee. Being mid-afternoon, there was no line at the window.

I paused, looking up. In my younger and more athletic

days, I would have attempted a leap to the counter as a way inside. Alas, that would be a vault too far, given my senior-status inflexibility. And from ground level, I was unable to see who might be inside. So it was serendipitous that at the very moment I paused beneath the window, who should appear but Heidi.

"*Guten Tag*, HHC!" she bent to stroke me.

Then came Natalia's voice from inside the café. Heidi responded, requesting a chai latte. And was my feline intuition serving me correctly, or was there a certain awkwardness in the way she stepped back from the window and was on her haunches again, lavishing unusual attention on me.

In recent weeks, during afternoons when I was dozing on the top shelf of the magazine rack, I had observed how Heidi had become a regular at the serving window. Usually in the mid-afternoon, when the café went through a lull. And when Ricardo was on duty.

They would have long conversations, with much laughter and teasing. She'd often stay at the window, waiting for other customers to come and go, lingering as long as it took to finish her chai.

There was no such chatter today. But after a while she was answering a question of Natalia's, which seemed to concern me. Soon she was lifting me up and placing me on the counter, where Natalia served up a saucer of warm milk, her dark eyes sparkling as she watched me lapping it up.

There was a pause while Natalia poured hot water containing an exotic combination of spices and ginger from a small metal jug. A look of earnest concentration on her face, before she replaced the metal jug on the counter with a decisive clunk.

Beginning to froth milk, she flashed a glance at Heidi.

"Ricardo likes you very much," she said with laser-like directness.

Color instantly rose to Heidi's cheeks. "I don't think so."

"Definitely," she held Heidi's gaze. "I know what he is like. Talk, talk, talk. Whenever he likes a girl, it is the same with him. Talk, talk."

Heidi was shaking her head.

"Even that first time he saw you, for the coffee testing," Natalia's eyes were resolute. "He keeps talking about chai. In front of everyone, he still talks. That's his way when he likes a woman."

"Maybe he was just nervous," said Heidi, raising a hand to brush back a lock which hadn't fallen to her cheek.

"And you have these long conversations …"

"Yes, but …"

"I have seen with my own eyes."

"In the afternoons …"

"He only wanted to go to yoga because of you. Never had interest before. In Barcelona I said to him once, 'Let's try this yoga' and he's like …" she hunched her shoulders, contorting her features in an expression of apathy.

"That doesn't mean he's into me. I've never encouraged …"

"If you play it cool," Natalia's expression was blazing. "He is only more keen. It drives him crazy."

"I would never do anything!" Heidi's voice rose in protest.

"There's something wrong with Colombians?" demanded

Natalia, her accent deepening with emotion.

"What?" Heidi was startled by the sharp turn in conversation.

"The skin?" She was pointing at her own. "Too dark for a German girl?"

"I never said ..."

"He's a good man! Intelligent. Hard worker," she frothed the milk furiously.

"Sure, he's all those things," Heidi was ambivalent.

Pouring milk into the cup, Natalia pushed it forcefully across the counter. "Then, what's wrong with him?"

Heidi's mouth moved soundlessly, as she struggled to get the words out. Before she blurted, "He's your boyfriend."

"Ricardo?!" It was Natalia's turn to be astounded. But her shock swiftly changed to hilarity. "He is my brother!" she snorted. "The little one."

"What?"

"*My* boyfriend, Federico, he is finishing exams in Barcelona. He comes here in six weeks."

"So Ricardo ..." Heidi was struggling to take this in.

Putting her elbows on the counter, Natalia leaned forward, fixing Heidi with a droll expression. "He likes you. If you like him," she shrugged, "and I think yes, then you can make each other happy. Like Federico and me."

Coming to the end of the milk, I lifted my head from the saucer and fixed Heidi with a blue stare. She was astonished. Bemused. Struggling to take it all in. But along with the shock, there was also a new sparkle in her eyes. She began to smile.

It was a short walk home to Namgyal. After an event-ful day, I took my time on the journey back. I slipped behind the row of stalls outside the monastery gates, pausing to take in a new and pungent aroma, where cast-off dill from a food outlet had been tossed onto the grass verge behind it. I stopped at the chin-height scratching post, formed by a gnarled tree trunk, to give myself a gentle jaw massage – both sides – and behind the ears.

It was late afternoon when I entered the gates to the paved courtyard. A few tourists were wandering in the distance, taking in the temple with its flight of red stairs leading up to elaborate Tibetan architecture, the tiers of roofs studded with gold ornaments stretching up towards the sky. Behind it all, the soaring, ice-capped Himalayas. In the slanting gold rays of the sun, the scene had a magic to it like a mirage that, rainbow-like, might dissolve away if you turned your gaze from it for just a moment.

Instead of crossing to the building which was my home, I stopped to sit some distance away, looking up towards the empty sill which was my usual vantage point.

Today, Rishi had discovered that the assumptions he had made about me being a threatening beast were quite wrong. In fact, I had turned out to be among his most vigorous defenders.

Heidi had also had her assumptions about Ricardo and Natalia revealed to be mistaken, their intimacy arising from the fact that they were siblings, not lovers.

In both cases, Rishi and Heidi had been held back from life and love by nothing more tangible than ideas. Thoughts which had grown over time to become as certain to them as facts.

"We paint the world with our thoughts," Christopher had said. "We apply broad swathes of color to this person and that object, without even realizing what we're doing. We do it unknowingly and all the time to everything and everybody, so that our entire experience of reality is like a painting, a creation of our own mind. We are all painters."

Today I had experienced the truth of that, only a whisker away. It was always easier to see in others, of course. To witness the dramatic change that had come over Rishi, when he began to perceive me in a different way. How Heidi's extreme awkwardness had visibly given way to emotions of an entirely different kind.

As I sat in the autumn sun, I was reminded of what Yogi Tarchin had said about the source of wonderment or awfulness, of beastliness or delight: *The delightfulness of lemonade comes from the mind of the being perceiving it as delightful. And whatever happiness is produced by mind … is only arising because of a previously created cause. The apparent causes of our happiness — like lemonade — are merely the conditions. What's actually happening is that we are enjoying the fruits of previously created karma.*

There was something deeply reassuring about the wisdom that the real source of wellbeing was not to be found in the outside world, but in one's own mind. There need be no dramatic change in circumstances to experience the greatest happiness. The only shift required was of one's own consciousness.

You can create powerful causes for positive experiences even just sitting here, Yogi Tarchin had said. *Celebrating your own happiness and the happiness and success of others.*

With the glow of the sun on my fur and face, I sensed contentment in this moment. Even more so, as I reminded myself that the contentment I was feeling didn't come from the sun itself, but from my mind as a result of previous kindness.

That contentment welled up all the more as I celebrated whatever good deed I had done, to be experiencing such happiness here and now. And knowing that, by celebrating it, I was creating the cause for future moments of happiness, my wellbeing increased only the more. What had started out as a passing mundane sensation was becoming magnified to one that was profound and dynamic, enveloping every part of my being to the very tips of my whiskers.

Celebrating is the great multiplier. And celebrating the wisdom that mind itself is the true cause of happiness – this is a multiplier beyond anything that might be conceived. I felt the truth of it deep down in my bones. The embodiment of wisdom so that even if, to the world, I may have simply appeared to be a cat sitting in the sunlight on an ordinary afternoon, my own experience of reality was quite extraordinary – that of vibrant and increasing bliss.

At which moment something apparently mundane, yet strangely magical, occurred. Up above at the window, the Dalai Lama appeared. A small silhouette to begin with, but growing in size as he approached. He paused, looking across the courtyard.

Many had been the time when, from where he stood now, I had watched the Dalai Lama crossing from the monastery, the temple or the gates. On some occasions, he had glanced up to see me at the window. This was the first time our positions were reversed.

Just by celebrating the actions of someone of a higher level than ourselves, we create half the amount of virtue that they have, Yogi Tarchin had said. *And by rejoicing in the virtues of Buddhas or bodhisattvas, we can attain a tenth of the benefits they gained, because their level of development is so much greater than ours.*

It would be easy for any being to rejoice in the kindness of His Holiness. And as His Holiness's Cat, where to begin? Perhaps how he had rescued me from certain death on the streets of New Delhi. Brought me back to Namgyal to share his home. For the countless hours we have spent meditating together. For the wisdom and humor and compassion he has constantly shared – that intangible but powerful *prana* I know so well, and that is felt by so many who come in contact with him.

Now, as I was suddenly struck by where that *prana* was coming from – and not as a mere idea – I felt caught by an upsurge of such powerful wellbeing that I was taken quite unawares. For there was only one place it possibly could come from!

Was it really true that, like any other external phenomena, the Dalai Lama was merely a contributing factor, a catalyst?

Could it actually be that the extraordinary awe so many beings feel in his presence – and which is among my greatest joys – arises in our minds as a result of previously created causes? If so, what did that say about the virtue we have created in the past, to feel such a force? About the fact that His Holiness, like Yogi Tarchin, has devoted his life to revealing the truth of this to others?

Having made this recognition, it was easy to feel the miraculous. For waves of profound gratitude, spontaneous and heartfelt, to flow from where I was sitting upwards to where he stood at the window. For the joy that arose to be amplified exponentially by the knowledge of how His Holiness embodied the wisdom that all is mind. And that our minds are wellsprings of radiant, boundless transcendence.

Reality had never appeared more wondrous and I had never been happier than as I sat on the pavers that autumn afternoon. And perhaps something of my inner transformation was evident to the Dalai Lama, because as our eyes met across the courtyard, he brought his palms together to his lips and smiled.

Chapter Eight

W<small>ITH THE WEATHER IMPROVING DAY BY DAY</small>, I <small>HAD BEEN</small> going to visit Christopher more often. Each time I emerged from the agapanthus and made my way around the side of the nursing home, before I could even see the door of his studio, I would hear sound of chamber music, a piano or a choir coming from within. Baroque music had never been so reassuring.

It would be wrong to say that Christopher was no longer painting. He was still utterly absorbed in his work. Whether standing, leaning heavily on the straight-back chair brought from the dining room or, more frequently these days, sitting in the chair, one thing continued to hold his attention – Amitabha Buddha.

Just as in the first days I had visited, when I had noticed him stare for ages at his picture of Caroline, before reaching forward to apply the tiniest speck of paint, so it was now with

Amitabha. So total was his concentration, he'd barely acknowledge me arriving and hopping on my chair, though I knew, of course, he was fully aware that his muse had materialized. From time to time, he might break away to mix some new paints on his palette or to pick out a different brush, before stepping towards the canvas with all the deference of approaching the Buddha himself, to make the most subtle of adjustments.

The oxygen lines running to his nose were now a permanent fixture. And while he was sometimes overcome by outbreaks of violent coughing, gasping and choking for air, something on a more profound level was also happening: he was withdrawing. In a quiet, unspoken but self-evident way, he was retreating from this world. As he sat in his chair for long periods staring at Amitabha, it was almost as if a transference were taking place – as though the less relevant or meaningful or even believable his diminished presence in this world felt to him, the more vivid and energized it became in the reality of Amitabha.

And what power it conveyed! The way that Sid, Serena and the others had responded on seeing the painting, and the immediate emotional connection they had felt had, if such a thing were possible, become even greater. Christopher had portrayed Amitabha wearing silk clothes and a jeweled crown. Youthful and vibrant, holding in his lap a vase containing the elixir of immortality, the Buddha of Infinite Life and Light was a portrait rather than a *thangka*, and with that had come glorious artistic freedom.

Red light blazed from Amitabha's body, with a power that

drew the viewer into a different dimension – red being the symbolic color of enlightened communication, as well as the bliss of wisdom. Just seeing it awakened a recognition that this infinite life, this wisdom, was coming not from Amitabha, but from one's own mind. He was merely the enabler – the external appearance who brought to awareness the boundlessness and purity of the primordial consciousness of any being who had the extreme good fortune to see him.

Through his brushstrokes, Christopher expressed so much of what I had heard the Dalai Lama explain using words. It was an artistic manifestation of the Dharma. In particular, the truth that reality is a creation of our own minds and, if we wish, each one of us has the capacity to create a purer, more benevolent and boundless reality than we usually consider to be possible. Just as His Holiness had told the famous pop star visitor on that dark monsoon day, the act of imagining how an ideal self might be is the start of its manifestation. Believing is seeing.

It was this truth towards which, in all the hours he sat looking at the painting, Christopher was being drawn. This truth in which he had become immersed at His Holiness's behest. The pure land of Amitabha, called "Sukhavati" in Sanskrit, the land of pure joy. Sometimes I would see his lips move and glance over to where he was holding the mala beads the Dalai Lama had given him in his right hand, as he recited the mantra of his *yidam*: *Om Amitabha hrih. Om Amitabha hrih. Om Amitabha hrih.*

WHEN HE WASN'T WORKING, CHRISTOPHER STILL ENJOYED the ritual of preparing tea for himself and milk for me, although it took him longer than in the past. He would still sometimes babble happy endearments to me about Babou the ocelot, about Vaske and Minou. Occasionally he'd recite a line or two of his favorite poem:

"Dear Pig, are you willing to sell for one shilling
Your ring?" Said the Piggy, "I will."
So they took it away, and were married next day
By the Turkey who lives on the hill.

MORE FREQUENTLY, HOWEVER, HE'D INVOKE ME AS HIS CELES-tial messenger, the envoy responsible for ushering him into the presence of the Dalai Lama – and thereby Amitabha himself.

"Picasso and Dali and Kandinsky may have had their feline companions," he would declare at such moments. "But which feline enabled them to feel the energy of loving kindness? Which propelled them, through their work, to seek transcendence?"

Which indeed? With milk placed before me, he'd hear no objections from HHC!

Sometimes, when I sensed he would like company, I'd jump on the chair beside him and the two of us would just sit, two sentient beings consciously sharing the moment together.

From his chair, the studio looked much the same as always,

completed canvases propped against the walls. Only now there were a few gaps. The *Blue Shadows* triptych along with the two other canvases were no longer there.

"What a windfall!" he would sometimes exclaim gleefully. "Who would have thought I'd make such lucrative sales at the very end of my life? That I'd clear all my debts! Now I can die a happy man."

The pile of brown envelopes that had previously occupied the shelf behind him were gone.

On another occasion, looking towards Caroline's portrait he said, "I had another letter from Caroline. Seems like she wants to visit." His tone was pensive as he looked towards me, "I don't have the heart to tell her that it's already too late."

ONE MORNING CHRISTOPHER WAS DEEPLY IMMERSED IN Amitabha, staring at the painting while reciting mantras. After a while he stopped, his gaze unwavering. The last few times I had visited, he hadn't got up even once to add to the painting. Not so much as a single daub. But now he was summoning all his strength, pushing himself from the chair, both arms trembling from the effort. He paused for a moment, gasping for breath, on the brink of a spasm of coughing. With both hands on the back of the dining chair, he somehow managed to steady himself.

I watched him turn to his paints and squeeze some from a tube, before taking great care in selecting a brush from a tub. Applying paint to the brush, he approached the portrait of

Amitabha before turning to me. "You know what this means, don't you, O Pussy my love?"

I didn't as it happened. I had no idea what he was about to do, much less its significance. But there was something decisive about his tone – and at the same time, unburdened. As if a door had been thrown open and he was about to step through.

Leaning towards the bottom right side of the painting, he signed it in definitive black paint before stepping back saying, "It is done."

As he faced me again, the light from outside had shifted in a very singular way, so that a shaft of sunlight directly struck the now-completed painting – and it reflected its color back onto Christopher. It wasn't only Amitabha who was dazzling red, but Christopher's face and body too. As he stood, ablaze in the reflection of the canvas, which in turn was a reflection of his own most exalted consciousness, the boundaries between Amitabha and Christopher became harder to discern. Where did one end and the other begin? They may have started out as canvas and painter but in that moment, the non-duality of the two could not have been more apparent.

"The most important commission of my life is complete," said Christopher.

WHEN I LEFT HIM IN HIS CHAIR A SHORT WHILE LATER, I paused to press against his leg. Even though he was reciting mantras, I felt his fingers and palm caress my neck at the same time that I inhaled the familiar pungency of oil paint on corduroy. For a few moments we held together in warm embrace.

I headed to the residents' lounge, to reprise my role as Therapy Cat – it was on just such a visit that I had first encountered Christopher. There was always joy to be had in seeing a roomful of dozing retirees suddenly come alive at one's mere appearance, with much wheedling and coaxing on the part of many of them just for a few moments' attention.

Nurse Chapman, strongly opposed to my presence to begin with, believing me to be a stray cat "riddled with disease" and likely to trigger all kinds of allergic reactions, had subsequently become my staunchest ally. After lifting me onto the laps of some of the frailest residents, so they could all have some Therapy Cat time, she announced that lunch was to be served.

One by one, the residents made the sedate move from lounge to dining room, many with walkers and several needing to be pushed in wheelchairs. From a window, I observed a female orderly walk down the path to Christopher's studio to tell him about lunch. Before hurrying back, anxiety etched on her face.

Moments later, the nursing home doctor was briskly following her on a return trip. And shortly after, two orderlies with a stretcher.

They appeared again after the longest wait. Christopher had been loaded onto the canvas between them. A sheet was drawn over his face.

I HAD WITNESSED A SEQUENCE THAT NOW SEEMED INEVITABLE, from the moment Christopher had added his signature to the painting. And in the strangest of ways, I felt relieved for him. Uplifted even. I had no doubt that he had departed this life on his own terms – not frail and frightened, but having completed his most meaningful and extraordinary work. His departure had been preceded not by weeks of slow and painful suffocation but, quite the opposite, by a journey of transfiguration as inspiring as it had been mesmerizing to witness. Through the skillful guidance of His Holiness, he had found his way to Sukhavati. He had even left the evidence of this on his easel.

But still. I would miss the strange, wild man with his paints and music and babbling endearments. I would miss our times together. And Edward Lear.

BEFORE GOING HOME, I WANTED TO RETURN TO HIS STUDIO. The door was open, but the room was in unfamiliar silence. Christopher's chair was pushed back at a strange angle, but there was no other sign of what had so recently occurred. I sat, breathing in the familiar aromas, taking in a place which had become a favorite part of my world.

Footsteps sounded from the path outside. I looked up to see Mr. Devi, Building Manager. A short, round man in an ill-fitting suit, accompanied by his foreman, Krish.

"My condolences, HHC!" Mr. Devi greeted me with regard in his tone. "I know you and Christopher were good friends. Right ..." he turned to Krish with a no-nonsense expression. "I promised Mr. Naidoo I'd let him have this room for accounts, as soon as it became available. His storeroom is bursting at the seams."

"Yes sir," his second-in-command was deferential. In denim jeans and taupe shirt, Krish commanded the variety of laborers, grounds men and other minions who kept the nursing home shipshape. "The chairs can go to the veranda and dining room, sir. That's where they came from." Looking in the corner he added, "The bench, fridge and kettle to the workshop."

"The paints, brushes and unused canvases," Mr Devi ordered, "to Occupational Therapy."

Krish nodded.

Mr. Devi glanced about the room, apparently satisfied by how quickly things were to be resolved. "Which leaves us only with the paintings."

"Municipal waste?" proposed Krish, always eager to problem-solve.

"This one must go next door." Gesturing to Amitabha, Mr Devi was eager to assert his higher knowledge. "The boss tells me it was commissioned by His Holiness. And there's another one," he scanned the room before his eyes settled on the portrait of Caroline. "To her office," he gestured to it. "She will contact the lady in question. As for the rest …" he glanced around with a despairing expression at all the canvases propped on the walls and strewn by the bench.

"Municipal waste?" repeated Krish.

"Hmm," Mr. Devi's expression was ambivalent. "If it was up to me, I'd agree. Very much so. But perhaps we must not act too soon. Someone may have a claim on one or two of them. An interest of some kind."

"Storage?" suggested Krish.

"One month, I think, would be quite enough. Is there somewhere you can squeeze them?"

"The garage, behind the tractor," offered Krish. "There's a shelf there. If we stack them, they will fit."

"You'll wrap them in something?" Mr. Devi squinted at the prospect of grease and dirt.

"Bin liners."

"If no-one makes a claim on them in the next month …"

"Municipal waste," Krish was decisive.

Mr. Devi turned to leave.

"When do you want the job done?" asked Krish. "This afternoon?"

"The painting of Amitabha should go next door right away. The boss will call His Holiness's office to let them know. As for the other stuff," Mr. Devi shifted his head from side to side, "maybe leave it a couple of days out of respect. Mr. Ackland was very popular with the other residents and the boss. We don't want to upset them. Mr. Naidoo will be happy to get his new storage room by next Monday."

Krish nodded. "Friday afternoon then," he confirmed.

As they left, I could already imagine Krish's men streaming in, collecting up canvases, moving chairs, packing away paints and brushes. It would be only a matter of minutes before whatever was in the room had been moved elsewhere. Before the studio was no longer the studio, but just an empty room.

Christopher Ackland's mandala would be completely dissolved.

DOWN AT THE HIMALAYA BOOK CAFÉ, THE EARLY AFTERNOON session was in full swing as I climbed up to my usual vantage spot on the magazine rack. I was surprised when Sid and Serena arrived together, heading to the banquette at the very back, closest to me. While Serena was in and out of the café on an almost daily basis, Sid was an infrequent visitor. Something in their manner suggested that business was afoot.

A short while later Heidi appeared at the front door, surveying the tables as if looking for somebody, then checking the banquettes one by one before finding Sid and Serena.

The three of them were soon deep in conversation. I recalled Sid overhearing Heidi's forthright exchange with Ludo after outdoor yoga. How upset she'd been by the gulf that had opened up between them, a chasm that had seemed too wide to bridge. Having come to Dharamshala with the express purpose of helping Ludo run the yoga school until the time came when he would have to step aside, Heidi's plans must have been thrown into disarray.

I wondered whether Sid was offering a suggestion for how to resolve things. A clever businessman as well as something of a diplomat, if anyone was up to the challenge it was Sid. But in the snatches of conversation that came my way, I kept hearing "Binita" as well as the names of her three daughters: Hema, Diya and Nisha. 108 Bougainvillea Street was also mentioned.

Heidi's initial demeanor had been subdued, but she

became more animated as the three of them chatted. At the coffee machine, Ricardo had noticed Heidi arrive and, when there was a lull in the line outside, he approached their table to take coffee orders – shortcutting the usual protocol of receiving orders from the waitstaff. He and Heidi held each other's eyes for a long moment.

All other things were eclipsed, however, with the arrival of Franc. Red-eyed and strained, Marcel following forlornly in his wake, he entered the café, walked straight through, and was heading for the private room upstairs when he caught sight of Serena, Sid and Heidi. Crumpling onto the banquette next to Serena, he didn't have to say anything.

"Oh, Franc!" Serena turned to hug him. "I'm so sorry. When?"

"Last night," his face was buried in her shoulder. Then pulling himself away, emotion tugging at his lips, "In her sleep."

"Well, that was something," she replied. "At least you didn't have to make any tough decisions."

He nodded.

"I'm so sorry, Franc," Sid reached over to squeeze his arm.

Heidi looked concerned.

"I'm just trying to hold it together," said Franc. "They say tears are like hailstones to beings in the bardo state. I spent the whole morning meditating."

"The best thing you could have done," Sid told him.

Serena stroked his arm, "Yes," she agreed. "Keep focused on the wellbeing of Kyi Kyi." She reached under the table to comfort Marcel.

Seeing what was going on, Sam had come down the steps from the bookstore. Sitting on the opposite banquette next to Sid, he offered his condolences.

It was clear Franc didn't want to stay. Being offered so much sympathy, he was struggling to retain his composure. Pushing himself up from the table he said, "I filled her bowls as usual this morning. Water and biscuits."

"Seven weeks," Serena nodded. "We'll remember her in our meditations."

There were murmurs of agreement around the table, while Franc stood.

"And if there's anything at all we can do, Franc?"

He turned away, nodding, before going upstairs, Marcel at his heels.

There was silence for a while after he left. Then Heidi, with an expression of bewilderment asked softly, "Seven weeks?"

"The maximum time we can be in bardo," explained Sid. "The state of consciousness between this lifetime and the next." Then, as her puzzlement continued, "When we die, the last thing we experience in this lifetime is the clear light of death. It's all that's left after body and normal consciousness dissolve away. A very subtle state of mind. At that time, if our response is *What's happened to me?* or *Where am I?* then those thoughts, triggered by whatever karma arises in our mind, create a new 'me'. A new 'I'. That 'I' initially takes the form of a bardo being."

Serena was nodding. "It's said that, through force of habit, bardo beings can be drawn back to what was familiar, like their old home, their loved ones. For that reason, we try not to disrupt their favorite places. So we might leave out our pets' bowls or keep blankets in their special hidey-holes. In some Buddhist cultures, they even set the table for the one who has passed, to reassure them that they have not been forgotten."

I thought of Christopher. If there was any place from this life to which he might be drawn back, it would be his studio. But within just days, his much-loved haven would be swept away, altered beyond recognition.

"This is all so different from what they say back home," said Heidi.

Serena's phone began buzzing. Excusing herself, she got up from the banquette to take the call outside.

"After grandma died, for weeks I used to go up to her bedroom. The others said I was being silly and that grandma was in heaven. But I was sure I could *feel* her there."

"Bardo beings," Sam was nodding, "are the opposite of us. We have to travel somewhere physically for our mind to be there. They only need to think of a place and they are there. They have the same subtle bodies we sometimes experience when dreaming."

"That must be confusing," said Heidi.

Sam nodded, "The time in bardo is said to be very confusing and noisy and we have no physical body to return to. We're drawn to beings with whom we have a strong karmic connection, who may be our future parents. But we might also be pulled back to the people and places from the life that just ended. We are tugged this way and that ..."

"This is why," Sid interjected, "in the bardo we can be

helped so much by people we were close to in our past life. If they meditate and can offer comfort and peace," he tilted his head to indicate upstairs, "as bardo beings we can be affected. In the midst of confusion and trauma, if we are reminded of what's virtuous, then in the bardo state, as in life, positive thoughts lead to positive experiences. And as an important time of transition, when we could go one of so many different ways, those thoughts have the potential power to guide us to a much better rebirth."

Heidi looked at the door leading to the stairs. "So that is what Franc is doing now?"

The two men nodded.

"In monasteries," Sam told her, "when a monk dies, they often hold special services and mantra recitation and *pujas*, or purification ceremonies, for them."

"Funerals?" queried Heidi.

He shook his head. "They're not really a thing in Buddhism. The focus is much more about the mind of the person who died. The mantras and pujas are for their benefit."

"In the West," she was shaking her head, "it's all about the body of the person and the grief felt by everyone left behind. Buddhism seems like the opposite. It's about the mind of the one who died. Because they still exist and need care."

"Exactly!" chimed Sam.

"Not so much about how sad *I* am. *My* feelings of loss."

"Which is right," said Sid. "Because we still have our lives. Our homes and loved ones. We aren't the ones making the perilous journey."

Furrows appeared on Heidi's forehead. "But what if you can't meditate? Can you still help the person in bardo?"

"We feed birds," Sid was nodding. "Or make offerings of any kind to other beings. And we dedicate the virtue from our acts of kindness to benefit the person in bardo."

"Makes sense," Heidi nodded, pausing to take this in. "I can see why Buddhists study this subject so much. When we plan to travel overseas, like to India, the more prepared we are the better. It seems to be the same with dying."

"You're right," Sam smiled. "And if you prepare well enough, you get to fly first class!"

Serena returned to the table, phone in her hand, with an expression of determined composure.

"That was Mum," she said, slipping back into the seat. "She's at Namgyal. Tenzin came into the kitchen to tell her that Christopher died this morning."

Around the table, the others were shocked.

Sid reached his hand across to Serena. Clasping it, expression shaken, she looked at him, "And His Holiness wants to see you."

"About Christopher?" his eyes widened.

"Seems that way," she looked surprised. Shaking her head she said, "Even though we were expecting this, it still seems unbelievable somehow. Only a few days ago we were sitting at his feet, drinking champagne ..."

THAT AFTERNOON, I WAS IN MY USUAL SPOT ON THE WINDOWSILL

when Sid was shown in to see the Dalai Lama. The portrait of Amitabha, on its easel, had been placed in front of a row of marigolds blossoming in tubs, the bright red of the painting contrasting vividly with the prolific gold and green of the plants behind. His Holiness was standing to the side of the painting as Sid arrived. After prostrations had been exchanged, both men clasping their palms together, His Holiness looked directly at Sid, "You have heard the news about our friend?"

"Yes, your Holiness," Sid was subdued.

"An exceptional artist," His Holiness turned, so that they were both looking at the picture. "He had no training in *thangka* painting. The symbols. The dimensions. That gave him much freedom of expression."

"Which he used to remarkable effect," Sid was appreciative.

"Yes," said the Dalai Lama. "Amazing, is it not? How you feel when you look at it," he pressed his palm to his heart. "This connection to the Buddha of Infinite Light and Life."

"Do you think he perceived Amitabha Buddha?" asked Sid.

His Holiness paused to consider this. "Based on his understanding of *sunyata*, and his devotion to the guru, the *yidam*, then …," His Holiness was nodding, "I think so. There are different ways to experience non-duality with the mind of enlightenment."

Sid looked both stunned and delighted.

Then the Dalai Lama was saying, "Mrs. Ponter says you already bought some of his paintings."

"Last week," Sid confirmed. "After Serena told me about *Primordial Dawn* and I came to see it in your reception room. I was very impressed. It was the first time I'd heard of Christopher Ackland. Then he came to Geshe Wangpo's class."

His Holiness listened as Sid explained how the group of students had visited Christopher at his studio. How he'd been working on the Amitabha painting. The reluctance with which he'd revealed the unfinished work – and the immediate impact it had had on all present.

When he had finished, the Dalai Lama told him simply, "I would like you to have this painting."

Sid looked astonished. "But you commissioned it!"

"For Christopher. To focus on."

"But … it's extraordinary!" Sid was finding it hard to grasp how the Dalai Lama could simply be giving it away at all.

"Yes. But many of my visitors are conventional monks. It may worry them," he explained, "to see an unorthodox work such as this at Namgyal. I have a duty to uphold the traditions of our lineages." His Holiness took a step closer to Sid. "Also, a painting like this may attain great value. We don't have many places where I know it would be safe. However," reaching out, he took Sid's hand in his own, "I think you know already where this painting should go?"

Eyes locked with the Dalai Lama, Sid swallowed. "Yes, I do," he confirmed.

HIS HOLINESS WORKED LATE THAT EVENING, REVIEWING THE final manuscript of the book Oliver had been translating. It was just him at his desk and me on the sill. With the passing hours, each of the orange curtained windows at the monks' residence went dark one by one, and eventually the temple lights were turned off too. The Namgyal courtyard and all the buildings were cast in the monochrome magic that appeals to we cats, as creatures of the night.

Gazing out across this rarely seen vista, I thought about the unlikeliness of what had happened: the deaths of two friends in the one day. Where were their minds right now, at this moment? And what were they feeling?

Kyi Kyi could hardly have better support for her time in the bardo. A peaceful death, followed by the devoted meditations of her dearest friend, offered hope that whatever positive karmas she had created in the past had the best possible chance of propelling her into a more favorable rebirth, wherever that may be.

Christopher, on the other hand, had lacked any spiritual cheer squad at the time of his death. Not only that, whatever reassurance he may have sought in the familiar could have led to dismay.

But did he need it? Or would his own faith in the practices be sufficient to see him on his way to Sukhavati? Indeed, was he already there?

From behind, I heard His Holiness push his chair back from his desk. I turned to watch him stand and give his weary arms a generous stretch, before turning to the portrait of Amitabha on its easel. As he did, he brought his hands to his heart in prayer. Moving his lips, although I didn't know the words he was saying, I had no doubt who he was saying them for.

Could there be a more auspicious benediction?

Across the courtyard, perhaps from a passing car, came the distant ripple of a piano arpeggio, along with the sound of a man laughing. The ephemera of a few passing seconds, it dissolved into silence as quickly as it arose. And whether it was the music or the laughter or a stray tincture of oil paint on the night air, for a while the silver courtyard was no longer deserted, but was the setting for a spectral illusion, accompanied by the memory of Christopher's deep, gleeful tones:

They dined on mince, and slices of quince,
Which they ate with a runcible spoon;
And hand in hand, on the edge of the sand,
They danced by the light of the moon,
The moon, the moon,
They danced by the light of the moon.

CHAPTER NINE

CHRISTOPHER AND KYI KYI MAY HAVE GONE, BUT THEY WERE not in any way forgotten. If anything, they were spoken of more than ever before. Whether in the Executive Assistants' office, the downstairs kitchen, or along the road at The Himalaya Book Café, I heard about acts of kindness carried out for their benefit, offering virtuous energy to propel their bardo beings towards the light.

Every week after their deaths, the small group of Geshe Wangpo's students who had sat at Christopher's feet, along with Franc and others from the café, gathered in the nearby garden under the cedar tree. That spot had been a favorite haunt for both Kyi Kyi on her daily walks, as well as Christopher. In the early evening they would recite mantras and verses of auspiciousness until nightfall, when they'd light candles, invoking blessings and luminosity on behalf of their dear friends.

Every seventh day after death is an especially important milestone for bardo beings. If they haven't yet found rebirth, they transition from one form of bardo being to another, a process offering the opportunity for positive change. If negative karma initially determines a more difficult rebirth, but one which hasn't yet occurred, the arising of positive karma on day seven can change that. This is the case on every seventh day after death, until day 49.

The benevolent actions, the propitious ceremonies and, more than anything, the way that Christopher and Kyi Kyi were held with such love in the minds of everyone in our little community was quite something to behold. And in its own way, deeply reassuring. When my own time came, dear reader, I hoped that I would receive the same devoted attention.

At the same time as the bardo processes were being followed, other different kinds of transitions were going on. Some of these were being made by those around me, especially those concerning 108 Bougainvillea Street. New deliveries were being managed. Urgent meetings were being held around the bookstore coffee table.

I was still none the wiser about exactly what Sid's former residence was to become. No doubt the truth would reveal itself in good time. I did know, however, that the future of Binita and her three daughters were bound up in it. And when they arrived in Dharamshala, I knew all about it. From being simply names spoken of in conversation, a more vivid picture of them emerged.

ACCORDING TO SERENA, HELPING HER MOTHER IN THE VIP kitchen, the four women had arrived in Dharamshala from New Delhi by train. Sid had offered to arrange transport from New Delhi for them and the few worldly goods they possessed. However, Binita was still embarrassed by how far they had fallen and wanted to remain as self-sufficient as possible, insisting they could make their way to Dharamshala on their own.

On the appointed afternoon, Sid and his driver had taken two cars to collect them from the railway station and drove them directly to 108 Bougainvillea Street. Surveying the opulence of their new home, Serena told Mrs. Trinci that Binita had been quite overcome with emotion, torn between tearful gratitude to Sid for delivering them from poverty, and shame that she had allowed her daughters and herself to become so dependent. The 21-year-old twins, Nisha and Diya, had needed no time to make themselves comfortable in their new surroundings, exploring the building from top to bottom, fighting over who should have which bedroom, and wanting to know if there were plans for a rooftop terrace. As soon as they discovered the wifi code, the pair of them fell into a deep digital trance on a veranda sofa.

By contrast, 23-year-old Hema's response had been markedly different. She seemed to resent everything about being here: the house, her mother, and most of all, Sid. Sullenly reluctant to do anything and responding only in curt monotones, she had soon closeted herself in a bedroom, nose in a book.

Hema had taken their troubles especially hard, Binita had told Sid and Serena later, when visiting them at home for what was intended to be a welcome dinner. With the girls watching TV – in itself a novelty after where they'd been – the three adults had sat in the tower upstairs, which offered a reassuring distance from which to survey the world.

It was not only the loss of all their comforts and privileges that had devasted Hema, Binita told the two of them. As her father's oldest daughter and apple of his eye, Hema refused to accept that Arhaan had had anything to do with their financial ruin. Worse, she chose to continue believing the myth her father had spread till his dying day – that his downfall had been brought about for one reason alone: betrayal by his former friend, Sid.

This was a myth Binita herself had initially believed, having no reason to doubt her husband. Even after his heart attack, when the extent of the family's calamity became terrifyingly real, she had ignored the messages from business friends and professional advisers, some discreet, some more overt, that Arhaan's version of events was a fantasy he alone had believed. The way he had overvalued assets as spectacularly as he understated debts; the exaggeration of commercial interest in his new ventures and scorning of risk. All of it to serve an image he had of himself as a hugely successful business tycoon. An idea that was to prove massively destructive.

"You just don't want to believe that the person you have given your life to, the one you love and trust, has told you so many lies. Time and again. Over and over," Binita told Serena and Sid. "Sometimes I wonder – did he believe his own lies? Did he have some kind of mental problem that somehow made him less liable?"

Not that it made any difference to what happened in the end. The family had still lost everything. But Binita had also lost her naivety about her late husband. She only wished that Hema could accept the truth and move on too.

THERE WERE MORE SNIPPETS IN THE WEEKS THAT FOLLOWED. How Binita and Heidi had met – an encounter of some significance, it seemed, which had gone well. How the women had attended a fitting for some special clothing. How Hema had, by chance, bumped into one of her closest friends from school, now a lawyer in Delhi. Assuming she understood how duplicitous her father had been, the friend had chattered knowledgeably about the dozens of lawsuits filed against Arhaan, while offering Hema her sincere sympathy.

Having heard so much about the newcomers, I wondered when I'd finally set eyes on them myself. As it happened, the first time was from a distance. Four Indian women, dressed in what looked like medical tunics, stepping through the open gates of 108 Bougainvillea Street. What was going on there, I wondered, failing to make any connection between them and the property's new residents.

Amid the ebb and flow of daily events, with one chapter in our world seeming to come to a close before the contours of the next were clear, other changes were afoot. Some were of the unplanned and unexpected kind – unforeseen, that is, unless you happened to be an astrologer.

EARLY ONE AFTERNOON, AS I WAS ENJOYING A SAMPLE OF THAT day's delicious *plat du jour* delivered by the ever-thoughtful Kusali, I became aware that we had a celebrity in our midst. Not one of the showy Bollywood types, who occasionally swept through the doors of the café with their entourage of fawning attendants. No, this one was of the far more intriguing kind. A man who might slip into or out of a restaurant without attracting any notice at all, but whose deep understanding of planetary configurations and what they signified filled many well-received volumes. The kind of person who might be anonymous to the masses, but who was sought after by some of the most powerful people in the world.

Being a cat of great discretion, I can't possibly tell you exactly who he is, dear reader. Let me just say that his name might bring to mind a large collection of trees. That with his twinkling eyes, white hair and beard he looked just as wizardly as you might imagine someone of his craft to be. That he is one of the pioneers of evolutionary astrology.

The one who advises all those Hollywood celebrities. Yes – *him*!

Around the bookshop coffee table, Franc, Sam and Sid had been holding another of their meetings. Several times, Sam had slipped surreptitious glances in the direction of the astrologer, who had been perusing shelves in the bookshop, before scanning the nearby community noticeboard.

The meeting coming to an end, Sam was unable to contain himself. Approaching the man, he asked him if he was who he thought he was.

The astrologer nodded his head in acknowledgement.

Declaring himself to be a true fan, Sam shook him by the hand and asked if he would mind signing copies of his books currently available in the shop – a request to which the visitor assented.

With some enthusiasm, Sam then introduced him to the owner of The Himalaya Book Café and the Maharaja of Himachal Pradesh as "a fellow Buddhist and pioneer of evolutionary astrology". Soon all four of them were sitting at the table, and a waiter dispatched to Natalia and Ricardo with a coffee order.

"*Evolutionary* astrology?" Franc honed in on how Sam had introduced their guest. "Is that different from a regular astrologer?"

"Evolutionary astrology is what you might like to think of as psychological astrology," the visitor's eyes twinkled behind his glasses. "All astrologers agree that our personalities and circumstances are reflected in our birth charts, right?"

The others were nodding.

"Well, if you accept the concept of rebirth, it makes sense that our personalities and circumstances are rooted in previous lives. If that is the case, what is a birth chart? I would suggest it is a map showing the variety of karmas that have propelled us into this life. We may find, in our natal configurations, clues about the main karmic influences we will be dealing with – a consequence of who we were and what we were doing in previous lives."

The faces around the table were rapt. Drawn ineluctably to the source of intrigue, it wasn't long before I ascended the few steps to the bookshop and was hopping up on the sofa between Sid and Franc. If the visitor was at all surprised by my appearance, he didn't show it. Rather, he seemed completely comfortable with a feline presence.

"I've often wondered about Buddhism and astrology," Franc was saying. "There always seemed to be a contradiction between the Buddhist view that we create our own reality and the idea of predestination; that no matter what you do, it is your fate to experience something or other."

"Ah yes," chuckled the other. "Astrological fatalism. That is not my approach. I'd see astrology as much more like offering a weather forecast to help us in our decisions. As individuals, of course we shape our reality through the choices we make. What interests me, especially, is what our charts reveal about our karmic treasures and wounds. What we bring to this lifetime.

"The idea of a consciousness that evolves through life-times," agreed Sam. "Seems much more interesting than fortune-telling."

Franc had been stroking me and my purr rose in throaty appreciation. He glanced at me for a moment before asking, "And pets. Do they have natal charts too?"

"Of course," the visitor's eyes followed his. "They have

consciousness, as we do. They may have been human in a previous life."

Indeed, dear reader. Yogi Tarchin had already revealed this very truth to Zahra and me.

"Is evolutionary astrology your discovery?" asked Sam.

The visitor shook his head. "There are a number of us with similar ideas. We use different words but speak the same language. It is a broad church. As you might expect, we came to the recognition around the same time!"

"A map of the soul's journey?" It was the first time that Sid had spoken.

"Quite so," agreed the other. "And whether you use the words 'soul' or 'mind', 'God' or 'dharmakaya' really isn't the point. Even if someone isn't convinced of rebirth as a literal fact, and would rather think of it as a metaphor, so be it."

"Is there *any* room," queried Franc, "for prediction in evolutionary astrology?"

"Absolutely!" the guest exclaimed, as Natalia arrived with the coffee order. "The birth chart itself is predictive of the challenges we face, as well as the resources we possess to meet them. And there can also be crystal-clear suggestions of timing. Transits and conjunctions which point to opportunities in one area of life or danger in another. The only thing I ever get preachy about ..." he lifted his coffee mug to his lips, "is that astrology is about symbolism, images and metaphors. It's not about literal facts."

Conversation continued about evolutionary astrology as a support on our inner journey. About Western astrology, as well as that practiced in the Himalayas and China. And the simple but striking notion that the coincidence between female and lunar cycles was probably the start of the connection between outer and inner, between the stars and the self, way back in primordial time.

Coffees had been consumed and shifting body language suggested that the gathering was drawing to a close. It was Franc who asked the almost throwaway question that was to have such momentous consequences. "So, what brought you to McLeod Ganj?"

The answer to this question was usually "the Dalai Lama" or a gathering involving Tibetan Buddhism in some way. But today's visitor answered, "It's not so much a 'what' as a 'who'"

Meeting their inquiring expressions he continued, "I've been in Delhi for a conference, and I found myself with a couple of days to spare. I decided to come to Dharamshala on what might be a bit of a wild goose chase. You see, I'm doing some astrological research and I was hoping to track someone down."

"And have you?"

He shook his head. "It's a long shot. He may not even be alive. If he is, he'd be quite elderly. I've tried all the most likely places down the hill in Dharamshala. No-one has ever heard of him."

"Are you able to share a name?" asked Sid.

"Sure," the visitor looked him in the eye. "Christopher Ackland."

"The painter?" Sid seemed surprised – as did Franc and

Sam. But none of them was more surprised than the astrologer. He looked incredulous. "You know him?" his eyes gleamed.

"Christopher died just over a month ago," Franc's voice was soft.

The visitor flopped back in his seat, dismayed.

On the sofa opposite, Franc turned pensively to Sid. "What would you say? We didn't really know him. Not that well."

"He was already very ill when we first met about two months ago," Sid told their guest. "He came to a class given by Geshe Wangpo, our lama at Namgyal," he gestured towards the monastery. "We knew about this extraordinary person."

"His painting, remember?" Sam prompted. *"Primordial Dawn."*

"Yes, exactly!" said Sid. "He had given a painting to His Holiness. A remarkable visual expression of a blissful meditative state. That was just before he came to a class, so we knew something about him before we met."

"He had to have oxygen lines," Sam gestured his nose.

"Poor guy," said Franc.

"Made quite an impact at class with his question about death," Sid shared a smile with Sam and Franc.

The visitor nodded, urging him to repeat it.

"I don't have the realizations to attain nirvana or enlightenment," Sid was paraphrasing Christopher. *"But I don't want to be reborn in samsara, with all its heartbreak and pain. Is there a third option?"*

"To which the lama replied?" prompted the visitor.

"Sukhavati. Amitabha's pure land. A reality that even those

of us who have delusion and karma can perceive. A place where we may continue our spiritual journey."

"And it just so happened that His Holiness had commissioned him to paint a portrait of Buddha Amitabha only days before," chuckled Sam.

There was a pause before Sid continued, "After class that night, a few of us waited with Christopher for his car to arrive from the nursing home. He had a certain ... charisma, wouldn't you say?" He looked from Franc to Sam.

"Definitely," Franc was nodding. "You encounter it in people who embody a particular wisdom. Authentic people who walk the talk."

"We went to visit him in his studio the next day," Sam was eager to continue. "He told us his story, about how he was becoming a recognized painter when he was a young man, but was overwhelmed by a fear of failure. How he gave up. Moved countries. And it was only when he got a terminal diagnosis that he began painting again, just for the love of it. He reckoned it was his finest work."

The visitor's eyes sparkled. Sam had confirmed something he already suspected.

"He had no money," said Sam, "until these two generous gents showed up."

"I was very happy to pay what I did for the painting," said Sid.

"As was I," Franc concurred.

"You own Christopher Ackland paintings?" the astrologer asked with excitement.

"Over there," Franc gestured to the wall next to the coffee machine, where the painting of rhododendrons was now framed and hanging.

The visitor turned, taking it in for longest while before shaking his head, "Extraordinary!"

"Why the interest in Christopher?" asked Sid.

The guest looked from one to another, seeming to decide how to respond, before saying, "Before I tell you about Christopher, let me offer you an astrological nugget about Vincent Van Gogh. One of the most famous and influential artists in history. While he was alive, he was considered a madman and a failure. Despite producing thousands of paintings, he only ever managed to sell just the one. After years of depression and poverty, he committed suicide in July 1890, aged 37.

"Almost exactly one century later, on 15 May 1990, his painting *The Portrait of Dr Gachet* sold for $82 million at auction. At the time, it was the highest amount ever paid for a painting. For a while after I first heard this story, I mulled over what happened to poor Van Gogh from an astrological perspective. Then I started wondering whether his natal chart, advanced by 100 years, might point to anything about that momentous event a century after he died.

"When I looked into the detail," his eyes gleamed, "I was amazed by what I found. There was a triple conjunction of the Moon, the lunar south node, and Jupiter in Sagittarius and in the sixth house. What's more, Jupiter was transiting, forming a square to his Sun on the very day his painting broke all records. There were other conjunctions too. They all pointed to something phenomenal going on."

"The charts still work after we die!" exclaimed Franc.

The astrologer nodded, "Forecasting tools for individual legacies."

"Like a ghost in a machine," murmured Sid.

"And you've done Christopher's?" Sam cut to the chase, leaning forward in his chair, along with Sid and Franc.

"After confirming the trend with a number of other people who achieved unexpected fame either late in life or after they died," the visitor smiled. "I asked myself: 'What about artists who are yet to become famous? From their charts, might we predict who they could be?'

"As a starting point, I looked for artists who had achieved early recognition, but for some reason had disappeared from view. Winners of prizes and exhibitions in their early lives who had never been heard of again. Artists whose natal charts showed some especially spectacular transits or conjunctions several decades later.

"Of the hundreds I looked at, Christopher's was one of a handful that really stood out. An alignment so eye-catching you couldn't miss it. I spent quite some time working on it. When I was certain, I tried tracking him down, starting in England. There weren't many clues. It seemed only by chance I discovered that he was somewhere in Dharamshala."

Leaning back in his seat, the visitor looked down at the table. "I am so very sorry to have missed him. I would like to have told him about the glories of his chart. The recognition that was coming his way."

"A fascinating perspective!" exclaimed Sid.

"Never heard anything like it," agreed Franc. "Yet it kind of makes sense when it comes to how people's reputations can dramatically change after they die."

"It explains something the Dalai Lama said," mused Sid. "Which I didn't understand at the time."

"Go on," prompted the astrologer.

"His Holiness commissioned Christopher to paint Amitabha Budda. More than anything, I think, to guide Christopher's thoughts in his final days and weeks. To help him to a state of non-duality with the qualities, the state, of Amitabha. After Christopher died, the Dalai Lama asked me to take the painting. He was concerned that the impressionist approach to the subject might be misunderstood by his more conformist visitors. He also seemed to imply," Sid lowered his voice, "that Namgyal Monastery wasn't the place for a painting of such great value. Magnificent as the artwork is, I hadn't thought it of particular financial worth."

"And it may not be," said the visitor. "Yet." Looking pointedly from Sid to Franc he asked, "Am I correct in thinking that you are the only ones to have acquired a Christopher Ackland painting?"

"And me," volunteered Sam. "He gave a painting to my fiancée and me. Wedding gift."

"Some gift!" The astrologer looked at him with regard before asking, "Do you know if he left any other paintings for sale?"

Sid shook his head. "His studio was dismantled as soon as

he died. Marianne Ponter is always under pressure for space. I heard that any paintings he left behind were going to landfill."

The astrologer rolled his eyes.

"We can double-check if you like," offered Franc. "The nursing home is just up the road."

"What *I* want to know," Sam eyeballed the visitor. "Is when Christopher's birth chart magic will happen? Are we talking years or decades from now?"

"Or like Van Gogh, a whole century later?" the visitor's eyes twinkled. Then he continued, his expression becoming more serious. "As it happens," he murmured, "just days."

All three men were astounded.

"Right now, the planets are making their way towards the most extraordinary configuration ever in Christopher's chart. An auspicious astrological conjunction that is rarely seen. Exactly how it plays out is something I can't tell you. What are offered are symbols, images, metaphors." The visitor nodded soberly. "All I do know for sure is that whatever happens, it's going to be big."

*

It was late in the afternoon, weeks later. From the top of the filing cabinet in the Executive Assistants' office, I watched Tenzin prepare to leave. He always followed the same routine, methodically clearing his desk, locking his drawer, shutting down his computer.

Opposite, Oliver was deeply engrossed in a rare Tibetan text discovered in a Himalayan cave and presented to Namgyal

Monastery that very morning. An original and previously unknown text, apparently written by none other than Lobsang Chokyi Gyaltsan, the first Panchen Lama.

"Well, I'm off," Tenzin collected his satchel bag from the desk.

Oliver looked up, "Evening at home?"

Tenzin nodded. "Next door first," he indicated the direction of the garden with the cedar tree. "Day 49 for Christopher and Kyi Kyi."

"Oh, is it?" Oliver glanced at his watch. "Then I won't be far behind."

He wasn't, dear reader. Nor was I.

The twilight gatherings had a special quality like no others. Brief, lasting no more than twenty minutes. Focused, with Christopher and Kyi Kyi the main objects of concentration, as mantras and special verses were recited. What set these times apart were the people who came and the spirit in which they came. A weekly coalescence of consciousness – close friends and relative strangers, seasoned meditators and people who had never before spoken a word of Sanskrit. Each one of them offering their support to beings who may still be passing through the bardo realms.

With Franc and Serena as chanting leaders on the bench, others sat on the lawn or on folding chairs, or stood at the back. The group began by reciting the verses of Lama Tsong Khapa's meditation practice – refuge, *bodhicitta* and the seven limbs. Next, they recited mantras quietly under breath, most especially the mantra of Amitabha Buddha – *Om Amitabha hrih.*

The Dalai Lama says that the best time for focused attention is when day meets night – dawn and dusk. And at that particular ceremony, the gathering of consciousness had never felt more coherent, nor the developing focus more powerful. Was it on account of this being the final such occasion? The significance of day 49?

According to the teachings, by day 49 any being in the bardo will definitely attain rebirth. No matter how tranquil or traumatic the journey, or how many transitions from one bardo form to another, by the seventh day of the seventh week the bardo period comes to an end for us all. The stage is set for a whole new realm of experience.

The fresh start brings with it a sense of turning the wheel. Our loved ones have moved on. Wherever their untethered minds may have taken them, they are now embarked on a new chapter. Which is a signal for those who remain. There is no further need to keep clothes in the cupboard, keepsakes of our departed friend, or other familiar items on display – at least, not for their sake. The pet basket and feeding bowls may safely be put away. Our loved one has struck out on a different journey. It is time for us to do so too.

So there is a sense of farewelling. Of gratitude for the lives that were shared, and mutual support for those left behind. Perhaps this was why more people were drawn to this final vigil than any before. From where I sat on the bench between Franc and Serena, I watched as more and more people arrived in the garden up the steps from the street, Sam and Bonnie handing out lit tealights. One by one, the group under the cedar grew larger and drew more tightly together.

There were staff from the nursing home, long-term sup-porters of Christopher's. Many of The Downward Dog School of Yoga students led by Ludo, as well as café regulars who had come to know Kyi Kyi over the years. Monks from nearby Namgyal and, of course, Tenzin and Oliver. The astrologer had got wind of the ceremony and had come to offer his wiz-ardly support. The voices were greater in number than ever, their offered chants more resonant. The rising Sanskrit chorus reached well beyond an invocation of blessings; the chanted repetition generated a specific energy – one already sparking into flame, becoming palpably felt.

The sacred language of *prana,* correctly motivated, has the power to dramatically transform from within. To uplift, to increase, to reach across whole dimensions of consciousness. And in the glistening eyes and moving lips of those gathered, I knew they were feeling it too. The effervescence had been sparked from somewhere deep within, but was soon racing up the spine with shivering effect. The current didn't so much grow as multiply into an electrifying, whole-of-body sensation. For the whole time that the mantras were repeated, the turbines kept turning, energy cascading further and further afield.

As Yogi Tarchin had revealed, when we remember that this sensation isn't being generated by the ancient Sanskrit or the magic of candlelight, but by mind itself, then the sheer joy of the moment is felt in its purest and most unbridled form. Our minds are enabling us to feel this. Virtue is the true source of inexpressible bliss.

We were in the final minutes, everyone chanting the Amitabha Buddha mantra out loud, when I saw him standing at the top of the steps flanked by two bodyguards.

Moments later, Franc and Serena noticed him there too.

His Holiness held up his hand, indicating that they should continue as if he wasn't there – which they did. But something had been communicated, because there were surreptitious glances from round the cedar tree, and secret smiles, and we all knew of his presence and the significance of what was occurring. If such a thing were possible, the radiance of that moment shone even brighter.

IT TOOK A WHILE FOR PEOPLE TO LEAVE, DEPARTING IN SILENT wonder. Wanting to continue abiding in this enchanted state, I vanished into a flowerbed, waiting for everyone to go.

After every other person had departed, there was one who lingered, evidently in no great hurry to leave. Heidi took her time to get up from where she had been sitting, before rolling up her yoga mat. No doubt, like me, she had wanted to stay with the sensation of what she had felt, to continue in the blissful *prana* evoked by this evening's special ceremony.

It was only when she turned towards the steps that we both became aware of movement on the pavement. Ludo.

He was alone and had evidently been waiting for her. She watched him come up the steps, pausing some distance away. "My dear Heidi. I owe you an apology," his expression was remorseful.

They had been like ships in the night for weeks since the argument, so Heidi had told Sid and Serena. Heidi had continued to lead the classes assigned to her at the yoga studio. Ludo took his. Apart from routine courtesies, they hadn't spoken.

With Heidi's permission, Sid had said he would speak to Ludo. Besides, he needed to square things away with him about 108 Bougainvillea Street.

"It was ... unforgivable for me to say what I did." Ludo's voice was solemn, "I am so sorry."

Heidi took a long time to respond. When she did, she said, "Thank you, Uncle. What you said to me though, was only what you believe. Your convictions."

"Yes," Ludo looked down. "But in affirming our own convictions, it is not necessary to denigrate the convictions of others. I understand your point of view. I accept it."

"Just as I accept yours," said Heidi. "The path of the yogi who aspires for complete mastery. It fills me with admiration. I just don't believe everyone is capable of it in this lifetime. Maybe not even me."

"You have great compassion, Heidi," he took a step closer. "Your heart is bigger than mine," his voice cracked with uncharacteristic emotion.

"Oh, Uncle!" She stepped over, embracing him.

For a while they held together, before he stepped away, taking her hands in his. "Sid has told me about the new venture."

She nodded.

"It sounds ideal for you."

"I can still take classes at the studio," she told him, eyes meeting his.

"I would like that very much,' he said. "As many from your roster that you can continue to take."

"I know this hasn't worked out the way you hoped."

"The way either of us hoped," he replied. "But what is the teaching of all yogis?" In the darkness, he prompted an oft-repeated adage from his classes: "Give of your best and then – let go!"

"Let go," she smiled. Then after a pause, "We agree on that."

"And on many other things besides," he took her by the arm. "Come. I have an eggplant parmigiana in the oven at home. Let's enjoy it together."

CHAPTER TEN

"*NOURISH YOUR BODY WITH YOGA STRETCHES ON THE LAWN.*" AT HIS desk, Tenzin was reading aloud from a thick, cream-colored invitation card that had arrived in that day's mail. "*Treat yourself to a five-star pampering from one of our professional beauticians.*" He looked across to where Oliver sat facing him, an identical card in his hand. "This invitation?" he asked mirthfully, as his eyes met Oliver's.

"Yes." Still somewhat pink from his cycle to work that morning, Oliver shifted in his chair. "I thought it would be good for Sid and Serena if one of us went."

"*Watermelon and cucumber elixir …*" Tenzin picked out another phrase, which he read in a humorous voice. "I can see why you want to go."

"It's more the yoga part …" Oliver interjected.

"Of course."

"And showing our support."

"His Holiness would insist on it!" Tenzin chuckled. "By the time you come back tomorrow, you'll be so rejuvenated we'll hardly recognize you."

"Laugh if you must." Opposite, Oliver was shaking his head with a smile, "I know you'd really like to be there; you just can't bring yourself to admit it."

Tenzin rested back in his chair and regarded his colleague with an amused twinkle. "My dear Oliver," he said. "My health and beauty regime is a walk in the evenings, followed by a shower. But I agree that it would be nice to support our friends. And if you're willing to subject yourself to all those lotions and potions …"

"I'll tell them it's a 'no' from you then," said Oliver.

"With regrets."

"Oh, you will regret it," said Oliver with a smile. "After I return from my five-star pampering."

DOWNSTAIRS SOMETIME LATER, THE UNMISTAKABLE CADENCES of Mrs. Trinci echoed from the kitchen. She and Serena had returned from an expedition to buy groceries and fresh produce for a VIP meal the next day. Okra, green tomatoes and other unfamiliar items were being carefully stored away. Who was the exotic visitor, I wondered, visiting His Holiness tomorrow?

"Oh, *tesorina*! My Most Beautiful Creature!" Mrs. Trinci soon had me in her arms and was placing me on a counter, before serving up a generous helping of double cream. "How happy I am to hear that you and Rishi are now friends."

"It *is* a relief." Across the kitchen, Serena was deep inside the fridge organizing items, before standing. "And quite a mystery how it happened."

Mrs. Trinci stroked me, as I lapped the cream with gusto. "How could the little boy resist such a being. Look at her, so soft and gentle."

Had I not still had half a ramekin of cream in front of me, I would have shot Mrs. Trinci a look of stern rebuke. Soft and gentle?! Those were hardly the qualities which had endeared me to young Rishi – quite the opposite. "Ferocious" and "ninja" would have been much closer to the mark.

Serena was preparing a plunger of coffee and Mrs. Trinci running through a check list on her phone, when there was a knock at the door. Sid.

"I thought I might find you both here," he said, stepping inside. "I've just been to Marianne Ponter." He pointed in the direction of the neighboring property.

"And?" Serena responded to the unusual energy about him.

"They still have Christopher's paintings!" he said, before an anguished expression passed across his face. "Well, most of them."

Over coffee at the kitchen bench, Sid described how he had taken the astrologer to the nursing home, where they had secured the earliest possible appointment with Marianne. They hadn't even reached the entrance before encountering a sight that filled them with dismay. Ranged across the driveway, held down by assorted roadside stones, were about thirty canvases in abstract style. Two laborers in overalls wielded rollers covered in whitewash. Under orders from Mr. Devi, their task was to apply a thick, smooth coat to every canvas, thereby rendering them good as new for the nursing home's art rehabilitation program. About ten of the canvases had already been thus treated.

Sid and his fellow visitor had ordered an immediate stay of execution, while Mr. Devi was consulted. A short while later in Marianne's office, the latter had explained his budget-saving brainwave to re-use the discarded canvases, rather than send them to landfill.

It was at this point that Sid, with all the majesty and mystery that a maharajah could muster, revealed the profession of his fellow visitor. Marianne and Mr. Devi were used to receiving visits from all manner of specialists, but were unused to one with knowledge of the occult. The astrologer had reprized his story of Van Gogh, relating the parallels with Christopher Ackland, and his hypothesis about the relevance of natal charts to individual legacies.

But what to do? Astrological forecasts were a perplexing matter for a manager who aspired to make strictly evidence-based decisions. Marianne Ponter's face was a vision of skepticism. Mr. Devi looked like he might now have misgivings about his order to whitewash Christopher's canvases, but given his boss's demeanor, he wasn't about to express them.

There had been talk of conjunctions and planetary alignments. The American visitor had communicated his expectations with an enthusiasm which hadn't been shared by all. Which had led to a discussion about the current status of the canvases. Had they really no worth and, if so, did that mean they were for sale? If their value was worth nothing more than that of the raw material, would the nursing home be willing to exchange them for, say, thirty new canvases?

At some point in the discussion, a memory had been triggered for Marianne. A particular recollection from her last conversation with Christopher – one to which I had been party. How she had sought to distract him from talk of debt, by encouraging him to imagine what it would be like if his paintings were worth a fortune. How he had responded with talk of philanthropy. More particularly – she smiled to recall it – The Sanctuary for Broke Old Bohemians.

Which was when Sid proposed a solution. Rather than follow through on the whitewashing order right away, why not keep the canvases for just one more month? By then, if there was no known change to Christopher's status in the art world, Mr. Devi's budget-enhancing idea should be implemented. On the other hand, if there had been some stellar breakthrough, Marianne would find she was the trustee to assets endowed to The Sanctuary for Broke Old Bohemians.

"I suppose there would be no harm in that," Marianne had been obliged to admit. "But being a trustee, and setting up a foundation, that's not something I've ever done."

Sid assured her that, having had long experience in such matters, he'd be very glad to assist.

By the time they left a short while later, agreement had been reached. The canvases had been removed from the driveway, carefully dusted, and allocated precious shelf space in the indoors stationery cupboard. A significant step up from the garage.

Sid and the astrologer had left the meeting well satisfied. While it was true that ten original Christopher Ackland's had been lost to posterity, twenty others had been rescued. And even the original ten could be salvageable, according to the astrologer, who had read of cases where masterpieces had been revealed beneath subsequent layers of paint.

Best of all was the hope the two men shared – which Sid now conveyed to Serena and Mrs. Trinci. "As our esteemed visitor observed," said Sid, "what were the chances that he would walk into that particular café, on that particular day, and find Sam, Franc and me at the very time he was trying to locate Christopher Ackland?"

"A sanctuary for bohemians!" Mrs. Trinci's eyelids fluttered dreamily. "I think I would like to go there in my old age. We would wear caftans, play music and dance by the swimming pool."

Serena regarded her quizzically. "You go for it, Momma!" she said.

Sid's expression was more earnest. "It does seem like a miracle," he nodded. "But if it were Christopher's intention, and if he had the karma for it to happen, who knows?"

THAT SAME DAY, DOWN AT THE HIMALAYA BOOK CAFÉ, I WAS sprawled on the top shelf of the magazine rack when Heidi arrived, accompanied by an Indian woman I immediately surmised must be Binita. Tall, forties, with finely sculpted features and wide brown eyes conveying sensitivity and wisdom in equal measure. She was wearing a striking amber sari, her hair tucked into an elegant braided bun, but it was the way she held herself that was especially striking. She had that indefinable bearing of someone at ease with herself and who expected the best from those around her.

In front of her, blonde, fair skinned, in white jeans and a pink scoop-neck top, Heidi led the way to the banquette at the back of the café – the one which was the quietest and closest to me. They sat, facing one another.

Binita met Heidi's eyes. "Much better," she said.

"All those vacuum cleaners," Heidi put her fingers in her ears. "Still. We must have it glistening for tomorrow."

"It will be," Binita nodded calmly.

Reaching for their phones, the two began going through a list of all the final arrangements being made, before discussing the opening day's special timetable. Binita, used to running a large house and staff, was unruffled by the many practical matters still needing attention. Heidi, experienced in leading a variety of different classes, knew how to devise a program to appeal to as many people as possible. The two of them, different as it was possible to be, made for a highly complementary team – as they seemed to be discovering.

After a while Ricardo appeared to take their coffee order. Suave in his pinstriped apron, he was in no hurry to return to the coffee machine, asking Heidi about what was happening on launch day.

Kusali's appearance sent him scuttling. "I'll take it from here," the Head Waiter said, before fixing his attention on Binita. "Is this your first visit here, madam?" he wanted to know, soon establishing that they shared a close mutual friend in the Maharajah of Himachal Pradesh. This was a Kusali I had never seen before, attentive as always, but his elaborate courtesies were accompanied this time, it seemed, by another kind of interest.

"May I recommend strawberry macarons to accompany your coffee order?" Kusali was saying. "The most refined and exquisite in all of India – with the compliments of our chefs, Jigme and Ngawang Dragpa."

After Kusali had left, Heidi looked at Binita and said, "He was flirting with you."

"He was not!" Binita protested, though there was a glint in her eye.

"Oh yes!" Heidi chuckled. "*Strawberry macarons*" she mimicked him. "*The most refined and exquisite in all of India. With compliments!*"

Binita snorted, glancing down at the table, then her sophisticated poise completely dissolved and she looked positively impish. "The coffee one," she nodded towards the machine.

"Ricardo?"

"Him," she confirmed. "*He* was flirting with *you*!"

"I know," said Heidi as she began telling her the story about the awkward encounter she'd had with Natalia, which had turned into something quite different.

"He *is* very good looking," Binita shot a surreptitious glance in Ricardo's direction.

"Yes."

"Well?" Binita raised her eyebrows.

"I've had a lot to come to grips with in the past couple of weeks. Now it's all about this," she nodded towards their phones on the table.

"He is checking you out," reported Binita.

Heidi glanced about the restaurant. "And Kusali is checking you out."

Binita met her eyes, suppressing a smile. "Makes me feel like a teenager again."

"And that's a bad thing?" asked Heidi.

"No. Not all bad," she was shaking her head. "It's nice to feel hope for the future again."

Franc and Sam stopped at their table while the two women continued their meeting – the four already having had discussions on 108 Bougainvillea Street. Sam announced that he had just pressed 'Send' on an email to everyone on the bookstore mailing list in Dharamshala, reminding them about launch day. Franc said he'd bring over his collection of Tibetan singing bowls later that day. Intrigued by the great variety of activities going on in Sid's renovated home, I decided that I must visit the place myself on the morrow, to investigate the grand opening.

Ricardo arrived with coffees at the same time as Kusali served the strawberry macarons – this time, given the presence of their mutual boss, without repartee. It was what Kusali did next that turned Binita's attention shelf-wards, with consequences more profound than I could ever have guessed.

As usual, the Head Waiter had brought a small bowl of that day's *plat du jour* for my delectation. Getting up for my late lunch, as I stirred, Binita noticed me for the first time. And pointed her finger, with an expression of delighted surprise.

"The cat!"

Seeing the impact my presence had on her, Kusali was quick to return to the banquette. "No ordinary cat, ma'am," he said, with a confidential expression.

Franc glanced at him, amused.

"This is ... the Dalai Lama's Cat."

While the others were nodding in agreement, the details of my living arrangements seemed of less interest to Binita than something else. "She's a Himalayan?"

"Yes," confirmed Franc.

"Rare breed?"

"That's right."

"Most unusual," she said, glancing at Heidi. "I must take her photo and send it to Yazhini, my sister. She has a gorgeous Himmie, just like this." She was evidently quite struck with me. "What a coincidence!"

"Where does Yazhini live?" asked Franc.

"Mumbai. But they used to be in New Delhi. That's where she first had Maya."

When I am presented with a few nourishing morsels to eat, usually nothing has the power to distract me. But hearing

that particular name, and spoken with Binita's particular into-
nation, I experienced a most extraordinary sensation. Lifting
my head quite suddenly to look at her, it was as though I had
been jolted by some invisible, giddying force. Awakened to the
unanticipated shift of a subterranean fault line that I hadn't
even known existed.

And as Binita held my gaze, with that mysterious, plum-
meting feeling, I wondered if she sensed it too.

You may have thought that given the importance of
launch day, with all the busy preparations leading up to it – not
to mention the continuing enigma of what, precisely, was being
launched – that I would have presented myself at the entrance
to 108 Bougainvillea Street early in the morning, ears washed,
whiskers preened, ready to observe the day's events with all
due heed.

Alas, dear reader, I did not.

Rising from my usual early morning meditation with His
Holiness, I was in a state of such tranquil clarity, my mind
completely free from all mundane musings, that I had no
thoughts about Bougainvillea Street, or anywhere else for that
matter. Enjoying every mouthful of a hearty breakfast, I took
myself out of habit to the Executive Assistants' office. There I
settled in my usual spot, aware of all the comings and goings in
that state of semi-wakefulness at which we felines are so expert.

It was only when Oliver arrived late, a bright green yoga
mat rolled under his arm, that I suddenly remembered.

"I'm going straight there," he told Tenzin, placing a backpack on his desk chair.

"For the five-star pampering?" Tenzin responded, in mock earnest.

"Don't be alarmed if a very slimmed-down, youthful-looking monk appears here later," Oliver told him. "That'll be me."

He was soon on his way and I was too, heading across the Namgyal courtyard, down the road towards The Himalaya Book Café, then making a left turn up Bougainvillea Street. From quite some distance away, cars were parked at the side of the road where the parking spots were usually empty. Small groups in yoga gear were walking towards the gates, the solid white posts on either side decorated with gold ribbons.

A new sign next to the gates was being studied by a few of the visitors. Sweeping gold lettering declared 108 Bougainvillea Street to be Sukhavati Spa.

"Sukhavati. Isn't that Buddha Amitabha's pure land?" I overheard someone ask.

"Sukhavati means place of bliss," said another.

"You know how 'dukkha' is dissatisfaction and suffering?" explained a third. "Well, 'sukha' is the opposite."

Reaching the gates, what met the eyes certainly looked like a land of bliss. A red carpet had been unrolled along the short driveway between loops of gold ribbon. Massive floral arrangements stood on pedestals to both sides of the open front doors. Inside the marble-floored reception area, staff in cream uniforms with gold braid were welcoming guests and sending them in a variety of directions. It seemed that a number of things were happening at the same time.

Avoiding the red carpet, I walked under a gold ribbon through a flower bed and round the side, where I could play the observer from behind a lush screen of lilies. Over two dozen people were unrolling mats of vivid colors on the front lawn. Oliver was among them, looking strangely unfamiliar in his yoga clothes. There were a few familiar faces from The Downward Dog School of Yoga, but most of the people were younger. It was a different group from any I had observed in McLeod Ganj, and there was a different atmosphere. Settling on their mats, some lying with their closed eyes and smooth faces to the sun, others stretching arms and legs while chattering in low voices. The sky was limpid as only late autumn skies can be, and the mountain breeze effervesced with the scent of pine. Never had a Himalayan morning seemed brighter with promise.

Heidi arrived to take her place at the front of the class, welcoming everyone to a yoga and meditation session. Latecomers continued to join in, as the very first outdoor class at Sukhavati Spa got underway. Once they were all engaged in their warrior asanas, facing the cedar forests with their arms outstretched, I crossed from flower bed to veranda unobserved, before slipping into the house. From the gleaming marble of the grand reception area, plush cream carpets led along a wide corridor and up a flight of stairs. Staying on the ground floor, I headed in the direction from which a sound was emanating – mysterious and resonant. The kind that makes one's whiskers tingle with curiosity.

The door into the room was ajar. In contrast to the lawn outside, the large chamber was in complete darkness, apart from the pink blush of Tibetan salt lamps ranged along all four walls. On the carpeted floor, people lay on towels and mats, some wearing eye pillows, all of them appearing to be in a state of deep relaxation. The warm air was rich with lavender. Silhouetted against the soft glow was a man it took me a while to recognize. It was Ewing, the piano player. He was leaning over one of the recumbent forms, holding a Tibetan singing bowl in his left hand, striking it softly with a wooden beater, moving it from over the head to the chest and finally placing it on the stomach of the person, where he struck it again, sending reverberations throughout their body. Only after the final haunting sound had faded away into complete silence did he remove the bowl, before stepping to the next person to repeat the chiming.

There was a hypnotic quality to the proceedings, the rhythmic gonging and its dreamy reverberations evoking a state not so much of drowsiness as of some other form of relaxation harder to define, one of lucidity but at a deeper level than usual. I settled onto the carpet, just inside the room, my body feeling delightfully heavy at the same time as my mind was, in some unusual way, free to wander.

Time passed. Quite a lot it seemed. So absorbed was I by what was happening, and so mesmerized, that I didn't even notice the approach of two people behind me, or one of them reaching down to collect me in her arms.

Serena. "HHC!" she whispered in my ear, kissing me. "I

hoped you'd visit!"

Yogi Tarchin reached to stroke my face. For a while, all three of us silently observed what was happening in the room, then Serena returned to the foyer and up the stairs.

She was leading the way along a newly wood-paneled corridor, when we were caught up in a profusion of heavenly fragrances. We turned the corner to a wider passage, from which doors on both sides opened into treatment rooms. Further along, people were waiting on sofas and in armchairs for aromatherapy sessions.

A young woman was emerging from one of the treatment rooms, touching her face. "That was amazing!" she told the therapist who followed her, a European woman in one of the elegant, cream uniforms. "What did you use?"

"Lavender, clary sage, patchouli," she replied. "We try to match the aroma to what our clients need. It's an intuitive thing."

"I feel I could float away with the wind."

Serena shared a look of happiness with Yogi Tarchin as she led him away. The beauty treatment space on the other side upstairs had the same layout as the aromatherapy area. The approach was all gleaming marble tiles, soft towels and subdued lighting.

"This is where your friends are working?" he queried.

She nodded.

"Are they settling in?"

"Better than we could have hoped," she whispered. "Sid always thought that Binita, the mother, would make the most of the opportunity, and she's been wonderful. We weren't so sure about the girls. They were part of the fast set in a big city, and the twins used to have this massive social media following. Binita wondered if they'd resent being moved to Dharamshala. After their financial disaster, they were too embarrassed to go online. Turns out, they're now posting images of themselves in this glamorous spa in the Himalayas. They're our most active marketers. It's amazing the bookings they've generated."

"And the older girl?"

"Hema has turned a bit of a corner too," Serena spoke under her breath. "She's fallen for the young architect who did this redevelopment."

"Love conquers all?" asked Yogi Tarchin, eyes twinkling.

Every one of the four treatment rooms were occupied, as was the waiting area with clients waiting their turn. "I see what you mean about the bookings," observed Yogi Tarchin.

"Let's hope it stays this way," said Serena. Then turning to lead him away, she told him, "You know, working on the spa launch has been a real eye-opener. Seeing the twins doing what they do with digital marketing, I mean. I feel so old."

"Age brings experience," Yogi Tarchin responded after a pause. "And with experience, wisdom. There will always be people more knowledgeable and enthusiastic about such things as social media. That's good."

Serena was following him closely.

"As leader, your job is to set things in motion, to create the organization. Others will take things forward, maybe even in ways you don't expect."

She was nodding.

"You and Sid have shown strong leadership with your spice pack business. Now with Sukhavati Spa. Perhaps there may be other ventures to come."

"You think so?"

As we turned a corner towards the staircase, the sound of voices rose from the reception area. Yogi Tarchin gave Serena an amused smile, before glancing at his watch and slipping into a secluded meditation recess. She nodded, before taking me down the stairs.

A steady flow of people were arriving down the red carpet. Franc and Ludo were among the group. Sam and Bronnie too. Evidently there was to be a gathering downstairs.

"We must find somewhere HHC will be safe," Serena approached Binita behind the gleaming reception desk.

Binita glanced about before spotting a wall recess, a short jump up from the counter and occupied by a glass vase. She removed the vase, laying down a dark blue towel from a hamper behind her. Then, having second thoughts, changing the blue towel for a cream one.

Serena held me up to the recess, where I was soon making myself at home, kneading the fluffy towel contemplatively, while taking in the view.

"Perfect cat-sized niche," Serena said approvingly.

Poised and regal, Binita conveyed the impression that the presence of a Himalayan cat presiding over reception was quite simply the *pièce de résistance* for an establishment such as this.

"I met this little one yesterday," she said. "I think she is very special."

"She is special to all who know her," Serena responded warmly.

As Binita held out her hand to caress my cheek, I remembered her reaction at the café. How she'd seen something in me that no-one had ever responded to before. And that what made me special to her had nothing to do with me being the Dalai Lama's Cat.

More and more people were entering the room. Waitstaff in Sukhavati Spa uniforms were circulating with fruit drinks, lemonade and sparkling water. Platters of pastries, fruit and other delicacies were being proffered. Serena and Binita were keeping an eye on the staff, while welcoming guests at the front door. Marianne Ponter asked if they could negotiate special rates for her residents. Sam and Bronnie were talking to Ludo about yoga during pregnancy. Right beside me, Franc was joking with Binita that he wanted to get the twins, Diya and Nisha, to do some social media posts for The Himalaya Book Café, saying he'd never seen half the people in the room.

There were further tides of guests as Heidi led her class, now ended, inside. Ewing shepherded his very mellow sound therapy group along the corridor. It was an unusually relaxed gathering, and although the room was full of people of every age and appearance, there was also the genial feeling of being among kindred spirits.

Down the stairs came people from the treatment rooms in a cloud of ambrosial fragrances, accompanied by three beautiful young Indian women. Walking with the same elegant poise as their mother, cream uniforms setting off their flawless features to perfection, they could have been models on a fashion runway as they descended.

Another guest arrived in somewhat of a flurry of activity – the astrologer. Gathering Sid and Marianne, the three of them came to join Franc who was still standing nearby.

"It arrived overnight." The wizardly visitor had printed copies of an article he'd received, which he handed to the three of them. "*A 70s Retrospective*," Franc read the headline aloud. "*Reassessing artistic currents fifty years on.*"

It was a full-page article, densely worded, but in an early paragraph he saw the name Christopher Ackland. "*Without question, one of the most overlooked artists of his time*," he read, excitedly. "*Ackland was the unrecognized pioneer of what emerged to become a whole new movement.* Who wrote this?" he queried.

"H A Wallace," replied the astrologer. "Royal Academician and highly respected art critic."

"*Whatever his subject, he brought to it a dazzling intensity*," Sid had taken up the reading. "Well, we know that." He continued, *Rewarded with early recognition, critics turned against his treatment of darker subjects and the artist disappeared from our shores, never to be seen again. It is one of our greatest tragedies that we never saw the mature work of an artist who was undoubtedly one of Britain's most outstanding impressionists. Ackland's fully evolved work would have been magnificent.*" Sid looked up from the page, eyes wider than I had ever seen them.

"Extraordinary!" said Franc.

"Our Christopher!" Marianne was shocked.

"The person who sent this told me about the sale of an Ackland painting from the Skea Collection. The reserve had been set at $50,000. After this review was published, the reserve was pushed up to one million."

Sid was shaking his head.

"Just unbelievable!" Franc smiled.

"You should know," the astrologer continued. "That reserve prices are only that. They can easily be exceeded. Sometimes, several times over. And the item being sold by Skea's is only small in size. Nothing like the scale of the canvases you have."

All three of them were turning to look at Marianne, in the sudden knowledge that she was now the custodian of, at the very least, a probable twenty million dollars' worth of rare paintings.

"I did have a new padlock fitted to the stationery cupboard yesterday," she told them. Before stating the obvious, "I don't suppose that really cuts it."

"I have a safe at home," offered Sid. "Fire and bombproof. You can store the paintings there until you decide what's next."

"Good idea," Marianne was nodding.

"How exactly we break the news to the art world that Christopher *did* produce mature work is something we'll have to think about," said Franc.

"Along with how I allowed ten of his paintings to be coated with whitewash," Marianne winced.

"That's all for another day," Sid reassured her.

"Looks like you will soon have your hands full with the new sanctuary," the astrologer looked brightly from Marianne to Sid. "For broke old bohemians!"

"If we do," Sid fixed him with an expression of warm regard, "it will be mainly thanks to you."

"Heaven knows what would have happened if you hadn't visited," said Franc.

"Oh, I think we all know that," Marianne was still looking embarrassed as she shook her head. "Doesn't bear thinking of." Then after a pause, "There was one other party involved in all this from the start." Turning, she gestured towards where I sat in my new hidey-hole, unaware that she had even noticed me.

"HHC!" exclaimed Franc.

"Christopher doted on her," said Marianne. "Called her by all kinds of names. Apparently, a lot of great painters, like Picasso and Dali, had their own cats."

"That's true," confirmed the astrologer. "The feline affinity."

"It was she," continued Marianne, "who inspired Christopher to give a painting to the Dalai Lama."

"Who in turn told him to come to class, where we all met," Franc was nodding.

"In many ways," Sid was enigmatic, as they stood regarding me with all due wonder. "None of this would be happening if it wasn't for HHC."

"She is so very much more than simply a cat," agreed Franc.

The astrologer regarded me, tugging his gray beard thoughtfully. "Her natal chart would be quite intriguing."

A SHORT WHILE LATER SID WENT UPSTAIRS, RETURNING TO halfway down the landing, accompanied by their guest of honor. The room was brimming with visitors. Serena chimed the edge of a knife against her glass to call for silence. Sid, every inch the maharajah, was soon welcoming everyone to Sukhavati Spa, introducing Heidi and Binita as Spa Directors, and Hema, Diya and Nisha as permanent staff. The three girls had joined their mother at reception, all of them radiant.

"This property has been in my family for many years, sometimes a home, sometimes business premises. Having seen how well it has all come together, I have no doubt that this is its most wonderful incarnation of all. A sanctuary where people can come to relax and heal, residents and tourists, whatever their age.

"I can claim none of this vision for myself. That came, very directly, from my kind and precious teacher, Yogi Tarchin." Turning he said, "It is our very good fortune that you are here with us today, Rinpoche, and an honor that you have agreed to say a few words to us."

Sid took several steps down, leaving the stage to his teacher. Yogi Tarchin took in the many people gathered around him and, like the Dalai Lama, it was as if even his gaze conveyed a blessing. In his gold shirt and fawn pants, it was as though a beam of sunlight was streaming onto the landing – bright and radiant, but intangible at the same time.

"That is a very kind introduction," he began. "But despite what this one would have you believe," he gestured towards Sid, "I never directed him to open a spa, much less one in the name of Amitabha Buddha."

There were chuckles as Rinpoche brought the audience into his confidence, a glint of mischief about his face. "What I did say to him is a suggestion I'd like to share with you today, because it is one of profound importance. We may think of Sukhavati pure land as a heavenly place of great joy. Somewhere we go when we die, if we have been good girls and boys. This is the simple idea, maybe a bit primitive. Because even if we were taken to a pure land with our minds as they are right now, with our restrictive idea of 'me', it wouldn't be long before we got a bit bored. Frustrated."

His suggestion was received with amused nodding.

"After three weeks, perhaps, we've had enough of all the light and love and we want to get home where things are not so comfortable, but more familiar."

There was some laughter around the room.

"So, if we are capable of evolved metaphorical thought, it is more useful to think of Sukhavati as a state of consciousness, because whatever is in our mind, we project onto the world outside us. Step by step, if we transform the way we think, especially by letting go of the self-grasping mind, we also transform our reality. Wherever we are, we create Sukhavati.

"If we wish for this, for heartfelt happiness and inner peace, a very good pathway is to focus more on others. For in giving, we receive."

With his shaven head and goatee beard, Yogi Tarchin not only had the appearance of an archetypal guru but the presence of one – by now he held the attention of everyone in the room.

251

"I know many of you already know this. Therefore what I told Sid, and what I want to suggest to you today, is that the *way* we help others is of the utmost importance. If our purpose is to develop our consciousness, to become capable of feeling the most profound states of joy, of Sukhavati, then we must be authentic. We can't be fake and expect things to work. Look at those beings we share our lives with, those for whom we already have genuine affection – and if they are in distress, then help them first."

When Rinpoche said this, I noticed the instant change in Binita's expression. Tears welling in her eyes and her lips trembling, as Yogi Tarchin clearly laid out Sid's motivations.

"It isn't necessary to make large philanthropic donations. To set up charities. To change the whole world – although this would be good! We are seeking to open our own hearts and minds first. So, we begin with those for whom we already have love and affection. Those with whom we already have a karmic bond. Then, based on an understanding of equanimity, step by step we learn to cultivate that same compassion towards others who are more distant."

On either side of their mother, the twins responded to Binita by drawing closer, slipping their arms around her waist, tears sliding off their cheeks. Even Hema gazed down, seemingly struck by the purity of Rinpoche's message.

"What we see around us," he ended, "is the expression of loving kindness. So it is fitting that it should be named after the pure land of the Buddha of Infinite Light and Life himself. Especially as we can celebrate in the presence of a very special representation of him."

Until then, I hadn't paid any attention to the red silk wall-hanging behind Rinpoche, with its elaborate motif and gold cord running down the side. But as Yogi Tarchin turned, taking the gold cord in his hand and exchanging a look with Sid, who nodded, I realized that the wall-hanging was only temporary. A veil, screening what lay behind. Tugging the cord briskly, both cord and red covering collapsed to the floor to reveal Christopher's painting of Amitabha Buddha.

The response in the room was an instant collective intake of breath, as people caught sight of him. Captivated by his immense, blazing red presence, one which seemed to reach out to each one of us personally, it was as though a charge had been ignited in the room, setting it ablaze with a particular energy. Drawing on the hopes and yearnings of everyone there, transmuting our every wish and aspiration. Whatever we had been feeling before, we were all caught up in a different sensation, one that seemed drawn from our very depths and brought dramatically to the surface, as the catalyzing power of compassion, the vitalizing force of loving kindness.

There were many glistening eyes in the room at that moment. Many evocations created by that sudden powerful connection – or was it reconnection – to this particular aspect of the enlightened mind.

And standing between Amitabha and the assembled gathering, a conduit to this state of exalted consciousness, was Yogi Tarchin. The guru. One who not only pointed the way to Sukhavati, but who embodied it, his very presence as unlikely and other-worldly as the Buddha whose portrait he had just unveiled.

"It is my very great pleasure," announced Yogi Tarchin, "to announce Sukhavati Spa formally open!"

EPILOGUE

I LEFT A SHORT WHILE LATER. NO MATTER WHAT ONE'S STATE of consciousness, a venue abuzz with animated humans is no place for a senior cat. It was quite enough to have witnessed the transformation to 108 Bougainville Street, and to know that the mandala of HHC now included the wondrous Sukhavati Spa. No doubt I would become familiar with its residents and explore its every garden bed and indoor hidey-hole in the days to come.

Back at Namgyal, in the downstairs kitchen, I found Mrs. Trinci and her sous-chefs hard at work preparing lunch for that day's VIP guest. Upstairs, the Dalai Lama was at his desk. I crossed to the windowsill and settled, surveying activity in the courtyard.

It wasn't long before there was a knock on the door and Oliver appeared to discuss arrangements for that day's visitor.

I recognized him immediately, dear reader. His single yoga session on the lawn at Sukhavati Spa had not transformed him – no doubt, as with meditation, more than one session is required. As he spoke to His Holiness, the words "Chargé d'Affaires" and "Alabama" were mentioned. Meanwhile, demure novices slipped into the room behind him to dust and polish.

As he was about to leave, Oliver glanced towards the windowsill.

"Oh," he remembered. "Some good news from the vet. The results of HHC's blood test came in this morning. All is well."

Blood test! Suddenly I was back in that chamber of horrors, where the vet had declared that the best of my life was already behind me. That I'd already had "a good life". That old age and decrepitude were all that lay ahead.

No doubt I should have been relieved that the test results were favorable. But of greater impact, at that particular moment, was the reminder of that horrible encounter and most unwelcome prognosis.

Both His Holiness and Oliver were gazing in my direction.

"Very good news!" His Holiness rose from his desk and was walking over.

Excusing himself, Oliver left the room.

"I am so glad, my precious one," the Dalai Lama sat beside me, leaning down to meet my eyes. Then, as happens so often, he responded directly to my thoughts. "When we know how quickly our health can change, how short our lives really are, then we find true purpose. Maybe we can rekindle the zest that comes quite naturally to kittens."

If I hadn't experienced the truth of this for myself, I may have found it hard to believe. But as His Holiness massaged my forehead with his fingertips, I thought how recognizing that one's best years – along with most of one's life – are now in the past, need not be a cause of depression. Quite the opposite. As His Holiness said, it is only when you fully understand the rare opportunity presented by each new day that you wish to make the most of it. The value of a life is determined not by its length, but by what you do with it. And there are always worthwhile things to be done.

Even when he received his terminal diagnosis, Christopher hadn't collapsed in a heap of depression. Instead, he had been enlivened as never before. Knowing for certain that his days were numbered, he had made peace with his past and given glorious expression to his passion. Working with a freedom and joy long denied him, he had produced his most transcendent work – aspiring even to non-duality with Amitabha Buddha.

If we wish to live with the joy of kittens, I had learned from my dear friends at The Himalaya Book Café, we also need to reach deep beneath the accumulated layers of disappointment and cynicism that have formed through the years. To be our own best friend and practice radical self acceptance. To shut down The Shitty Committee. If we are able to grasp the objective truth that the self we are so harsh to judge is nothing more than a concept, an idea with less substance than a passing, windblown feather, how liberating!

In our early innocence, when we perceive the world as a sensory playground, we find happiness in water, music, movement and light. I had observed something special from Franc, lying on the upstairs floor at the café with Marcel and Kyi Kyi beside him, transported by beautiful music. From Binita, traversing length after length of the swimming pool each day through the worst of her troubles, caressed by the waters and the sound of her own beating heart. From Christopher, so engrossed in his work that he lost his sense of self. If we wish to recapture our *joie de vivre*, we should do something, often, that makes our heart sing. Engage in an activity for no reason other than for the uncomplicated happiness it brings.

And if we remember, we may amplify that happiness by reminding ourselves that whatever bliss we experience comes not from the music or the water or the creative expression itself, but from our mind. It is the positive result of a cause created in the distant past, by the unknown being we once were. How fortunate are we! What a stroke of good luck to be harvesting the fruits of a life once well lived.

Recollecting this, and celebrating the true cause of happiness, magnifies our wellbeing. It also inspires us to live with greater virtue and kindness, to ensure that our happiness expands. What's more, by rejoicing in the good fortune of others, we not only create the opportunity to experience their attainments. When we let go of jealousy, we empower the purity of a vision free from the obscuring smog of duality. We release, a little more, our attachment to a separate self that can't be found.

As worldly-wise seniors, we can become benumbed by the ocean of suffering in which we find ourselves. Surrounded by so many worthy causes, each with its own urgent need, it is hard not to withdraw into ourselves, or for our benevolence to be reduced to a bone-dry exercise in bank transfers and charitable donations.

Yogi Tarchin had shown us how to live with authentic compassion. To first practice loving kindness with those to whom we feel connected at the heart. How powerful the strength of feeling when we help others with this motivation, whether through the hardships of this life or the bardo experiences that follow. And how uplifting to transmute suffering into transcendence. To reawaken the kindness which we were once able to give spontaneous expression to – and then do so again.

I had been reconnected to other long-forgotten instincts by Heidi, during that evocative twilight on the lawn of the Old Sanatorium. So acquainted had I become with the notion of HHC, Rinpoche, a cat with many roles and names, that I had unknowingly separated myself from the evident reality that I am air, water, earth and heat. As much a manifestation of nature as a tree, a waterfall, or any living being. Rediscovering the truth of this had been like a kind of homecoming. A reminder that the very fabric of my being connected me to all else on earth.

In the candle-lit mystery of the temple, Geshe Wangpo had explained how the end of our physical form need give no cause for fear. In the clear light of death, as in life, we create our own reality. Are we impelled by an instinct for a separate me, myself or I? Do we identify instead with the boundless radiance beyond all concepts with which we find ourselves face to face?

Alternatively, like Christopher, are we drawn to a particular form of transcendence, in a pure land such as Sukhavati?

"All is mind," His Holiness murmured now. And I had never sensed the truth of this more strongly.

There was a sudden commotion downstairs, as motorbike outriders, emergency lights flashing, swept into the monastery courtyard. They were followed by several four-wheel drive vehicles with tinted glass, one of which was flying the flag of the United States of America.

Beside me, the Dalai Lama looked down at the flurry of secret service agents and monastery security officials, taking in the busy-ness and importance playing out, as though it were a drama unfolding on TV.

"Arrival and departure, life and death, self and other – all is mere concept," he said with that ineffable luminosity of his, which not only captured all that I had learned, but which also showed how best to live in accordance with it. A state which included me and every other being in a field of radiant light, profoundly peaceful, with no beginning or end. "The more we let go of concept, my dear Snow Lion, the more we abide in our own true nature."

DEDICATION

Through reading, thinking and meditating

And the actions flowing from these,

May anyone who encounters this book

Purify all negative karmas and accumulate infinite virtue.

Blossoming under the guidance of precious teachers,

May we all have long life, good health and profound wellbeing.

By letting go of our selves,

May we taste the exalted joy of enlightenment.

Then may we, as Buddhas,

Support all sentient beings throughout universal space.

By manifesting spontaneously and effortlessly in myriad forms

*May we help those who experience their selves as separate
and suffering*

Quickly to realize their own Buddha nature,

So that all may abide in the sublime state

Of radiant compassion and boundless wisdom,

Non-dual great bliss and sunyata.

GLOSSARY

Abidharmakośa – a revered Buddhist text by 4th century writer Vasubandhu with detail on many subjects including cosmology

Amitabha Buddha – once an ordinary man who vowed to attain enlightenment to create a pure land – Sukhavati - where ordinary beings could be reborn. Amitabha is the Buddha of infinite light and life.

bodhichitta – for the sake others, the wish to attain enlightenment. The central motivation in Tibetan/Mahayana Buddhism.

bardo – the state of consciousness after one life has ended and before the next begins

dukkha – dissatisfaction or suffering, ranging from the most subtle to the most profound

Geshe – a monastic degree in Tibetan Buddhism the approximate equivalent of a PhD

khata – a white scarf, traditionally presented to an esteemed teacher/visitor from respect

kriya tantra – a class of practices where a person seeks to embody the qualities of a Buddha such as Green Tara or Medicine Buddha

mahamudra – the ultimate nature of mind and reality perceived non-conceptually. This is possible when a meditator has total control of his or her mind, a state known as calm abiding/ samatha.

maharishi – usually in the Hindu tradition, a greatly accomplished or enlightened person *mala* – a circular string of beads, like a rosary, typically used to count mantra recitations

mandala – usually an art work depicting key elements of a spiritual journey or cosmology. More loosely, a person's own world, cosmos, or experience of reality.

nirvana – a mind free from karma and delusions existing in a tranquil state beyond birth and death

non-duality – a state of consciousness with no distinction between the perceiver and the perceived

prana – the life force or energy which pervades all living things

puja – a ceremony typically used in Tibetan Buddhism to purify negativities and accumulate virtue

pure land – a state of consciousness characterised by blissfulness, virtue and wisdom

sadhvi – usually in the Hindu tradition, a woman who has renounced worldly activities to pursue a spiritual life

sadhu – usually in the Hindu tradition, a man who has renounced worldly activities to pursue a spiritual life

samatha – also called calm abiding. A state in which a meditator can focus on any object, effortlessly, with non-duality, for any length of time.

samsara – a mind propelled karma and delusion, thereby conditioned to seek rebirth

semchen – literally "mind-haver." Any being that possesses consciousness or sentience.

siddhi – paranormal powers that naturally arise from advanced meditation practices

Siddhartha Gautama – the birth name given to the historical Buddha of the 5th century BCE *sunyata* – the premise that all beings and phenomena lack intrinsic nature, being dependent on parts, causes and mind's participation

sukha – happiness, joy or bliss

thangka – a Tibetan Buddhist wall hanging depicting a Buddha or other object of concentration

tathagatagarba – Buddha nature, or the natural purity of mind, which can be transformed into Buddha consciousness

tonglen – taking suffering and giving happiness: a compassion-based meditation practice

tukdam – a meditation practice used in the immediate after-death state by an advanced meditator, who is able to transform the death process and remain in the clear light state for days or even weeks

vajra acharya – a qualified teacher of vajrayana in Tibetan Buddhism

vajrayana – the esoteric path in Tibetan Buddhism

yogi/yogini – a male/female whose life is devoted to meditation practice

yidam – a manifestation of the enlightened mind in the form of a Buddha with whom a practitioner may develop a connection. A yidam usually represents specific qualities to be cultivated, such as wisdom, compassion or power.

ABOUT THE AUTHOR

DAVID MICHIE IS THE INTERNATIONALLY BEST-SELLING author of *The Dalai Lama's Cat* series, *The Magician of Lhasa*, *The Secret Mantra* and other books including the non-fiction titles *Buddhism for Busy People*, *Buddhism for Pet Lovers*, *Mindfulness is Better than Chocolate* and *Hurry Up and Meditate*.

In 2015 he established Mindful Safaris to Africa, combining wildlife viewing and meditation sessions in journeys to unexplored places, outer and inner.

For more about his work go to: https://davidmichie.com/

Made in the USA
Middletown, DE
19 December 2022

19728991R00168